"We shouldn't be doing this, Clay. It's wrong for us to even think about it."

"Wrong?" Clay asked huskily. "To love each other for a while and find some warmth in the storm? Tell me, Jenny, how can it be wrong?"

He's under investigation! a small voice screamed inside her head.

But he's so...and I keep feeling...

The man's probably guilty of tax fraud, and you're the auditor!

Under normal circumstances Jenny would certainly have listened to that warning voice. But tonight it was drowned out by the roar of rising floodwaters, the sense of imminent disaster, the pounding rain beyond the window—not to mention the desire that had haunted her since she'd first looked at Clay.

These were definitely not normal circumstances.

ABOUT THE AUTHOR

Margot Dalton has been writing since she was able to read. Her first book was published by Harlequin in 1990. Since then she has written more than thirty contemporary romance novels. Three of her books have won the *Romantic Times* Reviewer's Choice Award, and her Superromance novel *Another Woman* was made into a CBS TV movie.

In 1996 Margot published her first title for MIRA Books. *Tangled Lives* was followed by *First Impression*—the first book in Margot's mystery series featuring Detective Jackie Kaminsky. *Second Thoughts,* the next Jackie Kaminsky title from MIRA, was published in March 1998, and *Third Choice* will be out in December 1998.

Margot lives in British Columbia, Canada.

COTTONWOOD CREEK
CREEK
Margot Dalton

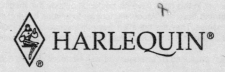

TORONTO • NEW YORK • LONDON
AMSTERDAM • PARIS • SYDNEY • HAMBURG
STOCKHOLM • ATHENS • TOKYO • MILAN • MADRID
PRAGUE • WARSAW • BUDAPEST • AUCKLAND

ISBN 0-373-70794-0

COTTONWOOD CREEK

COTTONWOOD CREEK

CHAPTER ONE

EVERY MORNING from April through October, rain or shine, Jenny McKenna and her grandfather went for a three-mile run. It was the best part of Jenny's day, even though she had to get up at five o'clock to do it, then shower and change afterward and battle early-morning traffic to get to work by eight.

She walked into the Revenue Canada building on a beautiful June morning still glowing from her exercise, went through the lobby and up to the vast third floor where dozens of desks, computers and file cabinets jammed the room.

Jenny had a makeshift office in one corner, formed by tall cork-and-metal dividers. All around her, other auditors and information officers were arriving and settling at their cubicles, pouring coffee and greeting co-workers.

"Hi, Lisa," Jenny said to her assistant, who shared the tiny space and was already sitting at her desk. "How are you this morning?"

Lisa rested her chin on her hand and looked up wistfully. "Not as good as you, obviously. Jen, you're positively radiant. Hey, and you're all dressed up. How come?"

Jenny set her briefcase on the desk and hung her

cardigan on the nearby coat tree. "Dressed up?" she asked, puzzled.

"You're wearing a skirt," Lisa said.

Jenny laughed. "Oh, that. I only have one pair of slacks that match this blouse. They needed pressing and I didn't have time this morning."

"Did you and your grandpa go for your daily run?"

"Of course. He sends you his warm regards."

"Your grandpa is so awesome." Lisa rummaged through an overflowing wire basket on her desk. "If I had enough energy I'd make a play for him, but I doubt if I could keep up with the man."

Jenny carried her cup to the nearest coffeemaker. "And you're...how old?" she asked over her shoulder. "Sixteen?"

"I'm twenty-three, as you well know."

"And I'm nearly thirty-one. Imagine what it's like for an old lady like me trying to keep up with Paddy McKenna."

"I doubt you have any problem," Lisa said, eyeing her enviously. "You're such a jock."

Jenny was a tall woman, slim and athletic, with auburn hair pulled back and held by barrettes. Her arms were lightly tanned, and her face was dusted with freckles. She grinned at being called a jock as she poured her coffee, then she returned to her desk, sat down and reached for a file.

Lisa toyed with her long blond ponytail. A thin, ethereal-looking girl, she favored flat slippers and long cotton dresses in pastel colors, and was a devoted practitioner of herbal medicine. And while her boss jogged every morning, she never left for work without consulting her daily horoscope.

Lisa and Jenny had been working together for more than two years. Despite their differences, they were a surprisingly efficient team.

"Jen," Lisa began.

"Hmm?" Jenny entered a series of numbers into her computer and frowned at the screen.

"If you could have a single wish granted, one thing in the whole world, what would it be?"

"An office with a window," Jenny said promptly. "Do you know the password to the McCrimmon files?"

"I think it's Tiger. Jen, I'm serious. What would you want if you could have anything at all?"

Jenny sipped her coffee and looked at her assistant. Lisa frequently asked questions like this, and Jenny knew from experience she wouldn't drop the issue until she'd gotten a satisfactory answer.

"Is money no object?" she asked.

"Not a bit. Sky's the limit."

Jen gazed thoughtfully at the tall divider next to her desk. "Okay," she said at last. "Then I want an office with a window."

Lisa pouted as she selected a file from her basket. "You're no fun."

Jenny sipped her coffee. "So I've been told."

The two started to work, and soon the only sound in their office was the click of keyboards and the rustling of paper. But as she shuffled forms and crunched numbers, Jenny found herself pondering her assistant's question.

Anything in the world...

Most women in her position would probably wish for a man and a loving relationship, but Jenny was finished with all that. She'd already had her chance at happiness with a man. In fact, she'd been loved by the best man in the world. There was no chance of finding anything so wonderful a second time, and the attempt wouldn't even be fair to some poor man who could never ever live up to Steve's memory....

She swung her gaze to the handsome face smiling from the gold-framed picture on her desk. Steve was in his climbing gear and lounging next to one of the Sherpa tents, the dazzling blue sky behind him.

Jenny looked at the photo for a long moment, her eyes stinging with tears, then turned back determinedly to her computer screen. But her thoughts remained elsewhere.

It wouldn't be a man she'd wish for, or a house filled with babies. Nor would it be a chance to travel to exotic places, although there'd been a time back in her college days when she would have loved to travel around the world with Steve. Nowadays, what she craved most of all was simply some space and freedom.

She got so weary of being crowded. She spent her day in a room with at least fifty other people, drove back and forth to work on roads clogged with traffic, ate in busy restaurants and lived in one of the fastest-growing cities in the western hemisphere.

Although Calgary was a sprawling city set between a mountain range and a vast sweep of prairie, Jenny sometimes felt there was no room at all to live. An office with a window, though she genuinely longed for this, wouldn't help very much because the window would look out on other office buildings, or teeming streets, or apartment buildings that blocked the view.

She sighed, causing Lisa to glance up curiously. Jenny met her assistant's eyes and gave her a wan smile.

"Open spaces," she said.

"What about them?"

"If I could have anything in the world, that's what I'd choose. Some space around me, and silence and peace. In fact, I'd like to be completely alone somewhere for about a year."

Lisa considered. "Not me," she said. "I like the city. Open spaces are too scary."

"Well, there you go. Different strokes."

Jenny returned to her keyboard and they continued their work in companionable silence.

THE RANCH OFFICE had a window facing west across the prairie, installed more than ten years earlier so Bridget could enjoy the view from her desk. She liked to see wildflowers in the spring and watch the winter sunsets spill across the snow.

But all traces of snow were long gone now. It was the middle of June and the prairie glowed with color. Yellow buffalo beans waved and nodded, pink wild roses bloomed in the coulees and blue lupines starred the tall grass. Cows grazed placidly, flicking their tails in the morning sunshine, their calves at their sides.

Bridget sighed wearily, took off her bifocals to rub

her eyes and twisted a strand of gray hair around one finger.

If only she could leave this place and walk across that waving sea of grass, disappear into the horizon and never come back. She could have a nice apartment in the city, cozy and self-contained, close to stores and movies and far from this vast, implacable sweep of land.

If only...

"I've been feeling sick for days," Teresa said from across the room as she opened a bottle of black nail polish. "I'm probably pregnant. Not that anybody cares," she added bitterly.

Bridget shuffled through the papers on her desk. "I don't think so," she said. "You're too thin to get pregnant."

"What does that have to do with anything?" Teresa's expression was belligerent. She leaned back in the office chair, tilting it dangerously on two legs. "Anyway, I'm not too thin. *I* just happen to have some self-control, that's all," she cast a meaningful glance at Bridget, then turned her attention back to her nail polish. She dipped the little brush in the container and began to apply the polish carefully.

Bridget watched in unwilling fascination. Whatever had happened to this younger generation? she thought. Where was the respect for elders, the automatic courtesy that had been part of Bridget's upbringing? When she was Teresa's age, she would never have spoken so rudely to a woman over sixty. But Teresa did it all the time.

The girl was in her early twenties, stick-thin and

pale, with black hair cropped close to her head and huge blue eyes ringed with shadows. She moved with a certain sensual languor, but Bridget suspected that it came not from smoldering sexuality so much as poor nutrition and general boredom with life.

"If I annoy you so much, Teresa," she said, putting on her glasses again, "why do you come over here all day and sit around bothering me?"

"There's nothing else to do." Teresa sighed heavily. "God, I hate this place."

She got up, shaking her fingernails, and slouched across the room to look out the front window. She wore boots, khaki trousers and a black shirt hanging loose, topped by a ragged linen vest. A long silver cross hung from one ear, almost brushing her shoulder.

"What's Michael doing today?" Bridget asked without much interest, looking down at the papers on her desk where the envelope lay. She touched it, then drew her hand back hastily.

Teresa toyed with the control on the venetian blind. "Good question." Her lip curled in annoyance. "His Royal Highness sent Mike off in some old truck to check fences about fifty miles away. He's going to be gone all day, so I'm left hanging around with nothing to do as usual."

"You should have gone with him and taken food for a picnic," Bridget said. "It would have been fun."

Teresa turned to stare at her in disbelief. "*Fun?* Riding around in a dirty truck through a pasture full of bull crap? That's your idea of fun?"

"When I was young, I would have loved to go off for a day on the prairie with my boyfriend."

Teresa hooted loudly.

Bridget flushed and began to feel angry, though she always tried not to let Teresa goad her into this kind of response. "I had a boyfriend, you know. In fact, I had a husband."

Teresa leaned against the door frame, studying her glossy black fingernails. "So what happened to him?"

"He had a terrible accident." Bridget touched the envelope again, eased back the flap to reveal the folded letter inside. "Two years after we were married, he was training a colt when it reared over backward and crushed him. He died in the hospital in Calgary two days later."

That had been more than thirty years ago, but Bridget still felt the pain as if it were yesterday. She remembered Hal's square, happy face, his strong hands and easy laughter, the way he used to hold her when she was young and slender.

"Bridey, you're as pretty as a wild rose," he'd whisper to her.

She would have said more, but Teresa's brief spurt of interest had already faded. She leaned forward to peer between the slats of the blind. "Well, well, if it isn't the king himself," she announced sourly. "Coming to pay us ordinary beings a social call."

"Clay's coming to the office?" Bridget asked.

"Big as life," Teresa reported. "Looking like he owns the world as usual, damn him."

She scuttled across the room, seated herself at the

other desk and put her nail polish out of sight in a drawer.

Despite her own misery, Bridget felt briefly amused. Teresa was a big talker, but she was afraid of her boyfriend's father just the same.

Not that anybody at the ranch had an actual reason to fear Clay Alderson. Unless, Bridget thought, they were doing something wrong…

Clay was quiet and intense, but he treated his employees with absolute fairness and was compassionate about their troubles.

Of course, Bridget had known him since he was a solemn, dark-eyed boy, when she'd come here after Hal's death to be the ranch's bookkeeper.

But he certainly wasn't a child any longer. Here on the windswept prairies of southern Alberta, Clayton Alderson ran one of the biggest cattle outfits in western Canada, an operation so large that the main ranch site resembled a small town.

Bridget looked at her desk again. The envelope seemed to be getting bigger, screaming at her from the mound of papers.

The door opened and Clay entered the room, pausing a moment to let his eyes adjust after the dazzle of sunlight outdoors.

He was a tall, well-built man in his mid-forties, wearing jeans, boots and a battered canvas jacket. Under the brim of an old gray Stetson, his eyes were dark and blazing with intensity, his tanned face weathered, with blunt cheekbones and finely sculpted lips. He had an air of authority, of power, that could be unnerving if you didn't know him well.

Or if you had a guilty conscience....

"Good morning, ladies." He turned to Teresa. "What are you doing today?" he asked.

"Nothing," the young woman muttered sullenly. "What's there to do around here?"

"Consuela needs some help in the garden and greenhouse. She's looking after all the bedding plants by herself because Jorge is helping with calf vaccinations for the rest of the month."

"You want me to help somebody plant a *garden?*" Teresa asked, her mouth dropping open. "Like, digging in the dirt and stuff?"

"It wouldn't hurt you." Clay leaned over Bridget's desk. "You look like you could use some fresh air."

Bridget smiled privately as she listened to their exchange.

Clay was the only person on the ranch who wasn't the least a little bit intimidated by this strange young woman. Clay's twenty-three-year-old son, Mike, had brought her home from the city last fall and announced casually that Teresa was going to "stay for a while."

Nobody knew where she came from or who she was, and it was difficult to understand Mike's attraction to the sullen, skinny girl. But then, Michael had never been an easy person to understand, either, not at all like his younger brother, Allan, who was a sunny-natured, happy-go-lucky type, well liked by all the ranch staff.

Clay turned to Bridget, and his face softened. "How are you this morning?" he asked with the grave courtesy that was as much a part of the man as his hard-hitting authority.

"I'm fine, Clay." She looked down at her desk. "Still going through the invoices for last week's cattle sale. We'll need a confirmation on some of these brand inspections before I can enter them."

"Okay. Anything else I should know before I leave for town?"

Bridget hesitated, biting her lip, conscious of the man's dark eyes on her.

"This came in yesterday's mail," she said at last, holding up the envelope. "I think you'd better have a look at it."

He reached for the envelope. "What is it?"

"It's a…" Bridget paused, swallowing hard. "It's a notice of audit from Revenue Canada."

"A tax audit?" He stared at her in disbelief.

Bridget nodded.

"But we've never been audited. The accountants always say there's not a figure out of place in any of your books."

Again she nodded, then stared down at her hands. She still wore her old wedding ring, but since she'd gained so much weight the past few years it didn't fit properly anymore.

I should have it enlarged, she thought, trying to turn the thin golden band. *It needs to be at least two sizes bigger.…*

"Bridget?" he was asking.

Even Teresa appeared to sense something in the room. She was watching Bridget with an avid expression.

"I don't know what it's about," Bridget muttered at last. "Maybe it's just...a random kind of thing." She waved her hand at the envelope Clay was holding. "They give the name of the person who's doing the audit. He works out of the Calgary office."

Clay glanced at the envelope. "I don't even know how they do this. Do you have to take all the books to them or what?"

"I think he'll come here and stay as long as it takes to examine the books," Bridget replied. "But I'm not exactly sure. Would you like me to call and find out?"

Clay checked the letter. "The auditor's name is J. D. McKenna, right? I'll go see him today when I'm in town." He glanced up again, his eyes so penetrating that Bridget shivered. "Do we have a problem here, Bridget?" he asked quietly. "Is there something I don't know?"

She shook her head. "I did the books last year the same way I always do. I can't imagine why we're being audited after all these years."

Clay hesitated, still holding the letter, then jammed it into his pocket and headed for the door. With his hand on the knob he paused to glance at Teresa.

"If you get a chance, drop by the garden and tell Consuela you're going to spend some time helping her this week. All right?"

Teresa didn't answer. When he was gone she made a rude face at the door and opened the drawer noisily to get out her nail polish.

"Who the hell does he think he is?" she muttered.

"He's the boss," Bridget said. "Clay's in charge

of everything around here, including the livelihood and daily activities of almost fifty people. And,'' she added, opening a ledger, ''he's also paying for your keep.''

''Well, he doesn't have to act so high and mighty. No wonder his wife left him.''

''Actually their divorce was a mutual decision. Clay and Eleanor are still friends. She and her husband even visit here sometimes.''

''I know, Mike told me.'' Teresa opened the bottle of polish and peered at it sullenly. ''But I still can't imagine any woman being married to him. He gives me the shivers. The man's like… a hawk or something.''

Bridget picked up a pen and a pile of invoices, but the tears blurring her eyes made it difficult to see the figures.

CLAY CROSSED the ranch yard, the letter burning a hole in his pocket.

A tax audit.

Why the hell was Revenue Canada suddenly interested in his business operations? He'd never had any problems with the government tax department before. Bridget had been handling the ranch payroll and doing the books at Cottonwood Creek since he was a boy. Her ledgers were taken on a quarterly basis to an accountant in the city who checked her numbers and paid the income taxes from a holding account.

But then, the business *had* experienced steady growth over the past several decades. Maybe the daily bookkeeping was getting to be too much for Bridget to handle on her own. Clay asked from time to time if she needed help, but she always insisted she was fine. She lived contentedly in her little cottage among the rest of the full-time ranch staff. He could hardly remember a time when she hadn't been part of life here at Cottonwood Creek.

He paused next to his truck, taking the letter out and frowning at it.

"Howdy, Clay. Heading to the city this morning?"

Clay turned to see his foreman approaching, coiling a rope as he came. Jim Cole was young and handsome, with a tanned face and clear blue eyes. Despite his boyish appearance, he was a seasoned veteran of the rodeo circuit and, according to rumor, a real devil with the ladies.

"'Morning, Jim. Yeah, I'm on my way." Clay glanced at the rope. "What's up?"

"One of the heifers in the West Quarter tangled with a porcupine yesterday. We had to snub her up in the round corral and take the quills out of her nose."

Clay grinned and leaned against the truck. "That must have been fun."

"She practically tore the whole place apart. But she's feeling a whole lot better now." Jim gestured with a gloved hand at the envelope. "Got a love letter?"

"Hardly." Clay's frown returned. "It's a notice of a tax audit."

Jim's eyes widened under the shadowy brim of his hat. "You're kidding. Are we in some kind of trouble?"

"Bridget doesn't think so. She figures it must be just a random check."

"So what happens?" The foreman leaned against the box of the truck. "Does Bridget have to take all the records into Calgary?"

"She says more likely the government accountant will come here and stay till it's finished."

Jim snorted and slapped the coil of rope against his leg. "No kidding? Some prissy little accountant's gonna come out here?"

Clay chuckled at the foreman's expression. "Apparently that's how it usually happens. And I'd sure hate to see this poor fellow wind up in the creek or on the wrong side of the bull pen."

Jim removed his hat and held it against his chest with a soulful look. "Now, who's gonna do a thing like that? We're always real polite to visitors, Clay. You know that."

Clay opened the door of the truck and climbed behind the wheel. In spite of himself he felt a little better when he pictured a government accountant in a suit and tie, picking his way across a manure-strewn pasture filled with big threatening Angus bulls.

"Clay, can you stop on your way into town and check the windmill out on Sagebrush Flats?" Jim asked, replacing his hat. "Dave says it's pumping sludge again. He thinks we'll need to pull the pipe and sink a new well."

"Damn." Clay forgot about the letter in his pocket. "Not another well. That sucker's almost four hundred feet deep. It'll cost a fortune to drill a new one."

His foreman shrugged. "The cows need water.

We'll be running out of surface water down there before the end of the month.''

"Okay, I'll check it out.''

Clay put the truck in gear and headed off down the graveled road that ran for more than twenty miles across ranch property. As he drove through fields of grass and cattle, he thought about all the things that needed to be done.

Fences, windmills, outbuildings and corrals, feed and water for several thousand head of cattle… The responsibilities were enormous, the problems never-ending.

And the staff had to be considered, as well. Difficulties always arose when you had a lot of people working together in an isolated setting. Many of them found it hard to cope with this vast lonesome prairie.

Clay felt a surge of contentment despite his worries. He'd always loved the prairie, loved the clean sweep of land and the distant horizon, the fierce storms that blew up from nowhere, the blazing summer days and crisp starry nights.

But a lot of people couldn't stand life on a ranch. His ex-wife had hated it so passionately that he still hesitated to think about marrying again, although he often felt lonely. If he ever got married again, the woman wouldn't be just a companion and sexual partner. Ranch life was so complex and all-consuming that she'd have to give up almost everything else to share it with him. There was simply no other choice. For he couldn't stop being a rancher; ranching was in his very bones.

But nowadays, it was the rare woman who chose

to submerge her existence in a man's life and occupation, especially—and here lay the irony—not a woman with enough independence of spirit to be interesting to a man like Clay. Such a woman got restless and disenchanted, and wanted more out of life. It wasn't fair for him to ask for so much sacrifice, and there was little pleasure in having a bored, discontented partner who blamed her husband for her lack of fulfilment—the way Eleanor used to.

Clay's face hardened when he remembered the horrible event that had precipitated their divorce, the thing he never allowed his mind to dwell on. But that nightmare was more than ten years in the past. And he and his ex-wife were much better friends now that she was remarried and living on the other side of the world.

The boys had been young adolescents when their parents divorced. Mike and Allan had stayed with him at the ranch and enjoyed their regular flights at Clay's expense to see their mother in Australia. Though it had worked out well for everybody, he wasn't prepared to risk marriage a second time, not when he had to bring a wife to this big lonely place.

He pulled off the graveled road, got out to open a wire gate, climbed back into the truck and headed across the prairie toward Sagebrush Flats, opening the window to enjoy the breeze on his face. As he approached the windmill, his gaze took in the herd of cows and calves grazing nearby; then he parked next to the tall metal structure, got out and walked over to the fence surrounding it.

A rattlesnake was sunning itself on the hard-packed

dirt. It coiled warily at his approach and slid off into the grass. Smiling, Clay watched the snake as it vanished, then rested his arms on the upper rail of the fence and observed the stream of muddy water trickling from the pipe.

The foreman was right. He should probably hire somebody to pull the well casing and sink a new one. But it was an expensive proposition, and if this damned city accountant came up with some unpaid taxes...

He returned to his truck, putting the coming tax audit firmly out of his mind. Instead, he went back to thinking about women and partnerships, and his older son's in particular.

Clay couldn't understand what Mike saw in the pale, lazy, bad-tempered creature he'd brought home to the ranch. The two young people slept together in Mike's room on the third floor of the big house, just above Clay's study. Sometimes late at night when he was reading or watching television, he could hear them fighting. Less frequently, he heard the telltale rhythmic creaking of bedsprings.

It still made Clay vaguely uncomfortable to know his unmarried son was sleeping with a woman in the bedroom Mike had occupied since he was a child. Especially a woman like Teresa, who seemed so cold and unpleasant. Clay wasn't overly disturbed by the morality of the situation, but he would have preferred a more satisfying relationship for his son. Mike had always been a shy lonely boy, not at all like his gregarious younger brother who had an endless string of pretty girlfriends.

Clay's thoughts returned to the sort of woman he

himself preferred. In his mind, a woman was most attractive when she smiled. He was drawn to warmth and humor, to intelligence and an optimistic outlook. When he tried to picture his ideal woman, it wasn't her face or body he visualized. He craved someone a man would feel eager to come home to because she was interested in him and genuinely cared what he was thinking and feeling. Somebody who could laugh with him and understand him, a *friend*, who could be trusted with his innermost feelings.

He wheeled the truck around and started back across the prairie, noting the small herd of mule deer grazing in the scrub brush next to the cattle. They flung their heads up at his approach, then turned and leaped up the hillside in graceful springing bounds, as light as a drift of feathers on the springtime wind.

"God," he said aloud, "I love this place."

Then he gripped the wheel and, after going through the wire gate, headed for the city more than ninety minutes away.

CHAPTER TWO

JENNY WAS SO ABSORBED in her examination of the McCrimmon files that she didn't hear what Lisa said.

"Hmm?" she murmured.

"I said, yummy. Double yummy." Lisa was gazing intently at something beyond the metal divider.

"Did Carl bring doughnuts again?" Jenny asked, leafing through a stack of tax memos.

"Not that kind of yummy. It's a man, and he's *gorgeous*. Omigod," Lisa added breathlessly. "I think he's coming here!"

Before Jenny could answer, a shadow fell across her desk and she looked up to see a tall man standing next to Lisa. He was lean and tanned, probably about forty, and good-looking in a rugged kind of way, dressed in jeans, boots and a Stetson.

Not unusual garb in Calgary, which still called itself a cowtown, but decidedly out of place among the throngs of office workers.

"I'm looking for somebody named J. D. Mc-Kenna," he said.

Lisa gazed up at him, apparently speechless, then glanced at Jenny.

"Well, that would be me," Jenny said. "How can I help you?"

"You're J. D. McKenna?" he turned to stare at her, and Jenny was acutely aware of the man's forcefulness. There was something a little intimidating about his dark, intense expression.

"Yes, I am. Please sit down." She indicated a folding metal chair next to her desk.

The man lowered himself onto it, then handed Jenny an envelope. "My bookkeeper just gave this to me. She told me it came in yesterday's mail."

Jenny couldn't help noticing his hands. Brown and hard, they were covered with scars and calluses. But they were well-formed, the fingers long and graceful. Jenny, who was always conscious of people's hands, found them surprisingly attractive.

She turned her attention to the contents of the envelope. "It's a notice of audit." To Lisa, she said, "This is the Cottonwood Creek file. Mr. Clayton Alderson. Could you pull it for me, please?"

Lisa took a manila folder from the cabinet, then handed it to Jenny and moved back to her desk, rolling her eyes eloquently as she passed behind their visitor.

Jenny gave her young assistant a warning frown, punched the code into her computer and brought a file onto the screen. "Here it is. Now, is there something you don't understand, Mr. Alderson?"

"I want to understand why we're being audited. It's never happened before."

His voice sounded taut and angry, and his big shoulders were tense. Jenny, who was accustomed to this reaction, gave him a soothing smile.

"It's just routine, Mr. Alderson." She glanced at

the computer again. "Your most recent tax return was flagged because of a revenue discrepancy."

"What kind of discrepancy? The ranch has had the same bookkeeper for almost thirty years, and we employ a city accounting firm to do the taxes. One of the company's accountants audits the books every year."

"I know. Your accountant is Saul Kleinschmidt at Barrow and Barchester. I've already spoken to him."

"You've spoken to my accountant?"

"Of course. I checked with him before issuing the notice," Jenny said calmly. "He said his last two annual audits have turned up the same discrepancy, and that it *has* been brought to your attention. It appears your operating profits at Cottonwood Creek have dropped off rather steeply the past couple of years, with nothing to explain the variance."

"What the hell's going on here?" Alderson leaned forward, his eyes blazing beneath the hat brim. "Are you implying there's something illegal about my business operation?"

Jenny met his gaze steadily, although she was surprised how much courage it took. "I'm not implying anything of the sort, Mr. Alderson. This isn't a personal matter, you know. I'm simply coming out to your ranch to check the books and see if I can determine why your revenues have been dropping."

"You think we're hiding income to cheat on our taxes? Is that what this is all about?"

His voice was soft, but the controlled anger in his tone made Lisa glance up nervously. Jenny, however, looked at the visitor with practiced calm.

"Mr. Alderson, your accountant has told you that revenues were down for two consecutive years. So this should hardly come as a big surprise to you."

The rancher made an abrupt dismissive gesture. "Saul said something about it, but I didn't pay much attention."

"Why not?"

"Because I've been dealing with this situation all my life. Revenues always go up and down in a ranching operation. Cattle prices fluctuate, there are droughts and blizzards and sickness to contend with, all kinds of things. On good years we plow the profits back into the business or land purchases, and try to leave enough in holding accounts to bail us out during the bad years. Ranching is a cyclical business."

"I understand that," Jenny said patiently. "And I'm sure there's nothing wrong with your books. We just want to find out what factors have caused this particular dip in revenue since it's happened two years in a row."

He watched her coldly. "So how do you propose to find out?"

"That's my job," she said. "I'll come to your place of business and go through every receipt and invoice. I'll check everything from phone bills to receipts for dog food. By the time I'm finished, we'll have a pretty clear picture of your entire operation."

"And how long will this take you, Mrs. Mc-Kenna?"

"That's Ms.," Jenny said automatically, conscious of his quick glance at the framed picture on her desk. "I expect the audit to take about three days, depending on how your bookkeeper maintains the company records and how much of the data is computerized.''

He watched her in silence.

''I'll need to have your bookkeeper at my disposal for most of the time I'm there,'' Jenny went on. ''And I'll also have to make reservations for accommodation nearby, if you could give me the name of a hotel.''

''A hotel?'' He smiled without humor. ''I don't think you have a real clear picture of my ranching operation, Ms. McKenna.''

''Well, then, perhaps you could fill me in.''

''The ranch site is more than ninety minutes by car from Calgary. There are no small towns nearby, except for a whistle-stop about forty miles to the north where there's a little strip motel, but I don't think you'd want to stay there. It houses a lot of oilfield workers, as well as the local saloon, and it's a pretty rough place.''

Belatedly Jenny realized that she should have checked all this before scheduling the audit. She'd just assumed there would be a hotel near the ranch if it wasn't practical to commute from home.

''If you like,'' Alderson said after an awkward silence, ''I suppose you could stay in the main ranch house. It's a pretty big place, and nobody lives there with me except my mother and my two sons and Teresa. We could probably find you a room with a private bath.''

Under other circumstances, Jenny would have been amused by the invitation. He was obviously reluctant to have her anywhere near his ranch, and yet courtesy forced him to offer her a room in the house.

"If you're certain it's no bother, Mr. Alderson, that would be very convenient for me," she said with a polite smile. "Lisa will make sure you're reimbursed for my stay."

He didn't return the smile. Instead, he got to his feet and took the notice of audit from her desk. "When will you be arriving?"

She looked at a calendar on her desk. "Next Tuesday morning."

"Do you know how to get there?"

"Your accountant gave me directions. They seem pretty straightforward."

He hesitated near her desk as if about to say something else, then nodded curtly and strode off through the rows of desks. As he passed, most of the women turned from their computer screens to stare at his broad shoulders and his proud carriage.

Lisa, too, sat with her chin in one hand, sighing as the tall rancher disappeared into the reception area. "Oh my," she breathed. "Oh my goodness."

Jenny opened a ledger, feeling vaguely annoyed. "I don't know what you're so excited about," she said.

Lisa stared at her in amazement. "Jenny McKenna, for God's sake, that's one of the best-looking men I've ever seen. And *so* sexy," she added, gazing into the distance again.

"Sexy?" Jenny's eyebrows shot up in surprise. "You're kidding. Lisa, the man was so angry, he was on the verge of being rude."

"I know. Didn't you find it exciting? All that male

anger, the tight jaw muscles, the clenched hands and piercing stare…"

"I don't find anything attractive about male anger," Jenny said. "And I certainly hope there isn't going to be some kind of battle when I start going through his books, because I just don't have the patience to deal with that nonsense anymore."

Lisa smiled wistfully. "I'd love to go out there with you. Are you absolutely certain you don't need help with this audit?"

Jenny shook her head. "I'm absolutely certain I need you here looking after things while I'm gone. Besides, sweetie, we can hardly have you out there in the wilderness mooning over some cowboy who might be facing criminal prosecution for tax evasion."

Lisa pouted. "I can't believe he's guilty of anything. Did you notice his tight little butt in those faded jeans when he was walking away, Jen? "

Jenny chuckled in spite of herself. "So because he's got a cute butt, he can't be guilty of tax fraud?"

"He didn't look like a cheater."

"They never do," Jenny said grimly. "Now stop distracting me. I have to get some work done."

"I'm going to look for Carl. We need some doughnuts." Lisa got up and started out of the alcove.

"You always tell me Carl's doughnuts are poison in a box," Jenny said.

"They are." Lisa paused by the divider. "But seeing that gorgeous man has roused all my base appetites. I want to satisfy one of them at least."

"Poor child." Jenny grinned without sympathy.

"I'm glad I'm old. It's such a relief to outgrow those romantic yearnings."

Lisa gave her a brief shrewd glance. She opened her mouth to speak, then smiled enigmatically and disappeared in a swirl of flowered cotton.

JENNY STAYED at her desk for half an hour after Lisa left for lunch; she knew her assistant would join a group of other young secretaries for sandwiches in the cafeteria and the chance to ogle the construction workers across the street. Finally, too hungry to work any longer, she replaced her files, cleared the desk and picked up her handbag. She headed out of the building and walked a couple of blocks to a little Italian restaurant she knew. Its great pasta made it a favorite lunchtime haunt.

The day was beautiful, mild and sunny, and the downtown area seemed less crowded and noisy than usual. But Jenny still found herself yearning for open spaces and solitude. She thought about Cottonwood Creek, where she'd be spending most of next week. How wonderful it would be to have an actual holiday at the isolated prairie ranch, instead of a difficult three-day stint of work where she'd probably upset everybody and be viewed as an enemy invader.

Jenny had done a lot of on-site audits and had few illusions about how pleasant her stay at Clayton Alderson's ranch would be. After two or three days, she'd probably be vastly relieved to get back to the city, to her own home and routine and her regular early-morning runs with her grandfather.

She entered the restaurant and was dismayed to see

that the place was full. Every table seemed to be occupied. She also became aware of a gnawing hunger that was becoming distressingly urgent. There was no other restaurant nearby that served anything she liked to eat, but she didn't have enough time to wait around for a table. As she hesitated, she noticed a man sitting alone at a table near the window, watching her. Clayton Alderson. He nodded curtly when she caught his eye, then got to his feet with obvious reluctance, spoke to a passing waiter and indicated the other chair at his table.

Jenny waited nervously as the waiter approached her.

"The gentleman asks if you'd share his table," he said. "He'll be finished soon."

"I don't know if..." Jenny hesitated, wondering what to do.

The situation was incredibly awkward. Clayton Alderson didn't really want her company any more than she wanted his, but to refuse the offer would be graceless and rude.

And if he was almost finished...

"All right," she said at last. "Thank you."

The waiter led her to the booth and she sat down, conscious of the rancher's dark eyes on her. He'd removed the cowboy hat and looked younger without it, much less forbidding. His hair was black and crisp, graying a little at the temples.

"This is kind of you, Mr. Alderson," she said. "I'm really hungry, and I don't have time to look for another restaurant."

"This place seems popular," he said in noncommittal fashion, concentrating on his food.

Alderson was more than halfway through a plate of spaghetti with meat sauce. He reached for a piece of garlic bread, and Jenny was conscious again of his finely shaped hands. For some reason she felt a deep unsettling shiver of emotion.

"Yes," she said. "I like to come here for lunch. They have the best pasta in the city."

He stabbed at the mound of spaghetti and swirled an expert forkful, putting it neatly in his mouth.

Jenny, who'd never quite mastered this trick, watched with secret envy and decided to have penne, instead of spaghetti. The last thing she needed was to splatter tomato sauce all over her blouse while this man sat and watched her.

She gave her order to the waiter, spread a checkered napkin in her lap and sipped nervously from a glass of water, wishing she could have gone somewhere else to eat.

"Do you live here in the city?" he asked.

Ah, so he's making conversation, Jenny thought. *Have to give him credit for that.* She rummaged in the basket of bread sticks and replied, "Yes, I have a basement suite in my grandfather's house over in Brentwood."

"So you're not married?"

"No," she said. "I'm not married."

He watched her thoughtfully. "Who's the man in the photo on your desk? A boyfriend?"

She felt a little annoyed by the personal nature of the question. But within a few days she'd be probing into all the deepest secrets of this man's financial life, so she supposed she couldn't really object to his polite inquiry.

"Steve was my fiancé," she said, staring down at the bread stick she'd grabbed. "He died two years ago during his second attempt at Everest. There was an avalanche that wiped out their high camp. It took three months to recover the bodies."

"I'm sorry." Alderson's voice sounded genuinely sympathetic. "That must have been hard for you."

"It was very hard," Jenny said quietly. "I still miss him."

"Are you a mountain climber, too?"

"Hardly." Jenny gave him a wan smile. "I go jogging with my grandfather every morning—that's about the extent of my athletic endeavors."

"You jog with your grandfather?"

"You may have heard of him. Paddy McKenna."

Alderson raised his eyebrows in surprise. "The triathlete?"

Jenny nodded.

"Everybody's heard of Paddy McKenna. I can't believe he's old enough to have grown up grandchildren. From what I've seen on television, the man's in great shape."

"He'll be seventy-two this fall." Jenny murmured her thanks to the waiter as he delivered her salad. "But," she added fondly, "he's got the mind and body of a thirty-year-old man."

"And you live in his house?"

"In the basement." she repeated, then dug hungrily into her salad. "I was the only child of an only child.

My mother's remarried and living in Florida, so Grandpa's all the family I have living nearby.''

"As I think I mentioned, my mother lives at the ranch with me," He grinned and his dark face was transformed. Jenny observed this with amazement, but his smile vanished as quickly as it had appeared. "She's quite a character, too.''

"In what way?''

"Just…colorful.'' He ate the last of his spaghetti and glanced at his watch. "She gets back from holiday today. In fact, her plane arrives in less than an hour, so I'd better head out to the airport.''

He got to his feet, dropped a couple of bills on the table and paused. "I guess I'll see you next week, Ms McKenna.''

"Yes. Tuesday.''

He inclined his head gravely and looked at Jenny for a moment with an unreadable expression, then took his Stetson from the other chair, fitted it on his head and left the restaurant.

CHAPTER THREE

THE CALGARY AIRPORT was as big, bright and bustling as the rest of the city. Clay stood in the arrivals area, looking at a huge mural of chuckwagons racing around a circular track. But the vivid images blurred and faded, replaced by a mental picture of the young government accountant as she'd sat across the table from him in the restaurant.

Somehow her youth and femininity gave an almost insulting quality to this legalized invasion of his privacy.

Jenny McKenna looked like the kind of wholesome athletic young woman who should be out on a college lawn somewhere, running around with a field-hockey stick. Beneath the silk blouse and neatly fitted skirt, her body had been strong and shapely, with high firm breasts and slender thighs. And her face had an open, honest, almost childlike look. She even had a cute smatterring of freckles across the bridge of her nose.

Under other circumstances, he would probably have found the woman quite attractive. Clay liked women who weren't artificial and overly conscious of their looks or their appeal to men. He would have enjoyed learning more about Jenny McKenna's life and her intriguing relationship with her grandfather—

and that handsome young dead fiancé whose picture was still displayed on her desk.

But knowing what the woman was about to do at his ranch, and how helpless he was to prevent it from happening, swamped all his interest and warmth in a hot wave of annoyance.

Clay moved away from the mural to study a monitor listing flight times. His mother's plane from Nevada was right on time, due in less than five minutes. He strode off in the direction of the arrival gate.

She was clearly visible in the stream of embarking passengers, her curly silver hair glinting under the fluorescent lights. As usual, she wore bright colors, this time an orange silk jogging suit and a lavish array of turquoise jewelry. She looked pale under her tan and almost too tired to tow her suitcase, but she beamed when she saw her son and waved enthusiastically. He hurried over to hug her.

"Hi, Mom," he said, conscious of how small and frail she felt in his arms. "How was your holiday?"

She withdrew from his embrace. "It was good right till the end, and then I'm afraid I really blew it. Clay, you can't imagine how exhausted I am. Let's just go home."

With a sinking feeling, he led her to where he'd parked his truck and stowed her luggage in the back. She refused to tell him any more about her trip until they were out of the city and heading across the prairie.

"Come on, what happened to spoil your holiday?" he asked.

Maura sighed, her gaze fixed on the expanse of rolling green pastures.

"Mom?"

"I was up more than twenty thousand dollars last night, Clay. I went back to my room and thought I'd go to sleep and come home a winner, but then I got a hankering to play just a little longer and maybe double my money, since my luck was running so strong. So I went back down to the blackjack tables and played till four o'clock this morning."

He felt a familiar weary impatience. "Oh, for God's sake. You promised me you weren't going to do that anymore."

"I know, I know," she said cheerfully. "But when I get down there to Las Vegas, I tend to forget everything I've promised."

"So what happened?"

"Well, my luck held right to the end, when I knew I had to go back to the room and pack for the flight home. So I bet fifteen thousand on a single hand, then doubled down on a four and seven. I drew a nine, which was pretty good, but the dealer hit twenty-one."

"You lost thirty thousand dollars on the turn of a card," he said flatly.

"Oh, don't sound so stiff and disapproving." Maura leaned over to slap her son's arm. "Twenty thousand of it was their money, you know. I'd only taken ten down there with me."

"You lost ten thousand dollars in a single trip to Vegas?"

"I'll just chalk it up to entertainment," she told him serenely.

Clay's hands tightened on the wheel. "Mom, how can you afford this? I know Dad left you with a good bank account of your own, but…"

"He certainly did," Maura said briskly. "And how I choose to spend it is none of your business."

"But if you—"

"I'm not talking about it anymore, Clay."

He glanced at her. Maura's head rested against the back of the seat and her eyes were closed. Clay knew by the stubborn set of her mouth that there would be no further discussion of his mother's gambling for a while.

Giving up, he drove in silence until she opened her eyes and smiled at him.

"You're looking unusually grim today," she said. "What's the matter, son?"

He shrugged. "Just the usual stuff."

"Like what?"

"Well, for one thing, we're going to have to sink a new well out on Sagebrush Flats. It'll probably cost a bundle."

"You've known about that well since last fall," she said calmly. "What else is bothering you?"

"Bridget just got notice of a full tax audit."

Maura sat up a little straighter. "Income tax, you mean?"

"Yeah, that's what I mean."

"For goodness' sake," Maura said thoughtfully. "I don't believe your father or grandfather ever had a tax audit in all the years they operated the ranch."

"I know. This is the first time ever. And I have no idea why it's happening."

She gave her son a keen glance. "Surely you must have *some* idea. Haven't you talked to them?"

Clay squinted at the long graveled road that narrowed from a ribbon to a thread in the distance, finally vanishing altogether into the limitless horizon.

"I went to see the auditor this morning," he said. "She's already talked to Saul Kleinschmidt. Apparently they're concerned about a drop in revenue at the ranch over the past two years."

"Why should they be concerned if our revenues drop?" his mother asked.

"I suppose they think we're hiding income somewhere to avoid paying taxes."

"Are we?"

Clay made an impatient gesture. "For God's sake, Mom! That isn't the way I do business."

"Then what's happening? Have cattle prices dropped that much?"

"No, they haven't. Prices have actually held fairly steady over the past few years."

Maura continued to watch him thoughtfully. "Well, then, have expenses increased? Did you buy a lot more land?"

"No. I assumed we *had* profits and Saul was putting them back into land payments the way we've always done. But when I talked to him this morning, he said there haven't been enough profits the past two years to do more than keep abreast of the lease fees."

"So what accounts for this drop in revenue?"

"That's what the auditor wants to find out. She'll come out to the ranch and go through all the books.

Apparently she'll look at every receipt to see why the income's been dropping.''

"She?" Maura asked.

"This government auditor is just a young woman," Clay said, frowning. "She looks like a schoolgirl."

"She can't be that young if she's got such an important job."

"Whatever," he said curtly. "But she can't be more than thirty."

Maura cast him a thoughtful glance. "Is she pretty?"

Clay tapped his fingers impatiently on the wheel. "Yeah," he said at last. "I suppose she's pretty. Tall and slim, kind of reddish-brown hair, freckles…"

"And she's a government auditor?"

"Her name's Jenny McKenna." Clay paused, watching a bull pacing along the barbwire fence, then turned to glance at his mother. "She's coming next Tuesday morning, and the audit will take about three days. I told her she could stay at the house."

"That certainly makes more sense than driving back and forth to the city or staying in that fleabag motel up at Silver Plains. Besides," Maura said cheerfully, "if she gets too insufferable, we can always put a couple of rattlesnakes in her bed."

"Jim Cole already suggested something like that. Maybe a little sight-seeing trip through the bull pasture."

Maura chuckled and closed her eyes again. But Clay had a brief disturbing image of Jenny McKenna's clear green eyes, her freckled nose and direct look. No matter how annoyed he was at the coming invasion of his privacy, he didn't like to think of the woman being frightened or humiliated.

He just wished she'd stay the hell away from his ranch.

"Maybe you trust people too much," Maura said, startling him.

"What people?"

"Accountants and bookkeepers." Maura looked over at him. "You never really question Saul's figures—you just sign on the dotted line."

"I'm a rancher. Cattle and horses are my job, not book work. I hire the best people I can find and pay them a whole lot of money to look after the numbers for me. What's the point if I'm not going to trust them?"

There was a brief silence. "Maybe Bridget needs a helper," Maura said at last.

Clay shot her a quick glance. "Yeah, I've sometimes wondered that, too. Even suggested to her, but she says no."

"Well," Maura said, "the woman's only a few years younger than I am, Clay, and bookkeeping for your ranch is a full-time job. She must be getting tired. Maybe she's begun to make mistakes."

I don't know," Clay said. "Bridget's always kept the best set of books in the district. She's a treasure."

"But her books are being audited this year," Maura said.

Clay shook his head. "There's got to be a reasonable explanation for all this. It could just be some kind of accounting error."

"I suppose it could." Maura turned to look at a

herd of broodmares with their new foals. "So what else is happening? Has that dreadful girl shown any signs of packing up and leaving?"

Clay shook his head. "Not much chance of that. Teresa seems to be settled for life."

Maura sighed. "I can't imagine what's going on in Michael's head. Of all the girls in the world…"

"I know. He sure picked a winner, didn't he?" Clay grinned sardonically. "I'm going to make her help Consuela in the garden. There are hundreds of bedding plants to set out."

Maura chuckled with genuine amusement. "Now, *that's* something I'll have to see. And how's my other boy?" she asked fondly.

"Well, you know Allan. We don't see much of him these days. He's traveling the rodeo circuit full-time. But he's home for a week or so now."

"He hasn't been hurt, has he?" Maura said anxiously. Sunny, blue-eyed Allan had always been her darling.

"No, that boy lives under a lucky star. He's actually won a few bull-ridings. On the weekend, he brought home two big trophies and a few belt buckles, and enough money to keep traveling for a while."

"I wonder if he's ever going to settle down," Maura said wistfully.

"Well, he's only twenty, and his college grades are pretty good. I wish he'd stay and do some work at the ranch like Mike does, but," Clay added, "I'd rather see him traveling the rodeo circuit than settled down with a girl like Teresa."

"So would I." Maura sighed again. "I just can't

think what Michael sees in her beyond some kind of awful sexual attraction.''

"I don't even like to think about it," Clay said frankly.

Maura leaned over to touch his arm in sympathy, then settled back in her corner again and fell asleep. Clay drove the last few miles in worried silence, glancing over at her small huddled form and the dark smudges under her eyes.

JENNY MCKENNA'S BASEMENT suite reflected her craving for open spaces. It was a big place, occupying almost the entire lower floor of her grandfather's sprawling bungalow in northwest Calgary. The sparse furnishings were in pale green, blue and yellow and all the walls were painted stark white. The high narrow windows were shrouded by curtains of filmy muslin to create an illusion of light and spaciousness.

The place was surprisingly attractive, but it was still a basement suite. Jenny stood in the middle of the room, unloaded her briefcase, sweater and handbag onto an armchair covered in flowered chintz, and looked around with a sigh.

She really should start to think about finding another place to live. Now that she'd scored a couple of promotions and her college loans were finally paid off, she could afford a nice apartment in a high-rise with a view of the city.

But Jenny didn't like to think about moving. She tended to form strong attachments and be reluctant to part with familiar things. Furthermore, when she finally left this place, she was going to miss her grandfather terribly. And Clementine would never be happy in some fancy apartment building. She liked to go out in the yard and play under the fruit trees.

Clementine was Jenny's cat, a sleek little gray tabby with white paws. At the moment she was sitting on a low table next to an aquarium, watching with apparent fascination as a pair of tiny green sea horses bobbed back and forth in their strange ritualized dance. Occasionally she lifted a paw to dab at the glass or at the top of the aquarium where a slit in the plastic mounting left the water exposed.

Jenny hurried over and scooped Clementine into her arms, patting the offending paw. "Bad kitty," she murmured. "Bad, bad kitty to bother Tristan and Isolde. See, Clem? They're dancing."

Jenny knelt on the floor and held her cat up close to the glass. Clementine hung boneless in her grasp, regarding the sea horses with an unblinking yellow gaze.

"They mate for life," Jenny told the cat, nuzzling her cheek against the warm furry head. "Isn't that sweet, Clem? And they dance together every day. Neither of them will ever dance with any other sea horse."

She watched, enchanted, as the two little animals completed their stately pas de deux across the bottom of the aquarium. The female seized a waving stalk of seaweed with her prehensile tail and held it like a maypole, glancing up coyly as her mate whirled solemnly around the swaying column.

The male was hugely distended, about to give birth. Jenny loved the idea of a species where the male actually got pregnant. It always tickled her to watch the sea horses who had, in her opinion, the perfect marriage.

"What's going on? Has that awful cat been bothering the fishies again?" a voice said from the open doorway.

Jenny looked up to see her grandfather standing in the foyer. Paddy McKenna was tall, lean and erect, with broad shoulders and a gleaming bald head fringed by silver hair. He also had cornflower-blue eyes and the sweetest smile Jenny had ever seen. As usual he was dressed in sandals, cotton running shorts and a T-shirt with a sleeping tiger emblazoned on the front.

He'd been widowed fifteen years earlier when Jenny's grandmother died of breast cancer. Jenny had been living here in the lower floor of his house since her graduation from college, an arrangement both of them found very satisfying.

"Hi, Grandpa. Clem's obsessed with the sea horses. *Bad* kitty," she said again to the cat, who gave her an inscrutable glance and licked her hand.

"She can't get at them, can she?" Paddy moved closer to the aquarium.

"No, the lid fits tightly and the opening is too small. But I worry all the time about her messing around this equipment with wet paws and electrocuting herself."

Paddy and the cat exchanged a long measuring gaze. "Serve her right," he said. "Besides, she's probably got at least two or three lives left. I saw her fall off the garage roof just a few days ago."

"Poor baby. Grandpa doesn't mean a word of it. He really loves you." Jenny hugged the cat, who nestled contentedly in her arms and began to purr.

Paddy snorted, then knelt beside his granddaughter to study the sea horses in their big saltwater aquarium. "Look at that poor guy," he said with a shudder. "I'm glad the idea never caught on with humans."

"The world would certainly be a different place," Jenny said with a grin, "if men had to bear and raise the children."

She watched the spiny little creatures who had finished their dance and bobbed off to separate corners of the tank.

"I love them so much," she said, "but I've felt guilty about owning them ever since they went on the endangered list."

Paddy got to his feet. "What can you do about it? Turn them loose somewhere to die?"

She looked through the waving seaweed at Tristan with his bulging stomach. "Of course not. That wouldn't make any sense, but these will be the last ones I own. I can't bear to think they're endangered in the wild. They're so beautiful."

Paddy smiled at her. "When's Tristan expecting his new babies?"

"They bred just before the weekend, so it should be early next week. I hope they're born before I go away."

"When are you leaving?"

"Tuesday morning." She frowned, remembering Clay Alderson's anger. "I think it's going to be a painful assignment, Grandpa."

"Well, come upstairs for dinner and tell me about it. I made stew and baked some sourdough bread."

Jenny brightened. "Really?"

He moved toward the door, glancing at his watch. "Just give me about twenty minutes to toss a salad together, all right?"

"Lovely. I'll change clothes and be right up."

Jenny set the cat on the floor. Clementine hesitated for a moment before she hurried to follow Paddy out the door, setting her paws daintily, her tail high in the air. He waited for the little cat to join him and closed the door after her.

Jenny watched them leave with a smile, then went into the bedroom to take off her blouse and skirt and pull on an old gray jogging suit. With a sigh of relief she slipped into some moccasins, read through her mail and fed the fish, then filled Clem's bowl and watered the plants. At last she took a carton of peach-flavored yogurt from the fridge along with a bowl of fresh-sliced peaches and carried them upstairs.

"I brought dessert," she said, sniffing the air with pleasure. "My, that smells good."

Paddy smiled at her from the stove. He'd changed into jeans and a sweatshirt, and had an apron tied around his waist. Two places were set at the kitchen table with yellow napkins and tall blue goblets. A bowl of blue and yellow daisies graced the table.

"Grandpa, it's beautiful." Jenny put the peaches in his fridge and seated herself, shaking a napkin into her lap. "What did you do today?"

"I had my swim and biked out to Cochrane and back, then went over to the seniors' center after lunch for a few games of cribbage." He removed the apron and sat down opposite her.

"Did you win?"

Paddy buttered a slice of warm homemade bread. "They're far too sharp for me, but I still love the place. They make me feel so young." He smiled at his granddaughter, saluting her with the buttered crust. "There was a sign on the bulletin board today, Jen. It said, 'Oh, to be seventy again!'"

Jenny laughed and took a bite of the bread, closing her eyes in bliss. "This is *so* good. I wish I could bake like you."

"It takes patience," he said. "A commodity you are regrettably lacking, my child."

"Hey, I'm getting better," she protested. "I'm a lot more patient than I used to be. In fact, I'm positively stodgy nowadays."

He gave her a thoughtful glance. "You're too young to be stodgy, Jenny-girl." There was a brief silence while he put oil and vinegar on his salad. "Tell me about this out-of-town job," he said at last.

"It's at a big ranch called Cottonwood Creek, about eighty miles southeast of the city."

"And why are they being audited?"

She shook her head. "You know I can't tell you any details, Grandpa."

"How long is this job going to take?"

Jenny finished her salad and reached for the bowl of stew. "At least three days. There's a huge volume of paperwork involved in running a business like that. All the payroll and expenses, depreciation on buildings and equipment, income from hundreds of individual sales of cattle, plus revenue from gas and oil wells and land rentals. It's very complex.''

"So will you drive back and forth every day?"

"No, I've been invited to stay at the ranch. But I'm afraid the invitation wasn't all that warm," she added with a rueful smile.

"I take it the rancher isn't thrilled about your visit?"

"That's an understatement." While she ate the rich beef stew, Jenny told her grandfather about the lunch with Clayton Alderson and the man's obvious annoyance over the coming audit of his books.

"Maybe he's the guilty party and he's afraid you're going to catch him," Paddy suggested.

"I doubt there's a guilty party at all," Jenny said. "It's probably just accounting errors. I think the man runs his empire like a supreme potentate and doesn't want anyone invading his privacy. Especially," she added wryly, "someone he probably looks on as a little snip of a woman."

"Oh, come on. You're no little snip," Paddy said. "You're a big strong girl, Jenny. A strapping wench."

She laughed. "Well, thanks a lot for that flattering description. You always make me feel better, Grandpa."

"So what's he like?" Paddy asked. "This rancher, I mean."

Jenny paused, considering. "Different," she said at last. "Not like any man I've ever seen."

"Different in what way?"

"Well, when he arrived, Lisa almost had a heart attack. She thought he was *so* handsome."

"Lisa thinks anything in trousers is handsome."

"I know. In fact," Jenny said with a teasing grin, "she frequently expresses admiration for your masculine charms."

"Well, *that*," he said placidly, "merely shows the child has excellent taste. What about you? Didn't you find this rancher attractive?"

"I don't know." Jenny frowned, considering. "I guess he's good-looking in a rugged kind of way. Tanned skin, white teeth, very intense dark eyes. Tall and well-built." She paused. "With lovely hands."

Paddy chuckled. "Sounds like Lisa wasn't the only one giving this fellow the once-over."

Jenny helped herself to more stew, feeling a little annoyed. "I didn't mean anything like that. I was just answering your question."

"Jenny..." His voice was serious.

"What?"

"It wouldn't hurt you to find a man attractive. There's nothing wrong with it, you know."

She looked down at her plate. "I'm finished with all that, Grandpa."

"Finished with it?" Paddy watched her shrewdly. "You're never going to fall in love and marry? No cute little great-grandchildren for poor old Paddy?"

"Oh, sure. Like you're concerned about great-grandchildren," she scoffed. "You're too busy breaking records in senior triathlons."

"That may be, but I want you to be happy, Jenny.

And I don't think you want to be alone all your life. You have too much to give."

She shook her head, still looking down at her plate. "All that ended for me when Steve died. I could never feel the same way about any other man. It wouldn't even be fair to try."

"That's ridiculous." Paddy said calmly. "There are lots of men you could love if you'd give them a chance and not shut yourself off from the world."

"Could *you* love somebody else? After all those years with Grandma when you were so happy together, could you love another woman?"

"Certainly I could." Paddy sipped from his water glass. "I get lonely too, you know. And your grandmother would have wanted me to find somebody, just as I'd have wished the same for her if the circumstances had been reversed. She wouldn't have expected me to be lonely for the rest of my life."

"Are you lonely?" Jenny asked, startled.

"Sometimes I am," he said. "Life is good, but I'd like to have someone to share the pleasures of my golden years. And you have a whole life ahead of you. It's ridiculous to spend it alone just because you have some romantic notion that you can never love again."

"Well, I don't believe I can," she said stubbornly. "Steve and I were soul mates. I could never love any other man the same way."

Paddy made an impatient gesture. "That's a lot of nonsense. Besides, Steve was—" He stopped abruptly.

"What?" Jenny asked, looking at her grandfather. "What were you going to say?"

"Nothing." Paddy began to clear the table. "Let's have some dessert," he said. "Did I see fresh peaches in that bowl?"

Jenny went to the fridge to get the peaches and yogurt, still thinking about her grandfather's words. But whatever Paddy had been on the verge of saying about Steve, she didn't want to hear it.

Instead, she changed the topic, asking him about his swim, telling him of Lisa's obsession with one of the young construction workers across the street from the office.

Soon they were talking and laughing again with their customary ease, and the strange little moment of tension between them passed without further mention.

CHAPTER FOUR

ON TUESDAY MORNING Jenny left home early and headed out to Cottonwood Creek, feeling her spirits lift as she drove into open country.

The sky was as gray as hammered platinum. While she drove, rain began to spatter the windshield of her Honda, increasing in tempo until she had to switch on the wipers to see the road. Her car radio issued warnings of stormy weather over the next few days and the possibility of flooding as the mountain water joined rivers already swollen by a record spring snowfall and heavy rains in April and May.

The towns and cities along the Bow River, the Milk River and the South Saskatchewan were apparently bracing for the crest of floodwaters. Volunteers, the radio said, were working frantically to reinforce dikes and pile sandbags near threatened homes.

Jenny looked around in astonishment as she listened to the radio. In a land so flat and barren, it was hard to believe flooding could ever be a concern. Most of the time, the prairie was so parched that summer winds carried suffocating clouds of dust into the horizon, and ranchers had to shuttle their herds back and forth between pastures to afford them enough water.

But this was always a country of excess. Too cold in the winter, too hot in the summer, too wet, too dry, too windy....

Jenny felt a brief pang of sympathy for the inhabitants, then thought of a man like Clay Alderson, who had to make his living from such a land. But he had lots of money, a fortune in land and cattle, and didn't need her sympathy. Besides, she had to remain objective about the job ahead of her.

She was out on the wide plains now, where there was nothing to see but the wet road in front of her, flanked by an endless row of power and telephone poles. Jenny looked around, relishing the spaciousness.

I should come out here more often, she thought. *On the weekend, I should just get in my car and drive until I'm in open country. It's so beautiful....*

But Jenny knew she'd probably never do that. Her life was too busy for her to find the time. On the weekends she had to do her laundry, help her grandfather with the house and yard and tend to her pets, shopping and housework.

Besides, if she ever came out here to walk or drive, it would be so hard to go back to the city again....

According to what the accountant had told her, this was probably Cottonwood Creek land all around her now, although it was almost another twenty miles to the main ranch buildings. She tried to imagine what it would be like to own such a vast sweep of land, and felt a twinge of envy for that handsome intense man who'd sat across the table from her, calmly eating his pasta.

To her left she saw a herd of buffalo grazing near the fence. The shaggy animals looked primitive and out of place, as if they'd accidentally wandered from the pages of history to stand near these rows of telephone poles. They huddled close together with heads lowered as the rain dripped from their massive shoulders and heads.

Jenny had read about the buffalo herd a few years ago in one of the city newspapers. They'd been acquired by the Alderson family in an attempt to protect and reestablish bison here on their native prairie. She recalled that it was a huge expense, because the animals required special fencing and handling.

In fact, the fence around the buffalo paddock looked to be about eight feet tall and heavily reinforced, while to her right the fencing was only a few strands of barbwire.

She thought again about the magnitude of this ranching operation and the complexity of the bookkeeping, and began to feel a little worried. Maybe three days wasn't going to be long enough, after all, to complete a full-scale audit. She wished she'd packed more clothes.

No point in worrying about that now, she decided. If necessary she could make a trip back to the city or have Paddy come out and bring her anything she needed. In fact, her grandfather would probably love an opportunity to visit a prairie ranch and go running on these open plains, far from cars and houses.

Finally she topped a rise and saw the main ranch buildings sprawled across the valley floor below. Despite advance warnings, she was still a little surprised by the size of the ranch. It really did resemble a small town, strung out along the winding banks of a waterway that must be Cottonwood Creek.

As Jenny drew nearer, she could see the trees that gave the creek its name, bending low over the water as they waved and tossed in the strong wind, their leaves wet with rain.

The ranch itself comprised acres of pens and corrals and long steel buildings that housed feed supplies, vehicles and machinery. Several rows of bungalows and wide mobile homes were ringed by tidy yards and white picket fences.

Small children in raincoats and rubber boots, played outside in the rain, laughing as they ran through the puddles. Vehicles moved around busily, mostly trucks hauling feed and fencing supplies, while cattle and horses stood quietly in the pens with rain glistening on their backs. It was a peaceful scene, and it felt almost surreal to stumble onto this place after all the miles of empty road she'd traveled.

Jenny passed the big ranch house, a three-story clapboard mansion with a deep pillared veranda, surrounded by more cottonwood trees and shrubs. Farther down the main road she came to a large square building made of rough logs, divided into two separate establishments. One was labeled Office, while the other appeared to be a postal outlet and general store dealing in work clothes, groceries and rented videos.

She parked and drew up the hood on her jacket, grabbed her briefcase and ran through the rain to the covered porch of the building. A couple of old cowboys in broad-brimmed straw hats sat on rocking chairs, watching her approach.

"Well, howdy," one of them said. "Lookin' for somebody?"

"I've come to see the bookkeeper." Jenny was glad she'd decided to wear jeans, boots and a sweater, instead of her normal office attire. She didn't feel quite so out of place.

One of the cowboys jerked a thumb over his shoulder. "Bridget's inside."

"You sure you want to waste your time with Bridget?" the other asked, giving Jenny a broad grin that revealed a couple of missing teeth. "We don't get to see many pretty young strangers around here. Why not set here a spell an' chat?"

The invitation sounded so warm that Jenny was both amused and flattered. "Well, thank you," she said with an answering grin. "Maybe later I'll be able to take you up on that."

"You do that," the cowboy told her. "You jest do that."

Jenny lingered for a moment to exchange small talk about the weather and the rising creek waters, then went into the office, took off her jacket and shook the rain from it.

A plump gray-haired woman got up from her desk and hurried to take the jacket, hanging it on a rack near the door.

"I'm Bridget Carlyle," the woman said nervously. "And you must be Ms. McKenna."

"Please, call me Jenny. So, how are you this morning?"

"Oh, I'm…I'm fine," the bookkeeper said, moving back to her desk.

But she didn't look fine at all. She looked pale and uneasy, making awkward little fluttery movements with her hands. Jenny watched the woman in exasperated sympathy, wishing her arrival didn't always reduce people to such a state of nervous tension.

Bridget Carlyle was probably about sixty, Jenny guessed, plump and sweet-faced, with a gentle smile and a pair of glasses hanging from a chain around her neck. She wore pleated slacks and a white blouse under a knit cardigan, and appeared to have taken some pains with her appearance.

Jenny became aware of a second person in the room, a thin dark-haired young woman with an alarmingly pale face and lips painted so dark they were almost black. She sat at another desk in a far corner of the office, watching the newcomer with a sullen expression.

"This is Teresa," Bridget said. "She drops in to visit me sometimes."

"Hi, Teresa," Jenny said.

The girl muttered something inaudible. Jenny was struck by Teresa's look of wariness and veiled contempt as she returned to the computer in front of her. She was playing some kind of video game and, ignoring the other two women, began to tap languidly on the keyboard.

Jenny turned back to Bridget. "Is there a place where I can work without being in your way?"

"Teresa, I'm afraid you'll have to move somewhere else," Bridget told the girl, "so Ms. Mc-Kenna…Jenny can use that desk."

Teresa again muttered something under her breath, got up and slouched outside, slamming the door behind her. Jenny watched her cross the porch without a word to the two old cowboys, who eyed her coldly. She headed off into the rain, hands in her jacket pockets, thin shoulders hunched, and wandered up the road toward the big ranch house.

"She doesn't have enough to do," Bridget said from behind Jenny. "She can't find anything to fill her days, so she hangs around bothering people."

"Who is she?" Jenny asked.

"Michael's girlfriend. That's Mr. Alderson's older son."

"Does Michael work at the ranch?"

Bridget nodded. "He's been on the payroll since he finished college. He brought Teresa here for a visit last fall and she just sort of stayed on."

"I see." Jenny looked at the long needles of water dripping from the porch roof. "It must be a hard place to live if you're not the kind of person who's happy with solitude and able to keep yourself busy."

"Yes, she doesn't seem all that happy here," Bridget said. "I don't know why she stays."

Jenny carried her briefcase to the empty desk and set it down while the older woman stood tensely, gripping her hands together.

"Now if you'll just tell me what you'll need," the bookkeeper said.

Jenny smiled. "You don't have to be nervous about

this, Bridget. I'm a perfectly ordinary person, not scary at all.''

Bridget smiled timidly. "Clay said you were nice, but still I've been worried about this ever since we got your letter.''

"He said that?" Jenny asked, startled. She felt her cheeks grow warm.

"Yes, he said he ran into you in an Italian restaurant somewhere after your meeting, and the two of you had lunch together.''

"Oh, he probably told you I was nice just to keep you from being scared," Jenny said, recovering her composure. "But I think you know, Bridget, that auditors like to eat bookkeepers for breakfast.''

She got the response she'd been hoping for. Bridget actually smiled, a shy grin that made her features light up. She really was an attractive woman, Jenny thought, hoping the bookkeeper could relax enough to make this job easier for both of them.

"I'll need your ledgers," she said, "and access to the files where you keep invoices and receipts. Also, I guess, the payroll records. That'll be enough to start with. Okay?''

"I've got everything ready." Bridget rushed to gather files and bound ledgers from a table along one wall, piling them on Jenny's desk. "And most of the files are on that computer, too.''

"You do full double entry?" Jenny asked. "Manual filing and computer?''

Bridget gave her a sheepish glance. "I just can't bring myself to trust computers. The thing could, I don't know, blow up, or something. Besides, our power supply goes out from time to time and stays off for hours. If the numbers weren't on paper, I couldn't sleep at night.''

Jenny tapped at the keyboard. A half-finished game of solitaire sprang onto the screen. She exited the game program, frowning. "People play games on the machine where you keep the records?''

"Yes, but nobody knows the password to the ranch files except Clay and me." With a furtive glance over her shoulder, Bridget scribbled it on a scrap of paper. "Here it is.''

Jenny hid a smile that was both amused and despairing as she looked at the paper. The password was "cotton.''

"Okay, I've memorized it,'' she said solemnly.

She tore the slip of paper into little bits and deposited them in the wastebasket. "Now if you could show me the program where the files are stored, and the ledgers for the first quarter of 1995, I can get started.''

Bridget opened the computer files and spread out the ledgers, taking half an hour to explain her bookkeeping system. Jenny, who'd been trained to do this, paid close attention and soon had a fairly clear grasp of Bridget's methods. To her relief she found that the records, although a little old-fashioned, were thorough and orderly.

"You've done a fine job of the books, Bridget,'' she said. "This shouldn't be a problem at all.''

Bridget's cheeks turned pink at the praise. "You really think so?'' she asked. "Because sometimes I think it's all getting to be…''

"What?" Jenny asked encouragingly.

Bridget shook her head and turned away. "Nothing," she murmured.

"Well, you should see the kind of bookkeeping messes I've had to untangle," Jenny said. "It'd make your hair stand on end. I always appreciate it when I find a nice neat set of books like yours."

Bridget seemed almost to glow. The telephone rang and she crossed the room to answer it, then had a brief discussion about hay bales and the rising water in the creek. At last she settled at her desk and began to enter a sheaf of bills while Jenny set to work.

Jenny loved this part of her job. Following an accounting path was like a treasure hunt. The numbers were clean and crisp, shining like beacons along a path, with profit-and-loss columns perfectly balanced at the end of the trail.

Human emotions could be tangled and murky, and motivations were often hard to understand, but you couldn't argue with numbers. To the trained eye they told a story fraught with danger and excitement, with hope and fear and triumph.

By the time an hour had passed, Jenny was beginning to form a picture of the way the ranch operated and was dazzled by its scope. She wondered if anybody, even Bridget who kept the books or Clay who ran the place, really understood how vast the operation was.

The ranch comprised seventy thousand acres, more than a hundred square miles of deeded family land, with an equally large area under lease. The cattle inventory held steady at almost three thousand head, and there were a hundred and fifty horses and three hundred bison. Fifty-six people were on permanent full-time payroll, and the number of part-time and seasonal employees could have formed a small army.

Expenses ran into the millions each year, primarily balanced by revenue from cattle sales, marketing of baled feed and huge rentals from the gas and oil wells on ranch property.

Jenny glanced at the plump little woman behind the other desk and thought of Clay Alderson eating his pasta with skillful twirls of a fork. Incredible, she thought, to realize that these two were mostly responsible for managing the business end of such a huge operation.

At that moment the office door opened, admitting a gust of damp wind and a noisy drumming of rain. Clay Alderson stood in the entry wearing a long yellow slicker that dripped onto the rubber mat. He carried a square tin patterned with flowers and kittens.

"Hello, ladies," he said, removing his hat and raincoat and setting the tin on Bridget's desk. "Polly sent me over with some doughnuts she just made."

Jenny looked up at him from behind the desk, momentarily at a loss for words. God, the man was handsome. In work boots, faded jeans and a denim shirt, dusty and liberally stained with grease, he was truly in his element, a man who belonged to the land.

"Hello, Ms. McKenna," he said quietly. "I'm glad you managed to get here safely in this weather."

"Call me Jenny, please," she said automatically.

"All right." He gave her a polite smile that didn't quite reach his eyes. "If you'll call me Clay."

"Jenny's already started on the books," Bridget

told him, opening the tin of doughnuts and sniffing at them appreciatively. "Polly makes the best doughnuts in the world."

"They certainly smell wonderful," Jenny said. She supposed Polly was the cook at the ranch house.

Clay Alderson took three mugs to the coffeemaker on the table, filled them and looked over his shoulder. "Cream and sugar?" he asked Jenny.

"Just black, please."

Bridget set a doughnut on her desk, then carried the tin to Jenny, who selected one of the warm sugary treats and bit into it with pleasure.

"Oh my," she said, "you're right. This is really delicious."

Clay brought her a mug of coffee and put it by the computer monitor. Again she was conscious of his hands, lean and graceful even though his fingers were stained with grease. He settled in a chair along one wall and sipped his coffee, booted feet extended, watching Jenny with a thoughtful gaze she found unnerving.

"What are you doing today?" Bridget asked him.

"I've been working over in the shed, trying to fix the big baler." He looked down at his hands. "Jack can't get the damned thing to knot, but I think we should have it figured out by lunchtime."

"Clay does most of the mechanical work around the ranch," Bridget told Jenny. "He's a genius with motors and things."

"I can see that," Jenny murmured, glancing up at him. "Your hands—" She fell abruptly silent, feeling awkward.

He watched her with that unsettling dark gaze. "What were you going to say, Jenny?"

"Just that you've got…" She floundered, staring at the computer screen to hide her discomfort. "I'm not surprised that you're good with mechanical things."

"He really is," Bridget said, munching hungrily on her doughnut. "Clay can fix anything."

The man continued to watch Jenny with an expression that made her feel increasingly nervous. She reached for another doughnut. "Is there any danger of serious flooding?" she asked.

He glanced out the window, frowning. "It's not looking good. If the creek keeps rising at this rate, most of our hay meadows will be underwater by the weekend. Which means," he added grimly, "that I'm probably wasting my time working on the baler."

"Oh, no," Bridget said. "Really, Clay?"

The rancher nodded and turned to Jenny again. "If we can't bale and sell the alfalfa, our revenues will be even lower this year. No doubt you'll be back to check the books again next spring."

"Not likely," she said, a little annoyed by his sarcasm. "After an audit as thorough as this one promises to be, I'm sure we can let a long time pass before we'll need to look at you again."

He met her eyes for a moment, then gestured at the desk with his coffee mug. "Has Bridget given you everything you need?"

"Yes, she's very well organized. I'm already fairly clear on the first quarter of last year." She paused. "But I'd also like to see the profit-and-loss statements for the six previous years just to serve as a basis of comparison.''

''That far back?'' Bridget looked alarmed.

''Is that a problem?''

Bridget and her employer exchanged glances. ''No,'' Bridget said. ''It's not a problem, but I'll have to go through the files in the storage room to find them. We keep the old records locked in a metal cabinet back there.''

''And the income tax forms for the past seven years? You've picked them up from the accountant's office?'' Jenny asked the rancher. ''I might want another look at them.''

Clay nodded. ''I've got them over at the house in a big cardboard box.'' He took a sip of coffee, watching Jenny over the rim of the cup. ''Saul said he'd be glad to come out while you're here if you need him for anything.''

Jenny shook her head. ''I can call his office if I need clarification, or e-mail him to have files transferred.''

''So you're all settled in?'' he asked. ''You don't need my help with anything else?''

Jenny gave him a polite smile. ''Bridget and I are getting along just fine.''

''Good.'' He set the empty coffee mug on the table, got to his feet and reached for his raincoat, shrugging into it. ''Then I'll get back to my baler.''

''Clay,'' Bridget said from her desk.

''Yeah?'' He paused with his hand on the doorknob.

''What about the creek? Are you really worried?''

He looked at her soberly. ''Sure I'm worried,'' he

said at last. "If the rain doesn't stop and the water keeps rising, some of those houses and corrals are going to flood."

Bridget's eyes widened in alarm. "What can we do?"

"Well, just in case, I've sent four of the boys to haul sand all day and bring out a load of sacks. If it gets bad, we'll have to get all hands busy filling and sandbagging, because nobody can come over to help us. All the ranches up and down the creek have problems of their own."

Jenny watched him in silence, wondering how he bore the weight of this responsibility on his shoulders. And in the midst of a flood he was also dealing with a full tax audit.

As if reading her thoughts, he turned to give her another of those cold, polite smiles. "I almost forgot. Polly wants both of you to come up to the house for lunch," he said. "If I get done with the baler on time, I'll see you there."

"Thanks, Clay," Bridget said. "Polly looks after them up at the ranch house," she told Jenny. "That's her husband, Joe, out there on the porch." She indicated one of the old fellows in the rocking chairs.

Jenny murmured her thanks for the lunch invitation and watched as Clay paused on the porch to chat with the cowboys. His face warmed and his teeth flashed white against his tanned skin. Then he was gone, striding across the porch to vanish in the flowing curtains of rain.

CHAPTER FIVE

THE RAIN STOPPED just before noon and the black clouds began to roll off toward the horizon, allowing a few rays of sunshine to glimmer through. By the time Jenny and Bridget left the office to walk up to the ranch house for lunch, the wet trees and swaying grasses along the path sparkled like diamonds in the midday light.

Jenny breathed deeply, loving the fragrance of sage and damp earth.

"Maybe there won't be so much danger of flooding if the rain stops," she said to Bridget who trotted at her side, trying to keep up.

Jenny smiled and slowed down, realizing that her legs were much longer than her companion's.

"It'll help a lot if the rain goes away." Bridget slowed her pace with obvious relief. "But that still won't stop the flood. Most of the water's coming down from melting snow in the mountains, and it's already on its way. The radio said they expect the water to crest by the weekend."

"Has the creek ever flooded like this before?" Jenny asked.

"Once or twice. I've been here more than thirty years and I can remember a few floods in that time, but not many.'' Bridget frowned at the rushing muddy water next to the path. "The creek's never been this high that I can recall."

Jenny thought again about Clay Alderson and the weight of responsibility he carried. "Are you worried about your own house?" she asked Bridget. "Will your basement flood, or anything like that?"

"I suppose it could. My cottage is pretty close to the creek. But I don't keep anything down in my basement," Bridget said, "except for some boxes of old clothes and things like that. I can easily move them upstairs. It's the hay meadows and the stock that are the really big worry, and all that machinery in the barns and outbuildings. Poor Clay," she added, her face puckering with concern.

Again Jenny felt an irrational guilt over the job she had to do. It was stressful enough to do an on-site audit at the best of times. But in a crisis like this, everybody at the ranch must see her as an unnecessary aggravation.

Still, when they arrived at the ranch house, the atmosphere was warm and hospitable. Maura Alderson, a regal-looking woman who, despite her diminutive height, strongly resembled her son, met them at the front door and smiled up at Jenny with frank admiration.

"My goodness," she said as she took their jackets and hung them in a closet. "Clay told me you were beautiful, but I had no idea."

Again Jenny felt that distressing touch of warmth in her cheeks.

These women had to be imagining things, or maybe

they got some obscure pleasure from teasing their guest. It was hard to believe Clay Alderson said such complimentary things about her to other people.

To *her*, he seemed anything but appreciative.

Jenny murmured something inane and followed her hostess into the living room of the ranch house, gazing around with a quick intake of breath.

The place was lovely, in the casual manner of homes belonging to people of wealth. The furnishings were massive, clearly chosen for comfort rather than style, upholstered in leather and grouped around a fieldstone fireplace that soared twenty feet to a cedar-lined ceiling.

Beautiful sculptures and art objects were displayed on oak side tables and bookcases, and western art adorned the walls. Jenny, who'd taken a few art courses in college, suspected that most of the paintings were originals. She longed to move closer and examine them but didn't want to be caught staring.

"My husband and I had most of the house renovated about twenty years ago," Maura said as Jenny looked around. "We knocked out some walls and ceilings and tried to modernize the place a little."

"It's lovely," Jenny said. "And you have so many beautiful things here."

"While Clint was alive we traveled a lot," Maura said casually, "and picked things up here and there."

Bridget moved through the living room with the ease of an accustomed guest. "So where is everybody?" she asked Maura.

"Polly's feeding us in the kitchen today. She said it didn't seem right to set a table in the dining room

when everybody's tired and dirty from packing sandbags.''

"Good," Bridget said. "I like eating in the kitchen.
Come on, Jenny, it's this way."

She led the way down a hallway floored in oak
parquet and covered with a Navajo-patterned runner
that matched the big rugs in the rooms they passed.
Jenny had an impression of space and luxury, of
warmth and solidness and a powerful sense of history.

The kitchen was filled with people, all talking noisily. Jenny entered the room with Maura and Bridget,
feeling awkward and conspicuous when all eyes
turned in her direction.

"Here she is now," Clay said, which gave her the
impression the group had been talking about her before she arrived. "Folks," he said, "this is Jenny Mc-
Kenna, the government auditor."

"Hello," Jenny murmured, smiling shyly at the assembled roomful of people and sliding into the chair
that Clay got up to hold for her.

"I don't know who all you've met," he began,
seating himself at the head of the table again. "Jenny,
this is my son Michael." He indicated a broad-
shouldered man on his left who looked like a younger
version of himself.

Jenny inclined her head in acknowledgment, and
when the young man smiled at her, she realized that
though they might be similar in looks, Clay Alderson
and his son probably had much different personalities.
Michael had a tense diffident look, with none of his
father's hard-edged confidence.

"And this is Michael's friend, Teresa," Clay said with a neutral expression.

Teresa lifted one corner of her black-painted mouth.

Jenny nodded. "Teresa and I have met."

"And my younger son, Allan," Clay went on.

"Howdy, ma'am," Allan said solemnly, leaning back in his chair and saluting her with a glass of milk. "I've just decided what to do with my life. I want to go to accounting school."

The room erupted in laughter, and Jenny smiled, as well.

Allan's appearance gave her a fairly clear idea of what Clay Alderson's wife must have been like. The rangy young cowboy was as blue-eyed and fair as his brother was dark, and he had an easy charm that was irresistible.

Even Clay grinned at Allan's joke, and once again his face was transformed. Then he continued around the table, introducing the rest of the group.

Jim Cole, the handsome blond ranch foreman, gave Jenny the sort of smile that indicated sexual interest. She murmured something noncommittal, finding Cole's reaction much less appealing than Allan's boyish flirtation. There was no room at all for emotional entanglements with the job she had to do, but Jim Cole looked like a man who saw romantic possibilities in any situation.

One of the old cowboys she'd met on the office porch was introduced as Joe Dagg, Polly's husband. Joe had removed his cowboy hat and had his gray hair neatly parted and brushed. The round tag of a tobacco pouch hung from his plaid shirt pocket.

He grinned at Jenny. "I've already met the lady," he said, glancing slyly over at his wife who stood near the stove. "In fact, Jenny says she wants to get to know me better."

Polly appeared behind his chair, hands on hips. She was a big woman with heavy arms, a shock of white hair and a kind, weathered face.

"You better not be flirting with no pretty young accountants, old man," she told him briskly. "And if I catch you hanging around that office, there'll be hell to pay."

"Seems like every guy in the room wants to flirt with Jenny," Allan complained over the guffaws of laughter, then gave Jenny another of his charming grins. "It's sure a good thing I'm man enough to handle all this competition."

Embarrassed by their boisterous teasing, which wasn't at all the reaction she'd expected from these people, Jenny glanced at Clay Alderson. He, at least, displayed no signs of wanting to flirt with her.

Instead, he frowned at his younger son. "That's enough, Allan," he said quietly. "Let's try to show our guest some courtesy, all right?"

Allan chuckled and subsided, but not before giving Jenny a cheerful wink.

"Dave and Myron and I filled two hundred and twenty-seven sandbags this morning after coffee break," he announced to the group, holding out his hands for Bridget's examination. "Look at my calluses, Bridget. I'm a wounded cowboy."

The bookkeeper snorted. "About time you did some work, you lazy pup."

But Maura leaned over to examine her grandson's callused palms, frowning at the fresh blisters. "Oh, dear. That must really hurt, sweetheart," she said. "You'd better come up to my room after lunch and I'll put some salve on them."

"Thanks, Gran." Allan made an impudent face at Bridget, then turned in his chair to smile winsomely at his grandmother, who patted his shoulder.

Jenny realized that despite his youth, Allan was practiced at manipulating women. His brother, Michael, on the other hand, sat staring at his plate while Teresa eyed the group with her usual sullen expression and said nothing.

Polly served lunch, which consisted of a green salad, a huge pot of chili and thick slices of fragrant homemade bread.

Jenny sampled her chili while Polly watched her closely from across the table. "It's delicious," she said. "Just wonderful."

Polly beamed. "That recipe's my own invention. I win the chili cook-off every year at the Wolf Hill rodeo."

"You didn't win last year," Allan said, reaching for more bread. "That new cook from the Bar S ranch won first prize."

"That's because he gave free beer to all the judges," Joe said loyally. "Polly's chili left his in the dust, and you know it."

Polly turned to her husband, her face softening with gratitude. Jenny caught the glance they exchanged

and smiled privately, warmed by the affection between the older couple.

At that moment she happened to catch Clay's eye
and found him studying her with an intent, thoughtful
expression she found unnerving. She looked away
quickly and listened to the conversation between Jim
Cole and Allan, who'd launched into a heated discussion about the upcoming Calgary Stampede.

"They should lower the entry fees," Cole was arguing. "It costs more than two hundred dollars to
enter one of the major events. Local cowboys can't
afford that kind of money."

"Then they shouldn't be riding in the Calgary
Stampede," Allan said, his mouth full of bread. "If
they can't play with the big boys, they should stay
out of the draw."

Jim's handsome face flushed. He stared at the
younger man in disbelief. "You think it's all right for
guys to come up from Texas and Oklahoma and win
all our prize money, just because they can afford the
entry fees and local cowboys can't?"

"It's not our prize money," Allan said. "The entry
fees make up most of the purse. If they enter, it's
their risk and their money."

"Like hell!" Jim exploded. "It's the added money
put up by the committee that makes the Calgary
Stampede one of the richest rodeos in the country.
It's not the damned entry fees."

"If they made it cheaper to enter, the Stampede
would be like any other dinky little amateur rodeo out
on the prairie," Allan said. "I think the only guys

who should enter the Stampede are the cowboys who can play in that league.''

''That's easy for you to say,'' Jim's face was red with anger. ''When you've got all the money in the world so you don't have to worry about two or three hundred dollars. It's just chicken feed to you, isn't it?''

Allan's usually good-natured expression turned hard, and Jim Cole's blue eyes flashed. Michael glanced nervously from one man to the other.

''Jim's right,'' Clay said quietly. ''Allan, you should learn to think about what you're saying before you're so quick to talk.''

''But I just…'' Allan glanced up rebelliously, then caught sight of his father's expression and stopped. He turned to his grandmother for support, but she ignored him, smiling at Teresa who was pulling a slice of bread apart and piling the pieces on a saucer.

''So, Teresa,'' Maura asked with wide innocent eyes, ''have you and Consuela finished setting out all those bedding plants?''

Teresa gave the older woman a venomous look and muttered something inaudible.

Maura leaned forward and said brightly, ''What was that, dear? I didn't quite catch it.''

''I said, it's too wet to work in the garden. The ground's a sea of mud.''

''Oh, dear, what a shame. Polly and I knew how much you were looking forward to it.'' Maura exchanged a mischievous glance with the housekeeper and returned to her bowl of chili.

Jim Cole helped himself to more bread, buttering

it with quick impatient gestures. But when he spoke, his voice was calmer and he seemed to have recovered from his argument with the boss's son.

"I estimate we're going to need at least ten or fifteen thousand sandbags," he told Clay, "just to protect the barns and machine sheds. More if we want to keep the water out of the hay meadows, too."

Allan groaned and looked down at his blistered hands.

Clay frowned. "The crest is supposed to get here by this weekend. Can we fill that many sandbags in four days, even with all hands working?"

Joe shook his head. "We can't have all hands filling sandbags," he said. "The cows and machinery got to be moved to higher ground just in case that big water comes. It'll take a lot of time."

Jim turned to the old cowboy. "Have you ever seen the creek this high, Joe?"

"It flooded real bad back in the fifties," Joe said replied, gazing out the kitchen window at the sky. "Made a hell of a mess, as I recall. But the creek wasn't moving like it is now. I don't like the look of this."

Michael said something in a low, tentative voice and Clay looked at him sharply. "What was that, son?"

"I said, maybe we should build some dikes. We could use tractors to move some of those old hay bales in place along the creek and cover them with dirt. Might be quicker than filling sandbags."

Clay studied his son thoughtfully. "Good thinking, Mike. It's worth a try, especially along the hay meadows. Pick a four-man crew and start working on it this afternoon, all right?''

Michael flushed at his father's praise and nodded eagerly, then glanced at Teresa who ignored him, still picking her bread apart.

''Hey, Mike,'' Allan said to his older brother. ''Can I be on your crew? It sounds a lot better than slaving all day filling sandbags.''

Michael hesitated. Jenny watched his thin dark face, wondering what the relationship was like between the two boys and if Michael would refuse his brother's request. Teresa, too, was watching intently

''Sure,'' Michael said at last. ''If you and Dave and Myron come over and work with me, we'll only need one other guy.''

Teresa's lip curled with scorn. She began to pick up the pieces of bread she'd piled and put them in her mouth, chewing with distaste as if the warm homemade bread were tasteless cardboard.

Bridget ate silently. Jenny watched her across the table, conscious of the tense, unhappy look on the bookkeeper's face when she thought herself unobserved. Bridget Carlyle seemed miserable, worried about something.

Maybe it was the flood, Jenny thought, or perhaps the stress of the audit. Although, judging from the tidy efficiency of the ranch ledgers, Bridget had nothing to fear.

Still, after a preliminary examination of the accounts, Jenny had already begun to develop a nagging suspicion that somebody involved in this ranching operation was in very deep trouble, indeed. She pushed the thought away, reluctant to draw any conclusions until all the facts had been explored.

"At least," Jim was saying to Clay, "this rain takes the pressure off that well at Sagebrush Flats. Both dugouts are full, so we shouldn't need to be pumping water into the trough until August at least."

"That's good." Clay glanced at Jenny again. "Because if Revenue Canada wants a lot more tax money from me, I don't think I can afford to sink a new well this year. Those cows will just have to go thirsty."

All gazes swung to Jenny, and she was uncomfortably reminded of her awkward position at the ranch.

"How's the audit going, anyhow?" Maura asked with the air of bright innocence that Jenny was beginning to recognize as a disguise for a sharp intellect. "Have you found any deep dark secrets in our books?"

"I've just begun," Jenny said quietly. "It's too early to tell anything about the accounts. But," she added, glancing at Bridget, "the ledgers have certainly been well kept."

Bridget flushed with pleasure. But her expression soon faded and she stared down at her plate again, looking worried and unhappy.

"How long will it take for you to draw some conclusions?" Clay asked.

Jenny felt a dangerous tug of sympathy. She was beginning to understand the man a little, and she could sense how much it frustrated him to have the audit proceeding on his own property, and have no choice but to wait for the outcome.

"I'd expected to finish by Thursday afternoon," she told him. "But I wasn't fully aware of the scope of your operation. I might have to stay through Friday afternoon. I hope that's not too inconvenient."

The words sounded lame even to her own ears. Her presence here could hardly be more inconvenient, considering how hard all of them were working to keep the rising creek waters at bay.

But Clay nodded courteously. "We'll be pleased to have you. Has my mother shown you your room?"

Jenny glanced at Maura, who shook her head. "We haven't gotten to that yet. I've put you upstairs in the yellow bedroom," she told Jenny. "I'm sure you'll be comfortable. Just have Joe bring your things up to the house, all right?"

"Thank you," Jenny murmured. "That's very kind of you." She cleared her throat. "I'm not sure that I have everything I'll need to stay the whole week, so I might have to call my grandfather to bring out a few things for me tomorrow."

"Your grandfather's Paddy McKenna, I believe?" Maura's eyes brightened.

"Yes," Jenny said.

"I'd love to meet him," Maura said warmly. "I've always admired him. In fact," she added, "I have a bit of a crush on him, just from seeing his photo in the newspapers."

Allan chuckled and patted his grandmother's shoulder. "Gran," he said affectionately, "you're so cute."

Maura ignored him, smiling at Jenny. "Tell your

grandfather to come for dinner tomorrow night,'' she said.

''Thank you,'' Jenny said. ''I'm sure he'll be pleased.''

Polly was serving huge slices of warm apple pie with wedges of cheddar. Jenny took a bite and wondered how much weight she was doomed to gain in her time at this place. She'd have to get up early tomorrow and go for a run. The thought of running on the prairie was so pleasant she found herself smiling.

Again she was conscious of Clay Alderson's dark intense gaze on her. She shifted uncomfortably in her seat.

He was unlike any man she'd ever met. Presiding at the head of his noisy table, the rancher had such a quiet commanding presence that everything seemed to revolve around him.

Involuntarily Jenny thought of her lost fiancé. At a meal like this, Steve would have dominated the conversation, telling stories of his adventures, dazzling all the women and charming most of the men with his exploits.

Jenny had usually been silent when Steve was around, obscured by the bright glow of his personality and his accomplishments. But it had been more than enough simply to sit next to him, to be the one he'd chosen.

Now, for the first time, she found herself wondering if Steve had seemed as wonderful to other people as he always had to her. She tried to remember what he looked like and could only recall his face in the photograph on her desk at work.

She realized with a little start of alarm that she'd forgotten to bring the photo with her, though she usually packed it whenever she traveled. She liked to set it on her bedside table so she could see Steve when she fell asleep in a strange place and remember how it had felt to be in his arms, kissing him…

Clay Alderson glanced at her again, his eyes piercing and faintly amused, as if he could read her thoughts. Jenny lowered her gaze to her plate, suddenly anxious for the meal to be over.

Numbers were so much easier to deal with than people, she thought wistfully.

In a roomful of talk and emotion like this, she often felt out of place and unsure of herself, but she was always comfortable with numbers. She could hardly wait to get back to the office, away from this crowd of people, and dive back into the ranch ledgers again.

CHAPTER SIX

MERCIFULLY THE RAIN showed promise of holding off at least for the rest of the day. Clay left the ranch house after lunch, fitting a hat on his head as he ran down the steps of the veranda and headed for his truck.

He had so many things to do that he couldn't decide where to begin. Workmen had to be given jobs, sandbagging crews needed to be assembled, contingency plans made in case of total disaster.

He climbed behind the wheel, his mind busy.

Mike's suggestion about building a dike out of hay bales was excellent, but it needed to be checked out carefully. If they were going to use last year's good-quality bales to stop the floodwaters, they might as well let the creek cover the hay meadow and destroy this year's crop, instead. Unless they could—

Somebody tapped on the truck windshield, interrupting his thoughts. It was Jim Cole, and Clay gestured for him to get in.

The foreman settled into the passenger seat and stretched his long legs, sighing.

"So what's the plan?"

"Well, I sure can't afford to spend any more time

tinkering with machinery," Clay said. "Not the way that water's coming up today."

"If Joe's calling for high water," the foreman said, "we'd better start building dikes. He's never wrong about the weather."

Clay drummed his fingers on the wheel, brooding about the sprawling ranch with its many corrals and outbuildings. "A flood is a hell of thing," he muttered. "The water goes everywhere and does so much damage. And afterward it's still not over, because you've got all that rotten sludge to clean up."

The foreman nodded in sympathy. "So what are you planning to do first?"

"I guess the main priority has to be the houses. Could you look after that, Jim? Get together a crew, take as many men as you need, decide which places are at immediate risk and start sandbagging to protect the houses along the creek. We'll try to keep water out of their basements and hope like hell they don't have to be evacuated."

"Okay. And I'll get Joe to take over moving all the stock and machinery."

"Thanks, Jim," Clay said. "I couldn't manage without you."

The foreman waved a hand dismissively. "Are you going to try Mike's idea for the hay meadows?"

"I'm about to check on that. And I think I'll ask Joe if he—"

Again Clay stopped abruptly, this time distracted by the sight of Bridget emerging from the house with the young tax auditor. They stood on the veranda talking to Maura, who looked cheerful and animated.

"She's quite a looker, that accountant." Jim eyed Jenny McKenna's tall slim body and auburn hair. "I wouldn't mind having a little of that down in my cabin to keep me warm at night."

Clay felt a tug of annoyance. "The woman's here to do a job," he said. "I think it's best to leave her alone, Jim."

The foreman glanced at his boss with a cheerful smile. "Come on now, Clay. You have to admit she's pretty cute, that girl. She looks like a real sweet armful."

"Yeah, she looks just fine." Clay grinned back. "And I want you ladykillers to keep away from her."

"Seriously?"

"You bet. I want all of you to leave her alone while she's here. If you're still interested when she gets back to the city, call her then."

Jim chuckled and pulled his battered Stetson lower over his eyes, sprawling in the passenger seat.

"Is that understood?" Clay asked.

"Yeah, sure," the foreman drawled, still grinning. "It's understood. But if that girl comes looking for me, I sure won't kick her out of my house."

Both men turned to watch Jenny and Bridget start down the path toward the ranch office. The day was warm and humid after the rain, and Jenny paused to take off her jacket, revealing a yellow T-shirt tucked into faded jeans. Her waist was slender, her breasts high and firm under the soft cotton.

Jim whistled softly. "I'll wait till next week like you say," he told his boss, "but then, watch out! That girl ain't gonna know what hit her."

Clay ignored the other man, his attention focused on Jenny as she moved down the path. Her hair shone red in the sunlight, blazing against her yellow shirt and the green backdrop of trees. He noticed the way she shortened her long stride to accommodate Bridget, and bent her head to listen to the older woman.

She's a nice person, he thought involuntarily, and felt a sudden pang of uneasiness.

Clay drove the foreman down to the barn to get his own truck, then headed over to the hay-storage sheds. These consisted of nothing more than a long roof supported on tall legs; the bales were stacked beneath.

These feed supplies were precious to any rancher. They helped him sustain his cattle in winter blizzards when the pasture was buried under three feet of snow, and in summer droughts when the native grass was parched and withered.

A rancher without an ample stock of baled feed was like a businessman with no operating capital, dependent on credit and the generosity of others for his survival. And Clay Alderson hated being dependent on anybody.

While he was considering, Michael parked a truck nearby and walked over to stand near his father, trailed by Allan and a couple of sturdy young workmen.

Clay glanced at his older son. "A lot of these bales are three or four years old, son," he said. "Not good for much except winter bedding."

"I know." Michael kicked one of the blackening

feed stacks with his boot. "So would it be okay to use them for a dike?"

"I think we might as well give it a try." Clay smiled. "Have you got any idea how you're going to build this thing, Mike?"

"I made a few sketches up in my room last night," Michael said. "I think if we start with a base of three, then two and a top course of one, and cover it all with dirt, it should hold if the dirt has a couple of days to dry."

Clay wondered what the surly Teresa had been doing while Mike was designing dikes. She hardly ever left the boy alone when he was off work. Instead, she pestered Michael without mercy until he finally yielded and took her into town to "find some action," as she said.

But Clay didn't want to think about his son's relationship just now. It distressed him that Mike, who was so shy and sensitive, had somehow tied himself up with a woman like Teresa. The relationship wasn't doing the boy any good, but Mike was of legal age and well able to make his own choices without interference. Still, there were times Clay had to force himself to back off and keep his opinions to himself.

He glanced over Mike's shoulder at the other three young men. "Mike's got a pretty good idea how he wants to build this dike," Clay told them, mostly addressing Allan. "So I'm putting him in charge and I want you guys to do just as he tells you. Okay?"

Both Dave and Myron nodded and agreed readily.

"Allan?" Clay asked.

"Sure," Allan said cheerfully. "I'll do just what Mike tells me. Mikey's the boss."

Clay examined his handsome younger son thoughtfully. "Good. Don't forget it," he said, then left the four men and got into his truck, watching in the rearview mirror as they went into the feed shed.

Clay had a hundred things to do, but as he drove back up the creek road, he stepped on the brake, then shifted his truck into neutral and parked. He got out and crossed to a little clearing enclosed by a wrought-iron fence.

The ranch cemetery was well tended, with wild rosebushes planted here and there among clumps of daisies nodding in the wind. Cottonwood branches hung low over the iron railing, casting the lichen-splashed grave markers into dappled shade.

Clay let himself in through the gate and began to walk. He saw his father's and grandfather's headstones, and those of uncles, aunts and his younger brother, Michael, who'd died of leukemia when he was nine.

He paused by a newer marker, a small stone of white marble grained with pink.

Suzanne Elaine Alderson, the headstone read. Beloved infant daughter of Clayton and Eleanor Alderson. 1984–1986. She Was the Joy of Our Lives.

Clay took off his hat and twisted it in his hands, staring at the gravestone. Tears burned behind his eyelids, even though it had been years since he'd last cried at Suzy's grave.

He glanced up restlessly and caught sight of the boiling creek waters, much higher on the banks than they'd been this morning. For the first time he wondered if the cemetery might be threatened along with the rest of the ranch. Clay looked at the quiet enclosure with its well-tended graves and Suzy's little marble headstone, then shook his head.

There were more important things to think about. He couldn't start allocating men and materials to protect the family graveyard when the waters might never rise that high. The concerns of the living were most important, after all.

Clay left the graveyard and drove to the main ranch buildings. He joined a crew of weary ranch workers near the barn who, along with their wives and children, were laboring to fill thousands of plastic sandbags.

He spent the afternoon with the workers, knowing it encouraged them to see their boss working just as hard as everyone else, fighting at their sides to save the homes along the creek.

But while he worked, his mind kept going back to Jenny McKenna and the job she was doing up there in the ranch office with Bridget.

He was no fool, and he realized now that he'd had an uneasy feeling in his gut for a long time about the state of the ranch finances. Something didn't smell right in those balance sheets. But he'd ignored the discrepancy, kept trusting his accountant and bookkeeper and telling himself if there was a problem he'd be told about it soon enough.

Now he recognized this as a careless, possibly even fatal mistake.

He should have hired an independent auditor to get

to the bottom of the matter long before the government intervened, and found out for himself why those revenues were dropping. But he was always so busy, and the thought of possible financial wrongdoing by somebody in his employ was so repugnant to him that he'd kept thrusting the problem aside.

Besides, Clay was unnerved by the presence of this government auditor, who was so quiet and competent, so strangely implacable despite her youth and wholesome good looks. Jenny McKenna was like a machine installed up there in his office, going relentlessly through the books.

And she was certainly no pushover when it came to men. Jim Cole might believe he could cozy up to her whenever he chose, but Clay had his doubts. The young accountant, though courteous, had a reserved manner that didn't respond at all to flirting.

Clay thought again about the framed picture on her desk. She must still be in love with her mountain climber, if she kept his picture where she could always see it. Another reason, he supposed, she didn't respond to flirting.

He actually found himself feeling a little envious of what the dead man had had. Because she was a true-blue thoroughbred, this Jenny McKenna.

Embarrassed by his wandering thoughts, Clay paused to lean on his shovel, remove his cap and swipe an arm across his damp forehead. He accepted a drink of water from a group of children hauling snacks in a wagon, then went back to work.

Clay shoveled sand into the damp plastic sacks with renewed energy, trying not to think about Jenny

McKenna's green eyes and shy smile or her tall lithe body and shapely breasts under the yellow T-shirt. Or that in a few hours he'd be joining her at the ranch house for dinner.

To say nothing of the fact that before long, this woman was probably going to tell him something about his ranching operation that he dreaded to hear.

JENNY WAS SO DEEP in her work, she didn't realize at first that Bridget was trying to get her attention.

"Hmm?" she said at last, glancing away from the computer screen to scribble a few notes in a spiral notebook.

"I'm leaving now," Bridget said, gathering up her sweater and handbag. "It's almost four-thirty. I want to go home and see if they've got any sandbags around my house yet."

"All right," Jenny said absently, looking down at her notebook. "Will I see you at dinner?"

Bridget shook her head. "I only go there in the evening for special occasions. Normally I make something at my own place or go over to the cookhouse."

"The cookhouse?"

"There's a married couple here who cook for all the single ranch hands. Their food's really good."

"That's right. I remember where you've entered the invoices for their supplies." Jenny thought about dinner with the Alderson family and felt a brief stirring of alarm. "So who's going to be at the ranch house tonight?"

Bridget considered. "It's hard to tell. Mike and Teresa usually go to town in the evening, and Allan likes to eat in the cookhouse with the ranch hands.''

Jenny thought about the big dining room she'd glimpsed through an open doorway, with its massive carved oak table and chairs. She tried to picture herself eating all alone there with Clay Alderson and his mother.

"Of course," Bridget said thoughtfully, "Polly tells me Maura likes to eat dinner on a tray in her room and watch television most weeknights, so it might be just you and Clay."

Please, God, Jenny thought fervently, *don't let it be just me and Clay. Please, please...*

"Is there anything else you need from me right now?" Bridget asked.

Jenny looked at the pile of forms and ledgers on the desk. "Not that I can think of. I'm going back through these older tax returns just now, and everything I need is right here."

Bridget paused in the doorway. "How long are you going to keep working?"

"Not long. Pretty soon I'll pack it in and go up to the house, I guess. Polly said dinner was be at seven."

"Just lock the door when you go out, all right?"

"Sure thing." Jenny smiled at the bookkeeper, who gave her a timid smile in return, then turned and headed out into the prairie afternoon.

Jenny got up and crossed to the window to watch Bridget walk away. The bookkeeper's shoulders were slumped and her pace was slow, despairing, as if she could barely summon the energy to put one foot in front of the other.

No wonder, Jenny thought, frowning as she went back to the stacks of ledgers. Because, by now there was little doubt in her mind that there'd been some serious wrongdoing at the Cottonwood Creek ranch.

The numbers were impossible to argue with. For years and years, as far back as she explored, the ranching operation had chugged along at a steady pace, smooth and well managed, with low-income years balanced by periods of prosperity in a fairly predictable cycle and, except for inflation, with expenses staying level.

But then in the last two tax years, profits had taken a sharp nosedive with nothing to explain the loss of revenue. Land purchases were down, expenses and payroll remained steady and cattle prices were up. Still, at least three hundred thousand dollars, possibly more, was missing from the revenue side, and Jenny couldn't find it anywhere.

She thought about Clay Alderson's explanation, that ranching was a cyclical business and he'd assumed the missing profits were being plowed back into land. This wasn't an outlandish concept for a man who ran his huge operation in such a hands-on fashion and left the bookkeeping to others. In fact, it might be completely honest.

Or it might be a clever defense, established in advance by the rancher to protect himself in case he was ever charged with tax fraud.

Jenny punched a few more numbers into the computer and frowned at the screen, thinking about the people who lived and worked in this isolated place.

Bridget had to have noticed the missing revenues,

even though it wasn't the bookkeeper's job to concern herself with profit and loss. Her only obligation was to keep the books in an orderly fashion, record the ranch expenses and revenues, and deliver all the numbers to the city accountant who filed the tax returns.

But she'd been doing the books for thirty years. Why hadn't she said anything when she saw the entries on the profit side dropping in recent years while expenses held steady?

It was difficult to imagine Bridget Carlyle stealing from her employer. During her career as an auditor Jenny had encountered a lot of white-collar criminals, and Bridget didn't fit the profile in any way. She lived modestly and alone, and was fiercely loyal to her employer.

Unless Bridget had some secret life, she was an unlikely embezzler.

Still, Clay and Bridget were the most probable culprits since they had the readiest access to the books. But a lot of other people lived in this place, and any one of them might be guilty of the crime. Cottonwood Creek's accounts were certainly insecure by modern business standards.

Jenny wasn't here to track down an embezzler, however. Her job was simply to determine whether something illegal had taken place and find out how it could have been done. At that point she would turn over her findings to federal officials who would conduct a criminal investigation and lay charges.

Jenny's head began to throb. She rubbed her temples with her fingertips and stared at the computer screen. The numbers were still a mystery to her, like a code she couldn't break.

But she was good at her job. In fact, she already had a glimmering of an idea, a trail to follow. The embezzlement of the ranch funds was so clever and elusive she couldn't yet tell where the revenues were vanishing, but she knew she'd find out before she left Cottonwood Creek.

It was just a matter of time.

CHAPTER SEVEN

WHEN AT LAST Jenny dragged herself away from the pile of old tax returns and left the office, it was past six and the prairie day had grown quiet and mellow. The light, too, had begun to change, deepening to a golden flood that spilled long shadows across the roads and fields.

She was deeply conscious of the light as she strolled up the path to the ranch house. Here in this open space it was almost a tangible thing, a part of the scenery, like the vast sky filled with puffy clouds and the distant horizon shrouded in a soft violet mist.

Despite her worry over the audit and the disturbing things she was finding, Jenny's heart swelled with pleasure at the space and freedom. A red-tailed hawk soared overhead, dipping and lifting on currents of air. The only sounds were the muted lowing of distant cattle and the rush of water from the nearby creek.

The creek seemed a little higher and wider than it had at noon, but the sprawl of buildings and corrals remained peaceful in the late-afternoon stillness. It was hard to believe that any real danger threatened.

Or that any kind of greed and crime existed here, Jenny thought grimly as she climbed the steps of the ranch house to the wide front door.

She hesitated, realizing that if she rang the bell, Polly would probably have to leave her work in the kitchen and come through the house to answer. After a moment she walked along the veranda, down the steps and into the back yard. Massed shrubs and rose trellises bordered a fieldstone terrace with a huge oval swimming pool.

She knocked at the kitchen door and smiled when Polly answered, her face registering astonishment.

"Well, Jenny, for goodness' sake!" the house-keeper said. "Why did you come all the way around to the kitchen door?"

"I thought I'd save you some steps. I know how busy you are." Jenny walked into the kitchen and sniffed the air. "What smells so good?"

"Venison in red wine sauce." Polly beamed. "And we're having potato croquettes and green beans with almonds. Are you hungry?"

"Starving. I can't wait." Jenny went through the kitchen, then hesitated by the door. "Did Joe get time to bring my suitcases up?"

"Your bags are right up there in the yellow room waiting for you. Just go down that hallway and take the back stairs. It's the first door to your left when you get to the second floor."

"Thank you. Should I..." Jenny paused awk-wardly. "Do they...dress for dinner?"

The housekeeper laughed, a rich booming sound. "My goodness, child, this isn't Southfork! If Clay's been doing a real dirty job," she added more gently, "he'll put on a clean pair of jeans before he eats, but you sure won't see any neckties or evenings gowns in the dining room.''

"Good," Jenny said with relief. "Because I'm not the evening-gown type."

Polly looked at her with obvious approval. "Anybody could tell that," she said.

Jenny smiled back, warmed by the older woman's friendliness. "Who's going to be at dinner, Polly?"

The housekeeper stirred a pot of bubbling sauce at the stove. "Well, Joe and I always eat dinner here in the kitchen, and Jim Cole's going down to the cookhouse tonight to eat with his sandbag crew. And Teresa and Michael have left for town."

She paused to taste the sauce and added a sprinkling of salt.

"All the way to Calgary?" Jenny said. "It seems like a long drive just for one evening's entertainment."

"Teresa gets restless," Polly said briefly. "She has a hard enough time filling her days here at the ranch. In the evenings she practically goes out of her mind."

Jenny thought about the bored discontented girl who was involved with Clay's older son. She had a brief flash of Teresa sitting at the computer where all the ranch accounts were filed....

"And Maura's having dinner upstairs in her room, watching the Cheyenne rodeo on television. Allan's eating with her." Polly gestured at a couple of trays on the table, already fitted with plates and heavy silver cutlery.

Jenny frowned. "So that means..."

"I guess it'll be just you and Clay in the dining room," Polly said casually. She carried a saucepan over to the trays, put venison medallions on the two plates and spooned sauce over them, then added the parsley-covered potato croquettes. "It'll be nice for him to have some company for a change."

Jenny heard the front door open and close, and the sound of booted feet on the hardwood floor. She murmured something and fled, running up the flight of back stairs to the yellow bedroom.

HER ROOM WAS as solid and beautiful as the rest of the house, with a fringed carpet on a floor of gleaming hardwood, an upholstered window seat that overlooked the prairie and a little stone fireplace with a Charles Russell painting above the mantel.

Jenny approached the painting and looked up in awe, wondering if it was an original. She hoped not, because it would be too intimidating to sleep in the same room with something so valuable.

As she hurriedly undressed and showered, she thought about the paradox of Clayton Alderson's ranching operation. This situation wasn't completely unfamiliar to her of course. In her job she occasionally saw similar places, businesses worth a lot of money but very short on operating capital.

If Clay ever sold his ranch, he'd be a millionaire many times over even after the bank debts were paid off. But as long as he held on to this sprawling place he'd probably find himself strapped for cash during the lean years unless he sold the family silverware or some of the priceless artwork.

Or hid some of the profits to avoid taxes.

She stared at the contents of her suitcase, wondering what to wear for dinner.

Not that she'd brought much to change into. It had never occurred to her that she might be dining alone with her host in a room decorated with Remington bronze sculptures.

Finally she settled on a simple white blouse and khaki skirt, brushed her hair and put on a pair of copper earrings, then descended the staircase reluctantly to the main floor.

Clay was already in the dining room, sitting alone at the head of the table and sipping wine. He wore a dark shirt, faded blue jeans and moccasins. Apparently he, too, had just showered, because his hair was damp and showed the neat tracks of a comb.

He didn't see her as she hesitated in the doorway, so she studied him for a moment, noting his sculpted face and well-shaped mouth, his brooding expression. Sitting alone in his beautiful old home, Clay Alderson seemed tired and strangely vulnerable. He looked up just then, and she felt a touch of embarrassment, as if caught spying on the man during a moment of unguarded intimacy.

"Hello, Jenny," he said, his eyes lighting with admiration as she came into the room. But the look was instantly replaced by his usual withdrawn courtesy.

"Hello." Jenny sat down and shook a linen napkin into her lap. "It looks like everybody's eating somewhere else tonight."

At least Polly hadn't set her place all the way down at the other end of the table. She would have felt awfully silly sitting ten feet from him and carrying on a shouted conversation. But her plate was at the side of the table, close enough to talk comfortably but far enough away to avoid any feeling of intimacy.

"I often eat dinner alone," he said. "Would you like some wine? Polly tells me it's zinfandel and goes well with venison."

Jenny held out her wineglass. "I'm really not much of a wine buff," she said. "White or red, that's about all I know."

He smiled and his face softened for a moment. "Me, too."

She watched as he filled the glass, slightly awed by the fine crystal. "There are so many beautiful things in this house."

"My family's lived here for a long time, and every generation has added something," he said.

"Every generation?"

"My great-great-grandfather arrived from Scotland in 1869, just two years after Confederation. At one time the ranch was almost half a million acres, running cattle all the way down across the Montana border. The spread's been whittled down considerably since then."

"It's still huge." Jenny sipped the wine and smiled at Polly who carried a pair of huge silver trays into the room. "Even after studying the books all day, I can hardly grasp the extent of the operation."

Clay watched as Polly set platters of food on the table. "These big old family ranches are pretty much a thing of the past. Nowadays they're mostly operated by American corporations."

"Anything else?" the housekeeper asked, picking up the now-empty trays.

Clay shook his head. "It looks delicious, Polly. Thank you."

"Just give us a shout if you need something. Joe's out in the kitchen helping me do the dishes."

Clay and Jenny both smiled at the cook as she left. A silence fell, broken only by the measured ticking of the big grandfather clock in the corner.

"It must be lonely," Jenny finally said, "eating in here by yourself every night."

He looked at her thoughtfully and she felt her cheeks warm. She hadn't intended to start such a personal conversation, but there was something about the man that unnerved her, made her utter things she wouldn't normally say.

"It's often lonely out here," he said, passing her one of the platters of food. "My wife used to hate it. She said no woman should ever have to live in such a godforsaken place."

Jenny was startled to see an expression of intense sadness cross his face. But the emotion vanished as quickly as it came, replaced by his usual air of reserve.

She was beginning to realize there were many aspects to this man, depths of emotions he kept carefully concealed. She looked down at her plate, wishing the meal was over.

"Your wife," she said awkwardly, cutting into one of the venison medallions with a bone-handled knife. "I assume she wasn't a ranch girl?"

Clay shook his head. "I met her at college. We

married when we were very young, and it was a mistake for both of us.''

Questions crowded Jenny's mind, but all of them threatened to carry their conversation to a more intimate level than she found comfortable. She opted for caution.

''What did you study at college?'' she asked.

''English literature.''

''Really?''

He grinned, and the weathered creases around his eyes deepened with amusement. ''You look so surprised. I've always liked reading.''

''So do I.'' She looked down again to avoid his smile. ''This venison is really delicious, isn't it?''

He murmured agreement, then said, ''I think Teresa feels the same as my wife. She finds the ranch a lonely place. Too lonely.''

Jenny raised her eyes. ''Teresa seems…not very well suited to life on a ranch,'' she said, then wondered if she was being presumptuous, passing judgment on somebody who was practically a member of his family.

But Clay nodded and fingered the stem of his wineglass. ''That's your opinion, too, is it?'' He sighed. ''I don't know what to do about Mike and that girl. I hate to see him make such a mistake.…''

Jenny chewed and swallowed another piece of meat, then finally decided to take a risk. After all, she was only going to be here for a few days, so it didn't really matter what she said.

''It seems odd,'' she said, ''that you let them live

together in your house if you don't approve of their relationship.''

He surprised her by nodding. "Yes. I've often thought about that, but my choices are pretty limited. If I forbid her to live at the ranch, Mike will leave. He's obsessed with Teresa for some reason. And I don't want him leaving, because this place is both his home and his future.''

Jenny listened, fascinated.

"If I gave them one of the cottages to live in,'' Clay went on, "I wouldn't have them under the same roof with me, but in a way I'd be giving their relationship my tacit approval. So I just let her keep staying here at the house as if she's a guest.''

"And keep hoping that eventually she'll leave, like all guests do?" Jenny asked with a smile.

He smiled back and their gazes met and held for a moment. Jenny was the first to look away, distressed by the girlish fluttering of her heart. But she found herself thinking about his well-shaped mouth…

"Have you called your grandfather yet?" he asked.

Jenny nodded, grateful for the change of subject. "I phoned just before I came downstairs. He's coming out tomorrow afternoon and staying for dinner. It was very nice of you to invite him.''

"That was my mother's doing.'' Clay reached for a roll. "But I'm looking forward to meeting him.''

"If I know Grandpa, he'll probably want to pitch in and help fill sandbags,'' Jenny said.

"Well, he'll be very welcome. We need all the help we can get.''

"You're really worried, aren't you?" she asked.

"It's a pretty serious situation. My first priority is keeping the houses dry and safe. But there's also stock and machinery and feed supplies to think about, and all of them will be at risk if the water gets as high as they're predicting."

Again she thought about the problems she was adding to this man's burden as she sat in his office and went through the ranch books. But she had to fight against this treacherous sympathy, because, she reminded herself, Clay Alderson might well be the author of those problems, and deserving of whatever happened to him as result.

She felt more at ease with a lighter topic, so she remarked again how delicious the meal was, then added ruefully, "But I'm going to need some exercise pretty soon. I've been eating more rich food than I'm used to."

"I think you told me you go running with your grandfather in the morning," he said, reaching for the silver butter dish.

Jenny was amazed that he'd remember such a small detail from their conversation in Calgary. "Yes," she said, "I usually do."

"So are you planning to go out for a run tomorrow?"

She hesitated. "I'd really like to, but I don't want to be in the way or anything. And I don't want to find myself…out in a bull pasture, or something."

He grinned in a way that made her think he was recalling a private joke. But then his expression became gentle and disturbingly intent.

"No," he said, "I wouldn't want that to happen to

you, either. How about if I take you out tomorrow and show you a safe place for an early-morning run?''

''Would you be running with me?'' she asked.

He chuckled, the first time she'd ever heard him laugh. For a moment he looked young, almost carefree. ''I'm not a runner, Jenny,'' he said. ''I get enough exercise in a normal day's work.''

She was suddenly conscious of his broad muscular shoulders, his lean body and callused hands. ''I'm sure you do.''

''But I'll be happy to drive you out on the prairie and show you a couple of safe trails if you like. How far do you run?''

''Grandpa and I usually do about two miles.'' Polly arrived just then with coffee and dessert, and Jenny smiled at her.

''All right,'' Clay said. ''I know just the place. What time would you like to go?''

''Is six o'clock too early?''

His eyes sparkled over the rim of his coffee cup. ''In summer, that's midmorning for me. I'll wait for you out front, all right?''

''Thank you very much.'' She began to eat her chocolate mousse.

''Anything else I can do for you?'' he asked courteously. ''Do you have everything you need?''

''Well…I forgot to bring a book to read,'' Jenny said, suddenly feeling a bit shy again. ''And I can't fall asleep without reading in bed for a while. I think I saw a library today when we were here for lunch.''

''It's in the room right next door and pretty well stocked. What do you like to read, Jenny?''

They spent a few minutes discussing books and favorite authors, a conversation that was particularly amiable because they apparently shared a similar taste in literature.

At last Clay pushed himself to his feet. "Well, this has been very pleasant," he said. "It's a treat for me to have such enjoyable company over dinner. But if you'll excuse me, I have to do some paperwork and then check on those sandbags. Help yourself to any of the books that interest you."

Then he was gone, padding silently out of the room in his soft moccasins, carrying his coffee cup, which he'd refilled. Jenny sat alone at the table and watched him disappear.

Her smiled faded and she looked down at the heavy linen tablecloth. The thought that crossed her mind was surprising. *If only I were here under different circumstances....*

CHAPTER EIGHT

SOON AFTER SUNRISE the next morning Clay walked along the banks of Cottonwood Creek in the slanting rays of thin daylight. He studied the horizon with a practiced eye and saw clouds building on the western horizon.

Probably going to rain before noon, he thought. That was all they needed, more water to add to this desperate situation.

By now he realized the flood really was reaching critical proportions. Cottonwood Creek was predicted to crest by the weekend. It was only Wednesday and the water boiled along, much higher than the previous day, already slipping over the bank in places.

Unlike the clear trickle that usually meandered through his ranch property, this was a muddy deluge, carrying small trees and scraps of lumber along with it, even a few carcasses of animals caught unaware by the flood.

Clay stood brooding at the edge of the high swift-flowing water, thinking about the precautions they were taking and the thousands of sandbags that still needed to be filled if they were to hold the waters at bay.

Mike's little engineering project over in the hay

meadow was looking more sensible all the time. Clay felt a surge of gratitude to his older son, along with a small stirring of relief. For the first time in years he had the feeling that somebody else besides Jim Cole was taking a bit of the responsibility from his shoulders. But the relief was only fleeting, because the welfare of this business and all its employees still remained in his hands.

He glanced east toward the hay meadow, squinting in the sunlight. From this distance the dike of soil and hay bales looked pitifully inadequate against the ominous rush of water.

Mike would have to start working his crew an extra shift through the evening, Clay decided. The boy could do without his nightly trips to town with Teresa for the next few days. In fact, Mike would probably be relieved to stay at home for once. Clay suspected his son didn't enjoy the city nightlife as much as his strange girl friend.

He glanced at his watch, strode over to a waiting truck and drove up to the ranch house, where he parked near the front gate.

The woman had agreed to be here at six o'clock, and he was right on time. But maybe she'd been joking. It seemed improbable that she'd actually want to get up so early and go out for a solitary run on the prairie.

He glanced at his watch again and tapped his fingers on the steering wheel, deciding to give her another five minutes before he left. While he waited, he thought about Jenny sitting next to him at the table in her modest blouse and skirt, with her hair freshly washed and shining, pulled back by those simple barrettes he liked so much.

In fact, he liked everything about this woman. The tall shapely body she tended to conceal rather than display, her level green eyes and thoughtful silences, her shy smile, the little pucker between her eyebrows when she was concentrating…

He'd even dreamed about her the night before. At the memory he was caught off guard by a sudden hot wave of sexual desire.

In the dream he'd been standing in the little cemetery next to Suzy's grave. He'd wandered from the graveyard and seen Jenny waiting under a cottonwood tree just outside the gate. She was barefoot and wore a white translucent dress, some kind of nightgown. He could see her breasts, high and pink-tipped, her narrow waist and flaring hips, even the triangle of auburn pubic hair only half-concealed by the shimmering fabric. She drifted toward him, wrapped her arms around him, pressed her half-naked body against his. They fell to the grass, as soft as velvet, kissing tenderly. He buried himself in her sweetness and felt such happiness that he'd wakened with a smile, his groin rigid with lust.…

Jenny appeared on the veranda at that moment and looked around uncertainly. Clay waved at her, suppressing the memory of his dream, and watched as she ran down the path toward him. She wore navy blue jogging pants, a plain white T-shirt and a pair of heavy-duty running shoes, and looked beautiful, her cheeks flushed.

"Hi," he said with forced casualness as she opened

the passenger door and climbed into the truck. "I was beginning to think maybe you'd been kidding about going for a run so early."

"I'm sorry I'm a bit late. I overslept, which is something I never do." She smiled. "Must be the prairie air."

Her smile would have made him forgive her anything. "No problem," he said, throwing the truck into gear.

"I hope you're not too busy for this," she said as they drove onto the road. "I'm already taking up enough of your time as it is."

This reminder of the tax audit hung awkwardly between them for a moment.

Clay turned to glance at her. She seemed even more natural than usual in her running clothes. He could see the freckles over the bridge of her nose, and the sweet curve of her mouth.

In spite of himself he recalled her womanly, erotic tenderness in his dream, and felt another stirring of arousal that made him look away quickly.

"I'll take you west to Prickly Pear Ridge and let you run back to the house," he said. "I drove it earlier this morning to measure exactly two miles. I also made a one-mile marker for you—a small pile of stones at one side of the trail."

"I really appreciate your going to so much trouble. Thank you."

"It's no trouble at all," he said.

She smiled again and peered out the window. "So I just stick to the trail we're driving on?"

"That's right. We've got a few cows and calves in

this pasture, but no bulls. You should be fine. How long does it take you to run two miles?''

''About fifteen or twenty minutes, and I'll need to do some stretching before I start.''

''Okay. I'll keep an eye on the trail, and if you're not back in half an hour or so, I'll come looking for you.''

She was examining the polished mahogany stock of the rifle hanging on a rack in the truck's back window. ''Is that loaded?'' she asked.

Clay shook his head and steered carefully around a couple of gophers sitting upright and chattering in the middle of the road. ''I never allow loaded guns in the vehicles.''

''Why do you carry them at all?''

''You never know what you're going to deal with out on the prairie. Maybe a coyote after a calf, or a horse that's broken its leg or been cut badly in barbwire and needs to be put down to end its suffering. It could be anything. A gun's a handy thing to have in the truck.''

She stared at the oiled rifle barrel. ''I really hate guns.''

''So do I, in the wrong hands,'' Clay said quietly. ''But out here a rifle's just a tool like anything else. I taught my boys to handle and respect guns before they were old enough to go to school.''

She nodded thoughtfully, then turned back to her rapt study of the glistening prairie.

He pulled the truck to a stop on a ridge, then got out and went around to open her door. But Jenny had already done so and in a moment had climbed down and was standing next to him, breathing deeply and gazing around in awe.

"This is magnificent," she said. "I've never seen anything so beautiful."

He looked at her glowing face, then at the sweep of land beyond her. The ranch buildings sprawled in the distance, dwarfed by the surrounding prairie. The horizon was visible all around them in a clear pure circle, and the sky soared overhead, pale green in the east with a pink tint near the ground, dark blue overhead. One star still glimmered high above the clouds building in the west.

"A lot of people hate this," Clay said. "They find it too barren, too open."

"Not me. I love it." She raised her face to the freshness of the wind, and her hair lifted and stirred on the breeze. "It's as if you can see from yesterday all the way to tomorrow," she murmured.

Clay swallowed hard, fighting a sudden urge to take her in his arms. When he turned away abruptly to show her the trail, a small bird flew up at his feet, drifted down onto the prairie grass and began to hop around anxiously.

Clay moved away a few paces to study the ground, then paused and gestured to Jenny.

She moved closer to him and looked down. As Clay held back some overhanging grasses she made a sharp intake of breath. For there, hidden so cleverly it was practically invisible, was a little nest woven of feathers and soft grass. Four brown-splotched eggs, no bigger than thimbles, lay in the nest.

"It's a horned lark," he said. "Don't they make a pretty little nest?"

"Oh," she breathed, leaning forward to study the eggs, her body pressing against his. "They're beautiful. I've never seen anything so…"

She looked up at him, her eyes shining with pleasure. Clay took her elbow and raised her gently, then gathered her into his arms.

When he kissed her, the feeling was just what he'd remembered from his dream, an embrace that comforted and excited him at the same time. He felt her mouth open, felt her firm body as it nestled against him.

His loneliness fell away, replaced by a great swell of tenderness and an aching lust. He wanted to hold her, devour her, search out all the innermost secrets of her body and leave her limp and sated with pleasure. And he could tell by her response that she wanted the same thing.

Then suddenly it was over and she was pulling away from him, turning aside in obvious embarrassment.

"I'm sorry," she muttered, hugging her arms and staring at the distant horizon.

The wind tugged a strand of hair from one of the barrettes and whipped it across her face.

Clay lifted the hair and held it back.

"Why are you apologizing?" he asked. "That kiss wasn't your idea."

"It's so unprofessional," she said. "You're the subject of a tax investigation and I'm the auditor. I should never have…"

Her cheeks were flushed with agitation and her body trembled. The intensity of her discomfort made him feel ashamed. She was right. He'd put her in an impossible position.

"I'm sorry, Jenny," he said. "It won't happen again."

She cast him an imploring glance. "Can we please just forget about this?" she asked. "Both pretend it never happened?"

"Sure," Clay said easily. "It never happened. Now, you'd better start running or you're going to miss breakfast, and I think Polly mentioned something about blueberry pancakes."

"Blueberry pancakes!" Jenny said with forced brightness. "Maybe I'd better run four miles, instead of two."

He smiled down at her, moved by her gallantry, her sweet nature, by everything about her. If he stayed any longer, he was going to kiss her again. And out here in the vast loneliness of the prairie, who knew what would happen next?

Because in spite of her abrupt withdrawal and her concern about professionalism, Clay knew she'd felt the same desire he had.

He wondered if any man had made love to her since that smiling mountain climber she'd been engaged to marry....

The thought of her lying in a man's arms made his groin begin to tighten again, and he knew it was dangerous to linger. Instead, he nodded more curtly than he'd intended, turned and went back to his truck.

"I'll see you at breakfast," he said, opening the door and climbing in. "All right?"

"All right. Thank you, Clay."

She stood alone on the ridge, her hair whipping in the wind, and watched as he drove away. When he was well down the trail, she began to bend and stretch in preparation for her run, getting smaller and smaller in the rearview mirror until all he could see was the white of her shirt and the rich flame of her hair against the bleached prairie grass.

JENNY RAN along the trail, her arms pumping, her breath coming in ragged gasps. She increased the pace, pushing herself, trying to quell the tumult of her thoughts by losing herself in physical effort. But she could still feel his arms around her, his mouth on hers....

You fool, she told herself furiously. *What an incredibly idiotic way to behave, throwing yourself at the man like some love-struck teenager!*

She could hardly believe what she'd done. This rancher was the subject of a government audit that she herself was conducting. There was a gross imbalance in his books, serious enough to result in criminal prosecution if it turned out to be deliberate.

And after lying awake most of the night thinking about the ranch ledgers—which was the real reason she'd overslept—Jenny was certain the revenue discrepancy was no accident, but a skillful tax evasion. Soon she'd discover just how it was being done. Clayton Alderson was the most likely culprit, and he would probably be on his way to jail once she turned over her findings to her superiors.

A new thought struck her, so chilling that she stopped and, chest heaving, stared into the distant horizon.

What if the rancher knew full well what was there in his books, and that she was going to track down his wrongdoing? Maybe he was deliberately pursuing her, trying to get her into bed so he could compromise the results of her investigation.

And she'd actually yielded to him, kissed him back like a love-starved fool.

Jenny moaned aloud, picturing the consequences if Clay Alderson wanted to make trouble for her. He could cause her to lose her job, be disgraced within the profession. And all because she'd been seduced by his dark good looks and the way he fit so well into this wild beautiful landscape.

Jenny's face set with resolve. She had to stay away from the man. She couldn't allow herself to be alone with him, not even for a moment, until she finished her audit and left the ranch.

She tried to remember Steve, to think about his handsome face and easy smile. But her lost lover seemed strangely distant now, so far away that his memory was like the scrap of a dream.

With relief, Jenny recalled that her grandfather was driving out to the ranch that afternoon and Maura was planning dinner for everyone. So there'd be no danger of another meal alone with Clay, or more of those conversations that seemed to flow so comfortably between them, weaving a dangerous spell of warmth and intimacy.

Maybe she could even talk Paddy into staying for a day or two at the ranch, helping with the flood preparations. Her grandfather would love filling sandbags, and there was little doubt Maura Alderson would enjoy having him as a guest. Then Jenny would have an ally in this strange seductive place, where all her emotional caution kept threatening to desert her.

She began running again, enchanted despite herself by the beauty of the morning. Near the ranch house the trail ran down along Cottonwood Creek, passing between the boiling waters and a small enclosure surrounded by a wrought-iron fence. Gravestones nestled among wildflowers and native shrubbery in a setting so peaceful and lovely that Jenny longed to stop and explore it.

Besides, she was reluctant to go back to the house and face Clay again.

She hesitated, looking around, then opened the gate and slipped inside. Many of the headstones were splotched with lichen, so old and weathered that the lettering was difficult to read. They were mostly family graves, ancestors of Clayton Alderson, some of whom had been dead for a hundred years.

As Jenny read the faded writing on the stones, she thought about the men and women buried here, the little children and grandparents, all locked in the same struggle with a vast implacable land. She would have liked to spend an hour wandering in the graveyard, but she recalled suddenly that Clay had talked about coming to look for her if she wasn't back in half an hour.

The last thing she wanted was to be alone with that man again this morning.

She hurried back toward the gate, then paused by a small pink-and-white marble headstone that looked newer than the others. When she read the inscription, Jenny realized with a start of surprise that little Suzanne Elaine had been Clay's daughter.

A child who'd died more than ten years earlier, when she was only two years old.

"She Was the Joy of Our Lives..."

Jenny stood frowning at the gravestone. Clay's marriage must have failed shortly after the little girl's death, because Bridget said he'd been divorced almost ten years. But she was certain nobody had mentioned this baby daughter. There was something lonely and disturbing about the little grave here in the silent freshness of early morning. The wind picked up and rustled through the grass with a mournful whistling sound, setting the wildflowers nodding.

Jenny shivered and turned away, leaving the cemetery and heading toward the ranch house at a brisk jog.

BACK IN HER ROOM she showered and dressed in jeans and a sweater, then went down to the kitchen where she found, to her relief, that Clay had already eaten and gone.

Maura Alderson sat at the table with her grandson, Allan, arguing amiably over a crossword puzzle in the newspaper. The older woman wore white slacks, a turquoise blouse and lot of expensive silver jewelry. She looked carefully made up and attractive.

"Good morning, Jenny," she said as her guest slid into a chair and accepted a cup of coffee. "Do you like crossword puzzles?"

"I love them." Jenny smiled her thanks to Polly who set a platter of blueberry pancakes on the table.

Allan looked up hopefully. "What's a six-letter word for a sour fruit used in jam? Gran thinks the second letter is a 'u,' but we're not sure."

"Quince," Jenny said after a moment's thought.

Maura crowed in delight. "That fits! See, Allan, I told you."

Jenny helped herself to a couple of pancakes, drowning them in syrup. "Polly's cooking is so wonderful," she said. "If I lived here, I'd probably weigh three hundred pounds."

"Not if you go running every morning," Allan told her. "Gran, what are you doing?"

Maura looked up guiltily from the paper. "Nothing," she said.

"You were checking the race results," Allan said. "Are you betting on the ponies again, Gran?"

"Maybe a little," the older woman confessed.

The boy looked at his grandmother thoughtfully. "I thought you promised Dad you weren't going to bet anymore."

"Oh, pooh," Maura scoffed. "Betting on the horse races is just an innocent bit of fun. It's my little hobby, that's all. Besides, what Clay doesn't know won't hurt him, right?"

She winked at Jenny, who looked down at her plate without making a response.

So Maura Alderson liked to gamble, did she?

Jenny wondered how expensive Maura's "little hobby" was. Maybe she'd ask Bridget when they were working together in the office and see what she could learn.

And she also wanted to ask about that tiny grave and its sad headstone.

"Yes?" she asked, realizing that Maura was speaking to her.

"I was asking what time you expect your grandfather to arrive."

Jenny looked thoughtfully at the woman's curly silver hair and artful makeup. "He'll be here around midafternoon, I think. He was hoping to go for a walk on the prairie before dinner."

"Well, then, somebody will have to show him around," Maura said with satisfaction. "And everybody else is so busy these days, I guess it's going to be me."

"That's very kind of you, Mrs. Alderson," Jenny said neutrally.

Booted footsteps sounded in the hallway, making her tense and grip her fork. But it was Mike Alderson who appeared in the kitchen doorway, his work clothes smeared with mud.

"Come on, Allan," he said curtly to his brother, who lounged at the table sipping coffee. "We need you out there."

"Okay, okay." Allan grinned at Jenny and rolled his eyes cheerfully. "Don't get yourself all upset,

Mikey," he said to his brother. "It's not good for you. I'll be along in a few minutes."

Mike turned on his heel and left the house. Allan got up and handed the unfinished crossword puzzle to his grandmother, then took a hat from a row of pegs near the door.

Jenny watched through the kitchen window as the young cowboy ambled out to his truck. She finished her coffee and got up, as well. "Well, I'd better get down to the office," she said. "Bridget's going to be waiting."

Maura watched her with an impassive expression. "Have a nice day, dear," she said. "We'll see you here for lunch, I suppose?"

"Yes, thank you."

Jenny smiled at Polly and headed outside. The wind was turning chilly and the sunlight had vanished, replaced by angry-looking gray clouds. A drop of rain splattered her face and she quickened her steps, heading for the path that ran along the creek.

She made her way into the sheltered green tunnel between the rows of cottonwoods. It was strangely quiet here among the trees. The only sound was the wind, sighing and moaning though the leaves overhead.

Suddenly a branch splintered next to her, shivered and broke apart. Immediately afterward Jenny heard a booming explosion. She looked around in confusion, trying to understand what had happened. Another burst of sound rent the stillness, so close it hurt her ears.

Jenny stared at the shattered tree and took a couple

of hesitant steps toward it. She touched the broken branch and studied the metallic object embedded in it. Then she looked wildly over her shoulder and began to run along the path to the shelter of the ranch office.

The sounds she'd heard had been gunshots, and the tree had been shattered by the impact of a bullet. The leaden slug was still lodged in the branch. As incredible as it seemed, she couldn't doubt the evidence of her own eyes.

Somebody had hidden in the trees along the trail with a gun, waiting for Jenny to pass by. And when she did, that person had fired two shots at her.

CHAPTER NINE

JENNY SAT behind the computer in the ranch office, her mind still whirling, her body gripped by occasional deep spasms of shock. But she hadn't said anything about the gunshots to Bridget, and she was already beginning to question her fear that she'd been the target of a deliberate attack.

It was just too incredible to think somebody had actually hidden in the trees and shot at her. The isolation of this place, complicated by the disturbing imbalance in the ranch ledgers and her agitation over her feelings about Clay Alderson—all those things must be combining to make her imagination work overtime.

She hadn't imagined the gunshots, of course. Or that splintered branch on the tree behind her with the slug embedded in the wood.

Still it could well have been an accident. Somebody out hunting birds or doing target practice, a couple of their shots going astray. In that green tunnel of trees along the creek, she would have been impossible to see.

Clay himself had just told her that a gun was a frequent necessity in the day-to-day work around Cottonwood Creek. But her memory of the rancher's words brought back an image of his big truck and the polished mahogany stock of that rifle in the window rack.

Jenny shook her head and frowned at the open ledger in front of her.

She couldn't believe that Clay Alderson would hide in the trees and fire a gun at her. It was too incredible, especially when, an hour or so earlier, the man had held her in his arms and kissed her with such passion and tenderness....

She moved uneasily in the chair, then looked up at Bridget who'd just brought her a mug of coffee.

"Thank you, Bridget," Jenny murmured. "While you're here, do you mind explaining to me how these cattle sales are handled?"

"Which ones?" Bridget pulled up a chair and settled next to Jenny.

"The sales made at auction. That seems to be where most of the cattle revenue comes from, isn't it?"

The bookkeeper nodded. "We sell a lot of our cattle through the big livestock yards over at Wolf Hill. They're hauled over there by truck and divided into lots before they're sold."

"The lots seem very small," Jenny said. "Considering how many cattle are sold at one auction."

"The cattle being sold at an auction have to be sorted according to size and condition, since a buyer will be bidding on them as a group. Sometimes there'll be no more than half a dozen cattle in a single lot, even though we may be selling two or three hundred head at that day's auction."

Jenny nodded her understanding. "And how does the ranch get paid for them after they're sold?"

"The buyer makes out a check to the livestock yard. The bookkeepers at the auction do a sales slip deducting their commission and expenses, then issue a check to Cottonwood Creek for the net amount."

This information registered in Jenny's mind with a sharp twinge of alarm. "So there's a separate check for each lot of cattle?"

"That's right. Whoever attends the auction on our behalf will bring home a whole handful of checks, sometimes as many as fifty. I enter the revenues into the ledger, and then Clay takes them to town and deposits them in the bank."

"But only you and Clay have signing power on the checks?"

"Yes. Both of us have to sign them before they're deposited or cashed. That's to prevent any of those checks from going astray between the sales yard and the ranch. There'd be no point in anybody stealing one of them, because he couldn't do anything with it."

Unless he—or she—was able to forge the signatures of the bookkeeper and the rancher, Jenny thought. Not a very difficult prospect for somebody who spent a little time around the ranch office, where signed documents were everywhere.

Or somebody who drew a regular paycheck from the ranch, also with both signatures.

"If one of those checks did happen to go missing," she asked aloud, "would you be able to trace it? I mean, is there a system in place to alert you that a check hasn't arrived?''

"Of course,'' Bridget said. ''The individual sales slips wouldn't tally.''

"Which sales slips are those?'' Jenny looked at the ledger again.

"The bookkeeper at the auction yard issues a sales slip for each lot of cattle, and a check for the same group. I match each check with its sales slip before I record it.''

"But if somebody took both the check *and* the sales slip before the auction receipts were turned over to you, how would you know the money was missing?''

Bridget looked shocked. "Nobody would ever do such a thing! Clay always goes to the cattle auctions himself, or sends along somebody trustworthy to take charge of the money.''

"Like who?''

The bookkeeper shrugged. "Whoever's got a free day and wants to go to town and spend some time at the auction. Maura, or Allan if he's home...'' She paused, thinking. "Sometimes Mike and Teresa like to go to the auction just so Teresa can get away from the ranch for a while. Most often Clay goes himself, to make sure he's satisfied with the price and the marketing. I even go to the auction sale from time to time,'' she added, "if I need to do some shopping in town.''

Jenny looked down at the ledger to keep Bridget from seeing her face. "If somebody did take both the sales slip and the check, like maybe a dishonest employee at the auction yard," she said carefully, "would the discrepancy still show up somewhere in your ledger? Is there a count before the cattle are shipped?"

"The trucker does a count," Bridget said. "He records how many cattle he's hauling because we have to pay transit insurance on every animal."

"And you balance that number against the auction revenues?" Jenny asked.

"Always. Sometimes their bookkeepers make a mistake, so we have to keep track of how many cattle we've shipped."

Jenny frowned. "I see. Well, it looks like a fool-proof system. A good thing," she added, "because the person coming home from that auction must be carrying a lot of money in checks."

"Sometimes as much as two or three hundred thousand dollars," Bridget agreed. "Nobody's anxious to have so much responsibility. That's why Clay usually does it himself, or gets Maura to go."

Jenny sipped her coffee and glanced at the plump bookkeeper who moved back to her own desk and selected a cookie from the tin on her desk.

"I guess," she said after a moment, "you've known Mrs. Alderson for a long time?"

"Maura? I've known her since we were girls together. She grew up on the next ranch."

"She's been very kind to me," Jenny said. "And she was awfully nice about inviting my grandfather to stay for dinner tonight."

"Maura's a gracious hostess." Bridget munched

reflectively on the cookie. "She's always been very generous."

"At breakfast today Allan was teasing her about betting on the horses."

Bridget's face clouded. "Oh, no, is she still doing that? She promised Clay she wouldn't bet anymore."

"Does she have a gambling problem?"

"I don't know how much of a problem it is," Bridget said. "But Maura does like to gamble, especially since her husband died. She got back from Las Vegas just last week, and I had the impression she'd lost quite a bit of money. Clay seemed upset with her."

Jenny decided not to press the issue further. "Maura's really fond of Allan," she ventured instead.

"Allan's always been her pet," Bridget said. "They're a lot alike. Maura spoils him, actually. Clay thinks Allan should stay at the ranch when he's not in school and work the way Mike does, but Maura keeps giving him money to travel."

"To rodeos?"

Bridget took another cookie. "Yes, it's a pretty expensive life-style. The entry fees are terribly high, and these modern cowboys fly all over the country to get from one rodeo to another."

Jenny considered this. She pictured Allan leaving the house that morning just before she'd gone down to the path along the river....

She shook her head to clear the image and took another sip of coffee. "This morning when I was out for my run..."

"Yes?" Bridget lifted a pile of invoices onto her desk and opened a ledger.

"I saw a beautiful little graveyard down by the creek. I hadn't realized there was a family cemetery out here."

"The Aldersons have lived here for a long time," Bridget said. "More than a hundred years."

"So Clay told me. The history of the ranch is fascinating."

"You should get Clay to show you some of the old ledgers," Bridget told her. "They've been kept since the late 1800s, and they're incredibly interesting. All the wartime rations and prices during the depression, everything's in there."

"I'd love to see them." Jenny paused, feeling awkward. "In the graveyard there's a little headstone…" She hesitated.

"Which one?"

"It must have been Clay's daughter. Suzanne Elaine Alderson, the inscription said. She died about ten years ago."

Bridget's pleasant face creased with pain. "That was such a terrible thing," she murmured. "Poor little Suzy."

"Why? What happened to her?"

Bridget shook her head warningly, looking toward the door. Clay came running up the steps at that moment and entered the office. He glanced at Jenny, his eyes dark and thoughtful under the hat brim.

She shivered and lowered her gaze in confusion, remembering that early-morning kiss so vividly she was afraid her emotions would show on her face.

But his voice was calm and noncommittal. "Hello, Jenny. I see you got home safely before the rain started again. Did you have a good run?"

"Very good, thank you," Jenny said, conscious of his eyes still resting on her. She punched some numbers into her keyboard and stared blindly at the computer screen.

Clay turned to Bridget. "Have you managed to get hold of the gravel-supply company, Bridget? We really need a few more loads of sand."

"I've been trying," she said. "But I keep getting a busy signal. I guess everybody's calling them right now."

"I suppose." He turned toward the door, then hesitated. "See if you can find us some more hands, too, would you? Call a few of the neighbors. Maybe somebody can spare us a bit of help. This thing is getting ahead of us, and time's running out."

"All right, Clay, I'll try," she said, reaching for the phone.

With one last glance at Jenny, which she tried to pretend she didn't notice, he left the office.

BRIDGET FINALLY got through to the sand and gravel supplier and ordered twenty yards of sand from a harried receptionist who said the ranch would have to send their own trucks since none would be available for several days.

She sighed and hung up the phone, deciding this message could wait until lunch because Clay wouldn't have time to dispatch a truck before then. Besides, he probably couldn't spare the extra hands who'd have make the trip all the way to the city and back.

That reminded her of his other request. She called several of the neighboring ranches to ask if they had workers to spare, but most of them were busy with the flood crisis or with normal early-summer ranch chores like haying and branding calves.

At last, she located a couple of smaller ranches on high ground, operated by families who could spare some of their workers and older sons to help the Aldersons. One of the boys even had a driver's license and was willing to leave immediately and drive the family's grain truck into the city for a load of sand.

Bridget dispatched him with relief and fervent gratitude, then hung up the phone and settled back to her work. She stole a glance at Jenny McKenna, sitting quietly across the room behind the computer.

Such a pretty girl, Bridget thought. And she's got a mind like a steel trap.

She was dazzled by the young woman's competence, her lightning-quick insights into the ranch ledgers and the neat methodical way she was following the trail of revenue and expense.

Bridget shivered and felt her eyes dim briefly with panic.

There was no hope at all that this young auditor wasn't going to find something amiss in the books. She was too smart, too dogged and quietly efficient. Before long, Jenny would know everything, and then Bridget's last hope would be gone....

She tried to concentrate on the pile of invoices, but the numbers kept dancing in front of her eyes. The only sound in the room was the click of the computer keyboard and the splatter of rain against the window.

Bridget put down her pen and looked at Jenny again, trying to remember how it had felt to be that young. The girl had such a clean delicate profile, with her straight little nose, full-lipped mouth and dainty chin. Her hair was pulled back and fastened neatly, and her cheeks still glowed from that early-morning run.

How could she possibly have stayed unmarried all this time when she was so pretty and so sweet-natured?

Clay had said something about Jenny McKenna being engaged to a man who'd been killed a few years earlier while…mountain climbing, yes, that was it. Something adventurous and romantic. That must be the explanation for Jenny's solitude. She'd loved the man and couldn't bring herself to care for anybody else.

Just like me, Bridget thought, her melancholy deepening. *After Hal died, I never wanted any other man. And I was about Jenny's age, too.…*

The thought made her feel closer to the young woman across the room. She certainly didn't hold any of her current problems against Jenny. In fact, she was going to be interested in what the auditor found at the end of her search, because she herself had no idea where or how the money had vanished. She just knew it *had* been disappearing, that the profit side of the ledgers had been dropping steadily over the past two years.

And she knew, of course, that she should have reported the discrepancy. But she'd been so afraid it would bring her own inadequacies to light, that everybody would realize she couldn't do her job anymore.

Now Clay was in trouble because of her, and this government auditor was going through the ranch books with a fine-tooth comb. God only knew what Jenny McKenna was going to find.

It's my fault, Bridget thought in despair. *It's all my fault....*

She slid open her desk drawer, took out the glossy prospectus for the gold-mining company and leafed through it with a shudder of revulsion.

Maura had been the one who'd brought her the prospectus and told her about the money people were making on this company's stock.

"It's a sure thing, Bridget!" Maura had told her in an exultant whisper. "I invested fifteen thousand just three months ago and it's worth almost ninety thousand right now. There are instant millionaires all over the place from trading in this stock. You can't go wrong."

Bridget had never been a gambler like Maura, but she'd been seduced by the lure of big money. She'd managed to save almost fifty thousand dollars during her years at the ranch—not nearly enough to make her dream come true.

Her dream was a home in the city, a nice little place with a yard for her two shelties and a garage for her car, close to the library and shopping and perhaps a movie theater. That was all she'd wanted for years. And Maura's glowing description of the gold-mining stock had made Bridget believe this dream could actually come true before she was too old to enjoy it.

With fear and trembling at her own daring, she'd invested five thousand, then ten, and been astounded at how rapidly the investment soared in value. Little by little she'd put more of her money into the stock and watched it double, then triple.

"I'd really like to tell Clay about all this money we're making," Maura had confided to her, "but he's so uptight about any sort of risk taking. Whenever he has spare cash, he ties it up in some stodgy old mutual fund. The boy has no sense of adventure. He's not a high roller like you and me, sweetie."

Just after Christmas, Maura sold her stock, cashed in a huge profit and advised Bridget to do the same. Bridget assured her old friend that she was about to sell, and Maura appeared to be satisfied with their secret flurry in the stock market.

But Bridget didn't sell. She kept hoping for just a little more profit since the stock was doing so well. Soon there'd be enough money to retire, buy the house she wanted and even have a bit left over to travel.

Late in January the share price began to fall. "A minor correction in the market," the analysts said.

So Bridget hung on, hoping for a recovery and another upward trend. When the stock fell past its original value, she was paralyzed by fear and dread.

Finally, just over a month ago she'd panicked and sold for twenty-three thousand dollars, less than half of her investment.

Bridget sighed and rubbed her aching temples. Jenny glanced up from her keyboard in concern.

"Are you all right, Bridget?"

"I'm fine." Bridget tried to smile. "Just a bit of a headache this morning."

"Why don't you go home and lie down for a while? I can answer the phone."

"It's nice of you to offer, but I'll be all right, Jenny."

Bridget thrust the prospectus out of sight in her desk, wondering why she didn't throw the dreadful thing away. It was over, after all. Her life was over, her future was ruined, her dreams were in shambles.

Since she couldn't afford to retire, she'd probably have to keep working at the ranch until she died. But once the government was finished with Clay's books, he wouldn't want Bridget Carlyle as his bookkeeper anymore.

She felt a clutch of fear that made her stomach heave with nausea. Where could she go? What could she do? Who would ever hire her again after her carelessness with these ledgers?

Bridget didn't realize she'd moaned aloud until Jenny got up and crossed the room to put an arm around her shoulders. "You don't look well, Bridget," she said. "You're so pale. Please go home for a while."

Bridget thought longingly about her little cottage with the dogs sleeping in their baskets and the tea-kettle whistling on the stove. "I can't," she said, looking around the room. "We're too busy right now, and Clay needs me to—"

"I can look after the office," Jenny said firmly, taking Bridget's elbow and lifting her from the chair. "You go home and have a nap. If any problems come up, I can always run over and ask you what to do."

Bridget hesitated. Her head was pounding fiercely and she felt on the verge of tears. "Are you sure?" she asked.

"Of course I'm sure. It's going to be lunchtime soon, anyway." Jenny got Bridget's raincoat, put it on her as if she were a child and gave her a hug. "You just go home and have a nice rest. After all, what's the good of having a tax audit," she asked with a smile, "if you can't at least get a little holiday out of it?"

"All right. Just an hour or two, perhaps," Bridget said gratefully, and went out into the rain, trudging up the road to her cottage. As she walked she thought about Jenny McKenna's green eyes and warm smile.

The girl was so nice. That was one of the worst things of all, the way this government auditor had turned out to be such a nice person.

Tears gathered in Bridget's eyes and trickled miserably down her cheeks, mingling with the raindrops.

CHAPTER TEN

ALONE IN THE OFFICE, Jenny stood at the window for a moment watching the bookkeeper's plump little form vanishing into the rain. At last she let the curtain drop and went back to her computer, resisting the urge to glance nervously over her shoulder whenever she heard a strange noise.

Only a tree branch scratching on the window or the saggy old veranda creaking in the wind, she told herself. There was nothing to be frightened of.

Nothing at all.

But she felt tense and jittery, probably suffering a delayed reaction to the shock of that gunshot so close to her body in the green tunnel of trees.

Jenny sat behind the desk and clenched her hands briefly into fists, looking down at the neatly trimmed unpainted nails.

Lisa always tried to talk her into going for a manicure, but Jenny resisted, saying she wasn't the type for manicures.

At the thought of her young assistant, Jenny felt an odd homesickness coupled with another sharp tug of anxiety.

She should probably leave the ranch today and tell the supervisors at Revenue Canada about her fear regarding her personal safety. Maybe somebody else could come out to Cottonwood Creek and finish the audit after the flood crisis was over.

For a moment Jenny had a guilty surge of hope, but suppressed it as quickly as it had come. She squared her shoulders, took a deep breath and brought up a new screen on the computer.

She, Jenny McKenna, was not the sort of woman who passed her problems on to somebody else. If there really was some kind of danger out here, she could hardly suggest that a different auditor come out and take over the Cottonwood Creek assignment.

Besides, her fears were ridiculous, she told herself firmly. It was just nerves, probably the result of isolation of the place and the tension over the rising creek waters.

And Clay Alderson himself, of course.

Bleakly Jenny remembered standing in his embrace, straining against him, so thrilled by the sweetness of his kiss that she forgot everything else. Clearly it had been too long since she'd been with a man. She'd believed that that part of her had died along with Steve, but she must have been wrong. Even if she could never fall in love again, she was obviously still susceptible to lust.

Now the memory of Clay's mouth and hands, his broad chest and shoulders and the muscular strength of his denim-clad legs was enough to make her writhe in her chair and ache with yearning.

Pure adolescent lust, Jenny derided herself, slapping papers around angrily. And she wasn't even immune to that emotion when it involved the subject of her own audit.

Shame added to her discomfort, making her hot and prickly with embarrassment. Finally she forced herself to open the ledgers and began to pound the keyboard with grim determination, trying to use work to keep all her troubled thoughts at bay.

Soon she was fully absorbed in the audit. When Joe Dagg stuck his head in the office and announced that lunch was ready, she looked up in confusion from her pile of ledgers, unable to believe that the whole morning was already gone.

She shook her head and rubbed her eyes, then gave the old cowboy a wry smile. "I'm really buried in this stuff, Joe," she said. "I think I'll just stay here and work through lunch, all right?"

His seamed brown face registered alarm. "But you gotta eat, Jenny! Why, you're practically skin and bones as it is."

Jenny chuckled. "Not really, but it's sweet of you to say so. I'll be okay, Joe. Really. Give everyone my regards, and please ask Mrs. Alderson if she'll send my grandfather down here for a visit when he arrives, all right?"

She felt vastly relieved by this new plan.

Refusing to go up for lunch at the ranch house had been pure impulse, but it was definitely the easiest course of action. This way Jenny wouldn't have to meet with any of the cowboys and parry their good-natured teasing, or endure Clay Alderson's penetrating gaze and the unsettling reality of his presence at the table.

Most important, she'd be spared the awkwardness of trying to eat while she wondered which person in that big ranch kitchen might have hidden among the trees and fired a gun at her as she'd walked by.

JOE REAPPEARED at the office less than an hour later with a foil-covered tray containing a hot beef sandwich smothered in gravy, a thermos of coffee and the familiar patterned tin full of warm gingersnaps and brownies.

"Clay wants to know if you're all right and if you need anything," he reported. "He was real worried when you didn't show up for lunch."

Jenny pretended to be deeply interested in the plate of food. Her stomach, in fact, began to churn and rumble with hunger as soon as she unwrapped the foil and a delicious aroma filled the office.

"Tell Clay I'm just fine," she said. "And thank you for the food. Please let Polly know how much I appreciate her thoughtfulness. And you, Joe," she added warmly, "slogging though all this mud to look after me. It's very nice of you."

The old cowboy beamed and ambled toward the door with his rolling bowlegged gait. "It's a pleasure. Now you have a real nice lunch, you hear?"

"Joe…"

"Yeah?" He paused with his hand on the doorknob.

"Quite early this morning, when I was coming down to the office through that double row of cottonwoods along the creek…"

Jenny kept her voice deliberately casual, pretending

to concentrate on cutting pieces from the slice of rich beef on her plate.

"Yeah?" he said again.

"I thought I heard a couple of gunshots. Could somebody have been doing a little target practice out there, do you think?"

Joe frowned and shook his head. "Not likely. That's too close to the trail, and everybody walks along between them trees. Too hard to see somebody on the path out there. It could be real dangerous, shooting a gun down near the cottonwoods."

The fried potatoes had crispy skins and were lightly drizzled with gravy. Jenny ate one, then nodded.

"I must have been imagining things. Maybe they were across the creek and I just heard the rifles. Is there a shooting range out there somewhere?"

The cowboy frowned and lifted his damp Stetson to scratch his head. "Not really. Allan and Mike sometimes like to set up a row of bottles across the creek and shoot at them for practice. Maura's pretty good at target shooting, and a few times even Teresa's gone out with them to take a few shots."

"I see," Jenny murmured, taking another forkful of potatoes.

"But Clay makes then clean up every damn bit of that broken glass when they're finished," Joe added with a grin, "so they don't like to do it very much."

"I don't suppose they do." Jenny was still trying to sound casual. "Well, I'd better get back to work. And thanks again for the food, Joe. You can tell Polly I was starving and she saved my life."

The old cowhand gave her a winsome smile, then

he was gone, splashing off across the ranch yard, leaving Jenny alone with her books again.

By midafternoon she realized Bridget was probably not coming back that day, although the bookkeeper had said she might lie down only for an hour or two. The poor woman must be feeling really terrible, Jenny thought with sympathy. She decided to close the office a little early and check on Bridget before she went up to the ranch house.

But she wasn't ready just yet to quit. It was late on Wednesday afternoon, two full days into her audit, and she was finally beginning to make some real headway. Doing a full audit, she often thought, was much like painting a picture, although people would probably have been surprised to hear a tax auditor's work described that way.

Yet it was strangely apt. She started out with a sort of blank canvas and a lot of numbers on paper. Gradually the multicolored scraps and bits, the statistics and invoices and deposits, the ledger sheets and tax forms, all began to fall into place. Put together, they made a clear picture of the business, often so clear that the owner himself was surprised by what he saw.

Jenny's artistic friends from college would doubtless have scoffed at her if she'd told them she felt like an artist, but it was the truth.

Involuntarily she thought of Clay Alderson and wondered if he might be planning to drop by the office for a cup of coffee and a visit. Clay would understand exactly what she meant by using numbers to make a picture of a business.

In fact, he seemed to understand everything she said almost before she voiced her ideas aloud.

With an uneasy flush of embarrassment, Jenny remembered that she wasn't supposed to be thinking about Clay Alderson in a personal way anymore. Especially since the image on paper that she was creating of this particular ranching business looked, increasingly, like a serious and highly damning indictment of its owner.

She'd gone through the records for five of the past seven years, building a profile of income and expenditure, carefully cross-referencing in every category. Now she was up to the last couple of years and she could see where the numbers had begun to shift.

Her instincts were proving to be accurate, but it was going to take a lot more work before she had something concrete enough to take back to the authorities for criminal investigation.

She flipped through the desk calendar, feeling restless. Two more days of studying the ranch books and she'd probably have everything she needed.

Just another couple of days...

Jenny gazed at the window where rain hissed and splattered, and slow drops of moisture trickled down the pane in wavering patterns. A new noise filled the silence, something unfamiliar, and she puzzled over it briefly until she realized it was the dull roar of the rising creek. It made her think of an animal on the prowl. Some kind of awful predator that was turning into a monster, waiting in the dark to devour all of them....

She shook her head. She was just being silly. This

ranch and its problems had nothing to do with her. In a couple of days she'd pack her things and leave. She'd never have to think about any of them again.

Shy young Michael and his sullen girlfriend, Allan's boyish charm and Maura's "little hobby," Bridget's obvious unhappiness. the meaningful flirtatious glances of the handsome young ranch foreman—and Clay Alderson's rare smiles that turned his dark face into sunshine...

Jenny moved restlessly in the chair, then looked up, startled, when the door opened and a burst of noise and color filled the office.

Maura, holding a yellow umbrella and wearing a red plastic raincoat, stood dripping cheerfully onto the mat. Next to her was Paddy McKenna in his waterproof green nylon running suit, his bald head bare and glistening with moisture.

"Grandpa!" Jenny felt almost weak with relief and love at the sight of the familiar craggy face. She ran across the room to hug him, then drew away ruefully when she realized how wet his clothes were.

"You're soaked," she said, looking at the damp patches on her T-shirt and jeans. "What on earth have you been doing?"

"See the welcome I get?" Paddy said to Maura, who beamed up at him. "After driving through rivers and floods to bring out her extra notebooks, batteries for her calculator and four pairs of clean socks? What an ungrateful child she is."

"Jenny is a lovely girl," Maura said. "We're all very fond of her." She gave both of them a bright knowing smile that made Jenny's cheeks warm.

Paddy tugged gently at a strand of his granddaughter's hair. "Well, I'm a little surprised," he said. "Most people aren't all that fond of the tax auditor, no matter how nice she is."

"We have nothing to hide," Maura said airily, "so it doesn't matter what Jenny's doing with the books." She glanced around the office. "Where's Bridget?"

"She wasn't feeling well so she went home to lie down." Jenny opened the tin and offered cookies to her guests. "Help yourself. I made a fresh pot of coffee just a little while ago."

Paddy grinned at her, his eyes crinkling with affection. "Settled right in, haven't you, Jen?" he saluted her with a gingersnap. "I knew you'd like being out here in the wide-open spaces."

Jenny sat beck down in front of her computer again. "So, Grandpa, how'd you get so wet?"

"Maura's been showing me around the ranch." Paddy sank into one of the chairs and crossed his long legs casually. "What a fabulous place this is. I'm really impressed."

"Your grandfather's already met the whole crew down there filling sandbags by the creek," Maura told Jenny. "He wanted to grab a shovel and start working right on the spot, but I said he had to come and say hello to you first. There'll be plenty of time for filling sandbags in the next few days."

Jenny laughed. "I'm surprised he listened to you. I can never get him to do a thing I say."

"Really?" Maura cast a sparkling glance at the older man. "You just have to know how to handle these stubborn men," she said placidly.

Startled, Jenny looked at them. She remembered her grandfather saying he was often lonely, and that he'd like to have a female companion. Certainly, Maura Alderson was attractive. Jenny just wasn't sure she wanted the woman to be her new grandmother.

If Paddy and Maura ever got together, what relation would she be to Clay Alderson?

She frowned, then abandoned the thought with an impatient shake of her head and turned to her grandfather. "How's Tristan?" she asked.

"That poor boy's as busy as a one-armed paperhanger in a windstorm. All the little horsies were born this morning just before I left."

Jenny laughed in delight. "Really, Grandpa? How many?"

"Dozens of them. Cute little fellows they are, too. Wait till you see them." Paddy smiled at his hostess. "Jenny has a pair of sea horses in a big saltwater aquarium. The male carries the eggs and gives birth, you know."

Maura nodded her approval. "I've heard that. A most sensible arrangement."

Jenny was still smiling at the thought of the crowd of tiny sea horses swimming among the waving fronds of the aquarium. Then she thought of her cat.

"How's Clementine?" she asked. "I hope you remembered to leave out lots of water and food for her if you're going to stay here until the weekend and help fill sandbags."

"You see why I can't seem to marry the girl off?" Paddy complained to Maura, rolling his eyes. "She cares more for her fish and her cat than she does about going on dates.''

Maura chuckled and cast Jenny a thoughtful glance that made her feel suddenly uneasy. She punched a few numbers into her keyboard and frowned at the screen to keep from meeting the older woman's eyes.

"So, Grandpa, have you met everybody?" she asked lamely, annoyed at herself for the question as soon as she spoke. Too late, she realized that she wanted somebody to mention Clay's name, to let her know where the man was and what he was doing.

Just like a teenage girl with a crush on the boy next door, she thought in despair. *God, I'm hopeless.*

"We watched Allan and Mikey for a while," Maura said. "They're working hard on their dike down at the end of the hay meadow."

"A fascinating bit of engineering," Paddy commented. "They're using those old bales like a dam to fill the gap, then covering them with heavy-gauge plastic and dirt. It's an ambitious project, but I think it just might work."

"Grandpa was a civil engineer before he retired," Jenny told Maura.

"I know," Maura said, munching on a cookie. Jenny wondered just how many other details about his life her grandfather had already shared with this woman.

"And I met Maura's handsome son down there with the sandbagging crew," Paddy said.

"Clay, you mean?" Jenny's heart began to pound. She peered at the screen, scrolling rapidly through a series of entries dealing with cattle sales.

"He was covered with mud and working like a field hand," Paddy said. "I could hardly believe the man was in charge of this whole vast operation."

"He certainly doesn't...put on any airs." Jenny had a mental image of Clay's muscular body, his legs braced, shoulders flexing as he plied the shovel. Her mouth went dry and her body warmed with another distressing flood of sexual desire.

"Have you talked with him much, Jen?" Paddy asked. "I really liked him."

Jenny was spared the need to answer when the office door opened and Bridget appeared in the entry, shaking moisture from her hooded raincoat, stepping out of her rubber boots.

"I'm so sorry, Jenny," she said. "I was only going to lie down for an hour or so, but then I—" She noticed the guests in the office and stopped abruptly.

"Paddy, this is Bridget Carlyle, our ranch book-keeper," Maura said. "Bridget, this is Patrick Mc-Kenna, Jenny's grandfather."

He levered himself from the chair and moved over to shake Bridget's hand. "Call me Paddy," he said, his eyes crinkling with humor. "Everybody else does."

"Hello, Paddy," Bridget murmured. She touched her hair nervously and hurried around behind the desk, her cheeks pink.

Jenny wondered if Bridget's flush was from her walk in the rain or from shyness at meeting this unexpected guest. Whatever the reason, she looked prettier than usual.

"Paddy's a famous local triathlete." Maura smiled

warmly at the visitor. "He holds the senior record for all of Canada."

"I know," Bridget murmured. "I have a lot of newspaper clippings about him in my scrapbook."

Paddy glanced at the bookkeeper in surprise and her color deepened. "Are you a sports fan, Bridget?" he asked.

She rummaged through the papers on her desk, avoiding his eyes. "Not really," she murmured. "I just… Sometimes I like to…" Her voice trailed off and she opened a drawer to peer inside.

"Well," Maura said briskly, getting to her feet, "it's time for us to be off. Jenny, I want your grandfather to get his things unpacked before dinner." She took the man's arm in a proprietary manner and tugged him toward the door. "Come on, Paddy," she said. "Let's leave these ladies to finish their work."

Paddy got up and followed her obediently, reaching over Maura's shoulder to help her open the yellow umbrella. They went onto the porch together, laughing.

Maura paused and looked back into the office. "Jenny McKenna," she said, "you didn't come to the house for lunch."

Jenny smiled awkwardly. "I was so busy here, right in the middle of a lot of things. I just wanted to keep at it."

"Well, you'd better not miss dinner," Maura said. "Polly's doing a roast with her famous Yorkshire pudding, and it'll break her heart if you're not there."

"I will be," Jenny promised.

"Good." Maura beamed at her, then flicked a

smile in the bookkeeper's direction. "You, too, Bridget," she said. "Can you come up for dinner tonight?"

"All right," Bridget murmured. "Thanks, Maura."

"Fine, I'll tell Polly that both of you are coming." Maura nodded with satisfaction and left the office.

Jenny got up and moved to the window, watching Paddy's tall green-clad body and the little woman in the red raincoat as they splashed off side by side toward the ranch house.

"Maura's being very…friendly," she ventured. "Is she always so outgoing?"

"She wants him," Bridget said flatly from her desk. "I can tell."

Jenny looked at her in surprise. "My grandfather, you mean?"

Bridget nodded. "There was never a man that Maura Alderson couldn't get if she wanted. But she is a very nice person," the bookkeeper added loyally. "Most people don't know how nice Maura is, deep down, because she seems so flippant all the time."

"But I'm not sure if…" Jenny paused and frowned at the raindrops splattering into muddy puddles in the ranch yard. Again she wondered if she and Clay were going to wind up being related in some complex embarrassing fashion. It would certainly be uncomfortable, in that case, if Jenny also had to be responsible for sending the man to jail.

But that wasn't true at all, she reminded herself. If Clay Alderson went to jail, it wouldn't be her fault. He'd simply be getting what he deserved for being greedy and trying to steal from the system.

Jenny McKenna had no sympathy for tax cheats.

But then, none of the people she'd audited in the past had held her in their arms and kissed her senseless.

As she headed back to her desk, she asked Bridget, "Are you feeling better now?"

The bookkeeper gazed at the window where the two older people had disappeared. "He's even more handsome in real life. Such a handsome man."

"My grandfather?"

Bridget nodded, her chin cupped in her hand, her expression dreamy. "I've got every newspaper article that was ever printed about him," she said. "When they had the triathlon in Calgary last year, I drove into town to see him, but the race area was so crowded I couldn't get anywhere close to the finish line. It was such a disappointment."

So Maura wasn't the only woman at this ranch interested in Paddy, Jenny thought. She stared at Bridget. The bookkeeper's face had colored with embarrassment again, and she obviously didn't want to pursue the topic. Instead, she opened one of the ledgers with a businesslike air, drew a basket of invoices toward her and began making entries in a determined fashion.

Jenny, too, settled in to work again, but from time to time she glanced at her wristwatch and found herself thinking nervously about the upcoming dinner at the ranch house.

CHAPTER ELEVEN

TEN PEOPLE SAT AROUND the big wooden table in the dining room, relaxing over dessert and coffee. All of Clay's family was there, as well as Jenny and her grandfather, Bridget, Jim Cole and even Polly's husband, Joe.

Maura, who usually preferred to eat dinner in her room, had dressed carefully for the occasion, Clay noted. She and Allan kept up a line of chatter so bright and amusing that he was able to forget his burdens for a little while and talk and laugh with the rest of the group.

Michael, he was pleased to see, seemed cheered by the success of his dike-building venture and was unusually expansive and talkative, although Teresa was her usual sullen self. Allan, of course, was at his best in situations like this. He answered his grandmother's witticisms with jokes of his own and flirted shamelessly with all the women, especially Jenny.

Clay glanced at the young auditor, seated next to her grandfather, whom Maura had placed at the other end of the table. Jenny had dark smudges under her eyes, and throughout the meal she'd avoided looking at him. Obviously she was embarrassed by what had happened between them early that morning. *Damn.*

Next to her Bridget was silent, as well, picking list-lessly at her food. Clay felt a brief twinge of concern. He suspected that something was seriously wrong in Bridget's life, and he knew he should find a few moments to talk with his bookkeeper and try to probe into the cause of her unhappiness. But it was a hard thing to manage just now. Jenny was always in the ranch office, so he couldn't talk privately with Bridget. And the threat of flooding was keeping them all strung out with tension and working like maniacs.

He frowned and stirred sugar into his coffee, then glanced up and caught Jenny looking at him. She flushed and turned away, bending nearer to Jim Cole, who was telling her a long story about his rodeo exploits.

She laughed at something the handsome foreman said, her face lighting for a moment, and Clay was surprised by a quick surge of jealousy.

If things were different, he thought, they could be alone somewhere like a normal couple, he and this young woman he found so attractive. He could walk and talk with her, explore her thoughts and tell her some of his. More than anything, even more than physical closeness and intimacy, he craved conversation with Jenny McKenna. He wanted to get to know her, learn how her mind worked and how she felt about things.

But there was a flood to deal with, as well as the dark specter of the tax audit casting its shadow between them....

Paddy McKenna looked across the linen tablecloth at his host, smiling with the genial warmth that seemed to come naturally to this likable man. "Well," he said, placing his hands flat on the table and addressing the whole group, nodding at Maura and her grandsons, "I've enjoyed a delicious meal and some good company, but it's still light outside and I'm in the mood to fill some sandbags before bedtime. Who'd like to join me?"

Clay got to his feet, folded his napkin and smiled gratefully at the older man. "It's good of you to offer, Paddy," he said, "but you don't have to do that. I'll excuse myself now and get back to work, but I'm sure my mother will be happy entertain you."

"I'm sure she would." Paddy tipped his wineglass gallantly at his hostess. "But as attractive as that prospect sounds, Clay, I'd really like to grab a shovel and see if I can't fill sandbags faster than young Allan here."

"Hey, I'm pretty fast with a shovel." Allan pushed his chair back and got to his feet, flexing his powerful biceps. "I got these muscles from riding bulls, you know."

"Ah, but I have age and guile on my side," Paddy said serenely, dropping an arm around the young man's shoulders and steering him toward the door. "I've learned how to pace myself and I'll bet you haven't, my boy."

The group laughed. Jenny got up, as well, joining her grandfather and the young cowboy. "I think I'd like to do some shoveling, too," she announced.

"All right! Come on, Dad," Allan said exuberantly. "Mikey and the other three guys can work on the dike tonight. Let's have a contest—the Aldersons against the McKennas. We'll see who can fill the most sandbags in three hours.''

''An old man and a young slip of a girl against two strapping cowboys,'' Paddy said thoughtfully. ''It hardly seems fair. We ought to spot these fellows another couple of workers so they have a fighting chance, wouldn't you say, Jenny-girl?''

His sally was greeted by a fresh burst of laughter, then everyone left the table and most left the ranch house, splashing through the rain to join the work crew down along the creek.

Mike and Jim Cole continued to the hay meadow and the team of men building the dike, while Clay and his younger son lined up next to Paddy and Jenny, picked up shovels and set to work.

Huge piles of sand had been dumped near the barn, along with mounds of plastic sacks. Men and women in mackinaws and slickers toiled steadily in the rain, filling sacks that were then tied by the older children, loaded onto wagons and hauled to the dike being constructed along the banks of the creek.

Clay soon settled in to the rhythm of the task, his mind wandering as he heaved and shoveled. So much to think about, so many eventualities to be considered and worst-case scenarios to be dealt with in the event that all their precautions weren't enough and the whole place was flooded.

''What will you do?'' Jenny asked quietly, working at his shoulder. ''If it's not enough, I mean.'' She gestured at the sandbag dike that was growing with such painful slowness.

Clay glanced down at her, surprised again by her

perception, and enjoying the sight of her as she labored at his side.

The woman was in wonderful physical condition. She worked as hard as Allan, strong and apparently tireless, her beautiful profile calm and withdrawn under the brim of her wet cap.

"I don't know what's going to happen," he said. "It's hard to think about, but I guess I have to, don't I? From the reports farther north, this water is going to be higher than anything we've ever seen before. We could lose everything."

The line deepened between her eyebrows. "Not the stock, surely?" she asked. "Haven't all the animals already been moved to higher ground?"

"Most of them." He gestured with his shovel toward the big round corral attached to the barn. "But there are some that'll be a real problem, like those Angus bulls and the horse over there. I'll have to decide what to do with them tomorrow, I guess."

She looked at the corral, where half a dozen bulls stood humped against the rails and a big horse trotted along the fence, gleaming like a phantom through the silvery fall of rain.

"Why can't you move them?"

"The bulls have various medical problems and need to be treated every day, and the horse is a stallion on loan from another ranch, standing at stud to a group of our mares. He's worth three hundred thousand dollars. I can't just turn those animals out into a barbwire field somewhere."

"Three hundred thousand?" She stopped working and leaned on her shovel, staring in alarm at the horse. "If he's on loan, can't you send him home until the danger's passed?"

Clay shook his head wearily. "I'd love to, but he comes from Texas and needs special handling. I can't spare the men right now. It's just one more thing to worry about." He wondered why he was confiding in this woman. She probably wanted only to be finished with her job and gone from his ranch.

But she seemed interested, looking in fascination at the big bay stallion pacing behind the stout rails of the corral. "Why does he need special handling?"

"He's vicious," Clay said grimly. "The most bad-tempered horse I've ever run across. He hates being in a box stall and he practically killed Jim in the round corral last week when we were unloading him. We picked him to stand at stud because of his conformation and bloodlines, but I hope he doesn't pass that temperament on to his foals."

"He tried to kill Jim Cole?" she asked, still looking at the horse.

"He's a striker," Clay said. "He rears up and flails with his forelegs. A big horse like that can break a man's ribs or split his head open with one blow. He has to be watched all the time."

Jenny grimaced and went back to work. Her jeans were damp, and she wore a waterproof nylon jacket borrowed from Allan, heavy gloves and a tractor cap pulled low over her eyes. Tendrils of hair escaped from the cap and were plastered to her wet cheeks.

Clay couldn't remember when he'd ever found a woman so attractive.

He wanted to ask her about the audit, find out if

she'd discovered any more information about those missing revenues, but something kept him from broaching the topic. At the moment, with the creek waters rising and the pile of sandbags growing so slowly along its banks, the ranch's financial affairs were far down on his list of worries.

"You're a good worker, Jenny," he said as she lifted and shoveled at his side with calm efficiency.

"I really like hard physical work," she replied. "Probably because my job is so sedentary."

"This kind of life seems to suit you," he ventured, bending to work in rhythm with her movements. "You're such a…"

"What?" she asked when he paused.

"Such a fine physical specimen, as your grandfather would say." He grinned at her and handed her another pile of sandbags. "You look like you should be a lifeguard or something, not an accountant."

"You know, I actually considered that occupation at one point during my teenage years, but it's pretty chilly work, being a lifeguard in Calgary. At least from October until April." She laughed.

His spirits lifted at the sound. Being close to her made him feel young and happy again, in spite of his worries.

"Tell me about your fiancé," he said a few moments later. "How did the two of you meet?"

"In college. My father died when I was fifteen, and a few years later my mother remarried and moved to Florida. I guess I was feeling really lonely and isolated. Steve was the first serious relationship I ever had."

"So the two of you went out together all through college?"

"Off and on." Her cheeks flushed, either with embarrassment or exertion, Clay didn't know. "Steve was kind of a restless type. He was always taking off for some adventure on the other side of the world, leaving me alone. I remember that we had quite a few arguments in those early years."

"But eventually you adapted to his life-style?" Clay asked.

"I suppose I had to." She handed over a couple of full sandbags to the children with their wagon and reached for another one. "If you want to have a relationship with a man like Steve, you learn to adapt to him because his goals and preoccupations tend to come first."

Clay wanted to ask her why any woman would choose to have a relationship with a man who put himself first, but he was reluctant to interrupt the easy flow of their conversation.

"What about you?" she asked, glancing up at him from under the brim of her cap. "You said you married quite young?"

"Far too young," he said. "At that age, I thought it was enough to be physically attracted to somebody and committed to the concept of a faithful marriage. I didn't understand how important other things were in a relationship."

"What other things?"

He frowned, thinking about the question as he worked in rhythm with Jenny's motions.

"Laughing together," he said at last. "Liking the

same things and having shared interests to talk about. That's what life comes down to ultimately. You can't survive on drama and excitement. It's all the little things that make you happy, and you really need to have somebody else who cares about them as much as you do.''

She was silent for so long he felt uneasy, wondering if he'd revealed too much of himself. But when she glanced up at him, her face was gentle and open, her eyes warm with understanding.

Clay caught his breath, fighting a familiar and almost uncontrollable desire to take her in his arms and kiss her, right there in front of everyone.

Night had begun to roll in, bringing a brooding heaviness damp with fitful gusts of moisture-laden wind. Flares glimmered along the row of laboring people, and the ranch's yard light cast a watery glow over the scene. Behind them the pile of sandbags continued to grow with frustrating slowness, strung out along the banks of the creek which boiled along, already three feet higher than its morning level and glinting like dull pewter.

Jenny put down her shovel and stood erect for a moment. She took off her cap to pull back errant strands of hair, then rubbed wearily at the small of her back. Next to her, Allan and another young man laughed aloud, indulging in some mild horseplay with Paddy McKenna. Inadvertently, they bumped against Jenny. She stumbled and would have fallen if Clay hadn't put out an arm to steady her. For a moment she leaned against him and settled into the protective curve of his body, so close he could smell the damp fragrance of her hair, feel her strong shapely body in his arms.

Clay tightened his grasp, loving the trustful way she rested against him and let him support her.

I could spend a lifetime doing this, he thought suddenly. *Talking with her, working at her side and holding her when she's tired.*

But then she drew away abruptly and replaced her cap, picked up her shovel and began working again without looking at him. He could see the tense set of her shoulders, her withdrawn profile, and he knew that sweet trustful moment was gone.

Once again she was a tax auditor and he was a man under a dark shadow of suspicion; nothing was going to change between them.

Aching with frustration and loneliness, Clay settled to work in silence as the night deepened around them.

NEXT MORNING it was still cloudy and cool, but the rain had stopped long enough for Jenny and Paddy to go out for their morning run. They jogged side by side, heading up the trail toward the ridge where Clay had first measured off Jenny's two-mile track.

"I think this is almost the halfway point," she said. "We should turn around pretty soon."

Paddy gazed at the vastness of prairie, washed with a pale glow of sunlight filtered through the bank of clouds overhead.

"What a beautiful place." He sighed. "You know, I didn't realize this kind of wild open country still existed."

"It's a different world out here," Jenny said.

"When you get far enough away that you can't see the ranch buildings, you begin to feel like you're the only human being on the planet. It's wonderful."

Her grandfather glanced over at her. "Do you really like it here, Jenny? Most people would hate this kind of solitude."

"I love it." She, too, looked at the sweeping expanse of prairie, the miles of dried grass swaying and rippling in the wind like an ocean of gold. "I've only been here a couple of days and I'm going to hate to leave."

"When will you be finished with your audit?"

At this reminder of the job she was doing at Cottonwood Creek, Jenny's throat tightened with anxiety. "By tomorrow afternoon, I think. We should probably be able to leave before dinner."

"But I'm not sure I want to leave that early." Paddy jogged at her side, squinting toward the horizon. "I'd like to stay and see them through this crisis, wouldn't you? They need all the help they can get. I'm planning to fill sandbags for the rest of the day, and all of tomorrow, too."

Jenny scanned the edge of the trail for her halfway marker, wondering if Maura Alderson had anything to do with Paddy's desire to stay at the ranch. She was reluctant to ask, however.

"I'd like to help, too," she said, "but I don't know if it's right for me to stay around after I finish the audit."

"Why?" Paddy cast her a shrewd glance. "Is there really some kind of problem with the books?"

"I can't talk about it, Grandpa," she said automatically.

"That means there's a problem." Paddy was silent a moment, keeping pace with her as she reached the pile of stones, turned and started back toward the ranch. "Has something been going on here that's seriously out of line?"

"I'm not sure." Jenny stared unhappily at the distant sprawl of buildings and corrals. "It's not my job to figure out who's been doing what. I only have to audit the books and hand the information on. Somebody else will follow up on it."

"But if there's something to follow up, it means they've got a problem out here. Other problems, that is, besides a flood that's about to wash them a few miles down the creek."

Jenny shook her head. "Don't press me, okay? I really shouldn't be saying anything about it."

"Sorry, honey," he said contritely. "I know this is awkward for you. It's just that…" Paddy stopped talking and the pair of them just jogged in silence for a while. A coyote spotted them and loped away, then paused on a distant hillside to look back, his feathery tail streaming in the wind.

At last Jenny spoke. "They're all such nice people, I know, so it's hard to think of any of them being involved in something illegal."

But she couldn't even say Clay's name aloud, let alone bring herself to think about how she was going to feel if this investigation of hers resulted in sending him to prison.

She remembered the way he'd looked the night before as he talked about love and loneliness, about the importance of being able to share his thoughts with somebody who understood how he felt.

She shivered and drew a sharp breath.

Paddy glanced down at her in concern. "Getting chilly?"

"I'm fine. But the wind is cool, isn't it? Even when you're running."

They approached the ranch buildings, where people had already begun to fill more sandbags in the early-morning light. Others were occupied with the regular ranch chores that still had to be done even though disaster loomed closer with every hour that passed.

Jenny showed her grandfather the bay stallion who paced restlessly along the fence rails in the corral next to the barn, his big muscular body glistening with dampness.

"Clay says that horse is worth three hundred thousand dollars," she said, "and they can't move him because he's so hard to handle."

"Poor Clay," Paddy said with sympathy. "What a heavy load of responsibility that man has to carry."

As if summoned by their words, Clay appeared in the doorway of the barn and waved at them. Paddy slowed to a walk and approached the rancher. Jenny hesitated, then followed, realizing it would look graceless to head for the house and leave them standing there.

"Good morning," Clay said, his eyes crinkling warmly as he smiled. "You two have a lot more energy than I do, shoveling sand half the night and then going out for a run at dawn."

"Jenny and I always enjoy our morning run." Paddy bent and stretched a couple of times, then grinned at his host. "But after I've had some breakfast, I'll be ready to start on those sandbags again."

"Paddy, you're the kind of guest a rancher loves to have," Clay said.

In his faded jeans, old gray Stetson and denim jacket lined with sheepskin, the rancher looked so handsome Jenny felt a treacherous surge of warmth.

"How about you, Jenny?" he asked. "Aren't you tired from all that shoveling?"

"Not really," she said. "I wish I could help today, but I won't be able to join the sandbag brigade until evening."

"Of course." Clay's smile faded and an awkward silence fell.

"Well," Paddy said at last, "I'd better head up to the house and hop into a shower. Maura said something about apple fritters for breakfast, and I want to get there before young Allan eats all of them."

Clay looked at Jenny intently, then glanced at the row of workers filling sandbags. "Will you finish the audit today?" he asked.

She shook her head. "Probably tomorrow. Has the creek risen again?"

"It's up another two feet overnight. We're reaching the critical stage already. At this rate the crest should arrive by tomorrow night and then at least we'll know the worst."

She stood helplessly, wondering what to say.

"I'm going to spend the day tending to emergency

preparations,'' Clay went on. ''I'm afraid I won't be around to give you any help.''

''That's all right,'' she said. ''I can manage.''

Near them the big stallion continued to pace, shaking his head and uttering low rumbles of anger that occasionally mounted to a challenging whistle. The sun, which broke through the cloud cover every now and then, rippled on his glossy hide and the bulging muscles of his hindquarters.

''Are you in a big hurry?'' Clay asked her. ''Do you have a few minutes to come into the barn and look at something?''

Jenny hesitated, then nodded. ''I guess so,'' she said.

He smiled, his weary face lighting with that sudden glow that always unnerved her. ''Good. Come with me.''

Trembling with excitement in spite of herself, Jenny walked with him into the barn.

CHAPTER TWELVE

CLAY REACHED BEHIND HER to close the barn door.
Jenny looked down at her feet, conscious of a whirl
of impressions. She smelled the mingled scents of hay
and leather, sawdust motes dancing in a beam of sunlight above the baled feed near the window, heard the
distant muffled shouts of the ranch workers and the
savage whinny of the stallion in the adjoining pen.

But all these things on the ranch seemed far away
and unreal at the moment. She and Clay were enclosed in this dark secret place, utterly private. She
felt both danger and excitement, as if she were more
alive than she'd ever been, her sensations keener, her
heart beating at twice its normal rate.

Clay was going to reach for her. She could sense
his yearning and her body's own reactions, and it
thrilled and frightened her. Not for years had she felt
such a powerful physical urge, such an aching desire
to feel a man's arms around her, his mouth moving
against hers.

But not this man! she thought in panic. *Not Clay
Alderson, of all people.*

Just as she was bracing herself to murmur an apology and leave the barn, Clay smiled at her and turned away, gesturing for her to come with him.

"Here's what I've been wanting to show you," he said casually over his shoulder as he walked toward one of the mangers.

Jenny followed nervously, watching in surprise as he leaned into a big hay-filled wooden manger and lifted something from its shadowy depths.

He extended his hands for her to see.

Enchanted, she forgot all her cautious reserve. The object on his callused palm was an orange kitten, no more than a ball of fluff with a white face and paws. His eyes were barely open, still milky blue in a tiny face that looked comically fierce.

"I found them yesterday morning," he said. "Two fluffy orange males and two little black females. I thought you might be feeling lonesome for your own cat and you'd like to see them."

"Oh, he's so sweet." Jenny moved closer to touch the kitten's soft little back. He spread his paws against Clay's hand and mewed loudly.

The mother cat, a big tabby, appeared around the corner of a box stall and gazed up at Clay, then rubbed against his leg.

"She doesn't seem to mind you handling her kitten," Jenny said, bending to stroke the big cat.

"This is Pebbles. She and I have known each other for a lot of years." Clay looked fondly at the cat by his feet, then replaced the kitten carefully in its warm nest. "But I don't know how to convince her she's going to have to move her family somewhere. If our dikes don't hold, this barn could be under four feet of water by Saturday morning."

"Oh, Clay," Jenny murmured, feeling another wave of sympathy when she saw how drawn and tired he looked. She put her hand on his arm.

He gazed at her with warm intensity, then drew her into his arms. For a moment they stood holding each other in the dim fragrance of the barn. She lifted her face blindly and waited for his kiss, but was startled and confused when the door opened suddenly and light flooded the barn.

"Clay?" one of the men called. "Are you in here somewhere?"

They sprang apart guiltily. Jenny turned away with forced casualness to look into the manger where Pebbles had stretched out full length and was contentedly nursing her brood.

"Over here," Clay called. "What is it, Sam?"

"We need you down by the creek for a minute."

Clay touched Jenny's shoulder and bent so close she could feel the brim of his Stetson brushing her hair. "Please don't go yet," he said softly. "I need to talk to you about something. I'll be back in a few minutes, all right?"

She nodded mutely, then watched as he strode from the barn and closed the door behind him. She peered down at the little family in the manger again, her heart pounding uneasily.

One of the black kittens had ventured across the soft expanse of their home and was now lost. She crouched in a far corner, mewing pitifully. Jenny picked the kitten up and held it close to her face, sniffing the warm milky fragrance.

"My goodness, so sweet," she murmured. "You're just so sweet." She replaced the little mite with her siblings, watching as she burrowed close to her mother's silken body.

Unable to resist, Jenny was about to pick up another of the kittens when she was startled by a sudden noise, the sound of a door opening and closing, a clatter on the wooden floorboards.

Clay, she thought. He must be back already. She forced a casual smile and turned to greet him, then froze in horror.

The big stallion loomed out of the dark shadows of the barn, his eyes glittering, his nostrils flared. He looked enormous at such close quarters, and his iron-shod hooves clanged hollowly as he threw up his head and began dancing toward her.

Jenny stood rigidly for a moment, her mind whirling. Then she began to look around for some way to escape. She was trapped at the end of a lane of box stalls and the stallion's huge body blocked her only path to freedom. The walls all around her were made of wide boards, with no projections she could climb.

The horse gave a shrill neigh, unnaturally loud and threatening in this enclosed space. Jenny could almost smell his rage and mounting frenzy. Horrified, she recalled scattered details of the things Clay had told her.

This stallion hated being confined in small places. He was a "striker"—one blow from his flailing hooves could break a man's ribs or crush his skull....

She backed against the manger, staring in dry-mouthed terror as the stallion approached her and stood quivering in the aisle, shifting from one foot to the other in rising agitation.

She tried to find her voice, to call out a plea for help, but her throat was closed with fear.

The horse snorted, baring his big yellow teeth, and kicked sharply at the side of the stall. Jenny heard the sound of splintering wood. Again she opened her mouth to scream but could only manage a strangled whisper.

Behind her the mother cat leaped from the manger and streaked off across the floor, alarming the stallion, who lashed out again with his hooves and narrowly missed poor Pebbles as she disappeared around the corner of a stall.

Jenny winced at the animal's awesome power. Suddenly he reared up on his hind legs and struck out with his hooves. He was close to her, almost on top of her. She could see his underbelly, the massive forequarters and heavy thrashing legs as he towered above her.

She flung herself into the manger, cowering next to the little nest of kittens. She covered her head with her arms as the horse thundered forward and lashed out with his hooves again. Foam from his mouth sprayed onto her head, and his breath was hot on the back of her neck.

The upper rail of the manger splintered and broke apart under the onslaught. Soon her frail shelter would be torn away, leaving her and the kittens exposed and helpless.

Finally Jenny found her voice and screamed. When

she peeped through her folded arms, all she could see were the black depths of the barn, a cloud of choking dust and the horse's wild glittering eyes and flailing hooves.

Suddenly the barn door opened, letting in a flood of light. A voice that shouted in alarm. Clay's.

The horse whirled and stood panting. His sides heaved, damp with sweat, and his head swung slowly from side to side. After a moment the animal gathered himself and thundered toward the door where a man's body was silhouetted in the opening.

Clay leaped aside, flattening himself against the wall as the stallion ran out into the sunlit corral.

Jenny began to climb stiffly from the manger. Clay hurried across the wooden floor and reached to help her, then took her in his arms, murmuring broken words of concern.

"Are you all right?" he said. "God, Jenny, how did that happen? Surely you didn't open the door and let him in?"

"Of course not." She rested in the circle of his arms as she struggled to regain control of herself. "I was looking at the kittens and he... All of a sudden he was just there."

"You could have been killed." Clay ran a hand over her face, stroking her body with anxious tenderness. "I don't even let any of the men come into the barn with that stallion."

"How did he get in here?" Jenny pulled away and brushed at her hair and clothes, then looked up at him searchingly. "Somebody had to open the door and let him in, then close it behind him. He couldn't unlatch that door himself.''

"It had to be a mistake," Clay said. "One of the men must have thought the stallion was supposed to be put inside this morning and didn't know you were in here. My God, sweetheart, I don't know how this happened, but I'm going to find out.''

Jenny ignored the endearment and looked up coldly at his dark features.

Do you really not know how it happened? she thought. *Or were you just conveniently outside and decided this might be a handy opportunity to scare off the pesky tax auditor?*

"Jenny," he asked, seeing the look on her face. "are you sure you're all right?''

"I'm fine," she said with forced calm, beginning to recover her composure. She pulled away from him and moved toward the door. "But I have to change and shower and get to work. I've got a whole lot of numbers to go through today. I'll see you later, Clay.''

Before he could say anything more, she let herself out the barn and hurried across the damp gravel toward the ranch house.

FOR THE SECOND MORNING in as many days, Jenny began her workday in tense silence, still agitated by the memory of physical danger.

Surely this was too much of a coincidence, she thought. Two terrifying early-morning episodes in a row, both potentially fatal.

Jenny glanced over at Bridget who was buried under a mountain of papers. Like everybody else on the ranch, Bridget looked tired and pale, on the verge of despair. To Jenny's concerned eyes it seemed that her office companion had even lost a little weight over the past couple of days.

Jenny began to feel a twinge of doubt about her own problems. Maybe she really was getting over-wrought and only imagining threats to her safety. For nobody around this ranch seemed particularly con-cerned about the ongoing tax audit. In fact, they all seemed to have forgotten the reason for Jenny's pres-ence and accepted her as a member of the community, a sort of temporary assistant for Bridget.

Under normal circumstances that would have suited Jenny just fine and made her job a lot easier. But these weren't normal circumstances. Those gunshots on the path yesterday, that sudden appearance of a savage horse in the barn…were those things really just ac-cidents, the result of a group of people too busy and anxious to be concerned with safety?

Or did they indicate a cunning intellect, someone who knew exactly what she was doing at Cottonwood Creek and what she was going to find, and wanted to silence her?

She stared blankly at the screen, where she'd en-tered all the receipts from cattle auctions for the past three years in a huge spreadsheet program.

Of course, if a tax thief was at work here at the ranch—and Jenny was almost certain she would find that to be the case—then getting rid of the auditor wouldn't accomplish anything. The tax authorities were relentless. Before long they'd have somebody else on the case, and the embezzlement would be found.

So why threaten the auditor?

She nibbled on the end of her pencil, frowning.

What if somebody had systematically funneled away a good portion of money and planned to run away with it? In that case, getting rid of her made sense. She hadn't yet filed any of her suspicions because her actual findings to this point weren't conclusive. If she were to vanish or meet with an "accident," the guilty party would have enough time for a clean getaway.

When she realized this for the first time, she felt a chill of terror right in the core of her body, making her stomach churn with nausea, sending little ripples of fear along her spine.

Jenny already knew the amount that had been embezzled. It was about three hundred and fifty thousand dollars, siphoned from the ranch revenues over the course of the past two years, funds that had vanished so completely only a skilled auditor could ever hope to track them through the intricacies of the bookkeeping system.

But Jenny was very skilled, and she was hot on the trail of the missing funds.

"Poor Clay," Bridget said, gazing through the window with a frown of concern. "I worry about that man. I really do."

"Why?" Jenny leaned over to follow Bridget's gaze and saw Clay laboring with the others by the mountain of sand.

As the creek rose and rain clouds began to threaten

again, all their preparations looked woefully inadequate. The long sandbag dike looked almost like a plaything built by children.

"He's getting so worn out," Bridget said, still watching her employer. "And he's been carrying a load of worries for such a long time. He needs a rest, that boy does."

"What kind of worries?"

Bridget shook her head, wrapping a gray curl idly around her finger. "Seems like lately there's never enough money to go around for some reason. He's always a little broke. And he's worried about what might happen to all of them after the flood." Bridget looked down at her desk, writing aimlessly on a scratch pad. "You know, Clay hasn't been the same since Suzy died," she murmured.

"I've wondered about that," Jenny said. "Nobody's really told me what happened to her. Clay won't—"

"I haven't seen him smile and look like his old self," Bridget interrupted, "except for a few times since you came. He really likes you, Jenny."

Jenny thought about those embraces they'd snatched. Once again she considered the possibility that Clay could be deliberately pursuing her to keep her from reporting his financial wrongdoing. It seemed so cold-blooded and manipulative, not at all her impression of the man.

But of course she'd been wrong before about a man.

Gradually, as she worked at this place and watched how Clay Alderson lived his life, she was coming to realize that her handsome fiancé hadn't been at all the man she'd presumed him to be. Steve's daring hadn't been true courage, but the behavior of a reckless and foolhardy man. Clay's quiet strength and concern for others, his constant shouldering of such a heavy burden, made Jenny realize just what a self-absorbed playboy her young lover had been.

This new knowledge hurt enough to bring tears to her eyes when she lay in bed at night, but it was also strangely liberating.

At her request, her grandfather had brought, along with the clothing and personal items, Steve's framed picture for her to put on the bedside table, but she'd never unpacked it. It was stored facedown in the bottom of the suitcase, and for the first time in years, Steve didn't smile at her when she awoke.

She was ready to go on with her life. And irony of ironies, she'd even begun to fall in love again. She finally admitted this truth to herself in the silence of the office, while rain began once again to hiss and splatter on the windows and drum onto the roof of the veranda.

And of all the people to fall in love with, she'd chosen the one man she shouldn't have. A man who her findings might well reveal to be a criminal.

She got up to pour coffee for herself and Bridget, then carried the patterned tin filled with Polly's fresh peanut-butter cookies to Bridget's desk. The older woman cast a wistful glance at it, then waved Jenny away.

"I've decided to lose some weight," she announced.

"Good for you." Jenny patted her shoulder. "I won't eat any of them, either. We'll just drink our coffee and be slim and healthy."

Bridget gave her a grateful smile. "I never thought I'd hear myself say these words to a tax auditor, but I'm going to miss you after you leave, Jenny. It's so much nicer having you here than Teresa."

Jenny returned to her own desk. "I wonder why she stays here when she hates it so much," she said thoughtfully.

"It's a mystery, all right." Bridget frowned, then opened another ledger.

A mystery.

Jenny settled by her computer and stared at the screen, thinking about those missing funds totaling more than a third of a million dollars.

Certainly enough money to make it worthwhile for Teresa to hang around the ranch, if she was involved in some kind of conspiracy to lift funds from the business. The girl seemed lazy and greedy enough to try something like that, and she was probably clever enough, as well.

But that would mean Michael was also caught up in the wrongdoing, and Jenny could hardly believe such a thing of Clay's older son. For one thing, Michael seemed shy and genuinely sweet, also very committed to the welfare of the people at the ranch. And, in Jenny's opinion, though the boy seemed to be firmly under Teresa's thumb, he loved his father too much to steal from him.

Allan, now, was a different matter, so charming and self-centered, so cheerfully, openly manipulative that nobody would ever suspect him of doing anything underhanded.

And Allan was his grandmother's darling—beautiful, mischievous Maura Alderson, who had a gambling problem and who gave money to her younger grandson so he could pursue his expensive life-style.

Jenny shook her head. She knew what this line of thinking was all about. It was an attempt to think of everybody who might have embezzled the funds so she wouldn't have to consider the most obvious suspect—Clay Alderson himself.

With every passing hour it was harder to see the man as a thief. She pictured him pointing out the bird's nest in the tall grass, holding the kitten on the palm of his hand, lifting his head to laugh while the wind stirred in his crisp dark hair, teasing Bridget with a cheerful grin.

Jenny's breath caught in her throat. *I really love him,* she thought in horror. *God help me....*

But the man's trying to kill you, an inner voice whispered. *If he can't get you into bed to shut you up, he'd just as soon kill you.*

No! Clay wasn't like that. He'd never hurt her deliberately.

And as far as trying to get her into bed, she suspected that most of their physical encounters had been her idea, not his, resulting from her overwhelming physical attraction to him. What was the man to do when a female guest kept throwing herself into his arms at every possible opportunity?

Humiliation washed over her. She winced and

moaned softly.

Bridget looked up in alarm. "Jenny, are you all right?"

"I'm fine," Jenny muttered. She blinked and tried to concentrate on the computer screen. "I'm just really tired and worried, I guess."

"I know. We all are," Bridget said grimly. "Every single one of us."

Jenny nodded agreement and went back to work, trying to think clearly as she studied the spreadsheet.

CHAPTER THIRTEEN

THE MISSING FUNDS had something to do with the cattle auctions, but Jenny still couldn't understand how the money had been stolen. The ranch system for tracking the auction funds had several built-in safety mechanisms, including double endorsements on the checks, the tally of lots sold that matched with money issued by the livestock yard and a total from the trucker's bill of lading that listed every individual animal hauled to market.

Yet according to her spreadsheet, the number of cattle shipped over the past two years was down by almost five hundred head, and the average revenues from cattle sales were off by three hundred and sixty-five thousand dollars, which closely matched the revenue discrepancy.

But the invoiced expenses for feed supplies, veterinary services and other routine maintenance items remained constant, indicating the ranch was carrying a stable inventory of cattle. Because, of course, if fewer head were being shipped, it should be costing more to maintain those extra animals on ranch property.

She frowned and brought up the auction data again, almost hoping to find an error in her figures. Before she could concentrate on a new column of numbers, the door opened and a man entered the office, shaking rain from his windbreaker, removing his cap to show a tousled head of blond hair.

It was Jim Cole, the foreman. He nodded at the two women and settled onto an old vinyl couch, extending his legs with a weary sigh.

"Poor Jim," Bridget said. "Would you like a cup of coffee?"

"Bridget, that'd be the nicest thing anybody's done for me all day."

He watched gratefully as Bridget got up and brought him a mug of steaming coffee. When he reached to accept it, Jenny saw that his brown hands were trembling badly.

Again she felt guilty, sitting here snug and warm at the computer tracking financial discrepancies while all these people were fighting to save their homes and livelihood.

But the government wasn't paying her to go outside and ply a shovel.

As if reading her mind, Cole looked up and gave her a brief smile. "I sure wish I had your job, Jenny. It's not much fun out there, filling a thousand sandbags every day and knowing damned well it's not going to be enough."

"It really won't be enough?" Bridget asked.

He shook his head and sipped from the mug. "The Flemmers and the Klatzes upriver are both washed out. Lost everything. Clay thinks we've got maybe eighteen or twenty hours before the crest hits down here."

Bridget grimaced, then hurried around behind her desk to get the tin of cookies and offer it to their visitor. The ranch foreman took a careless handful and ate hungrily, turning on the couch to glance at Bridget. "Clay wants you to see if you can get a cattle liner in here sometime today. We need to move the last of the stock up to dry ground."

Bridget nodded and reached for the phone. "He was hoping he wouldn't have to do that," she said as she dialed.

"I know, but we can't afford to wait any longer. We need something big enough to take fourteen Tarentaise heifers and half a dozen sick bulls, and a separate compartment for that damn bay stud out there because Clay doesn't want to risk trying to get him into a trailer. He'd probably kill somebody, and we need every hand we've got right now."

Jenny tried not to think about the big stallion's maddened eyes and crashing hooves. She frowned at her computer. "Jim," she said abruptly.

"Yes, ma'am?"

"When cattle are shipped to auction, what happens to the trucking slip?"

The cowboy stared at her in disbelief. "My God, you're even bothering with little things like trucking slips?"

"It's my job," she said quietly, "to bother with everything."

"What do you want to know about the trucking slips?" he asked.

"Everything. Where they come from, who fills

them out and how, and where they go after the cattle
have left the ranch.''

Jim Cole glanced at Bridget, who was talking to
somebody at the trucking firm, trying to order a cattle
liner for delivery within the next few hours. He rolled
his eyes at the bookkeeper and looked for a moment
like his old teasing self.

''The slips…well, they come from the trucking
company,'' he said, turning back to Jenny, his grin
fading. ''Every trucker carries a book of shipping bills
in his cab. After the cattle are loaded, he fills it out
with the date and the number of head he's hauling,
then signs it and gets it countersigned by the shipper,
which is us.''

Jenny nodded, making a note on her yellow pad.
''What happens to it then?''

''Whoever loads the cattle brings the slip up here
to Bridget. I guess she files it away somewhere. Right,
Bridget?''

The bookkeeper glanced up and nodded absently,
still listening on the phone.

Jenny indicated a pile of papers in a box at her
feet. ''And then when the cattle are sold, Bridget sta-
ples the trucking slip to the auction yard's statements
for each lot and files them all away in a folder for
that month's auctions. Right?''

''I guess so.'' Cole shrugged and got up, ambling
across the room to pour himself more coffee. ''Whatever she does, it seems to work pretty good. We've
never had any problems before.''

''Bridget is very efficient,'' Jenny said. ''I can't

believe how well she runs this office and does so much work all by herself.''

Bridget hung up in time to hear this. Her worried face softened at Jenny's praise.

"Did you get something?" Jim asked.

Bridget sighed. "I hate fighting with those people. They seem to have no idea what we're going through out here. She glanced down at her notes. "But they can spare a cattle liner this afternoon. It'll come around five o'clock."

The blond cowboy got to his feet, reached over to hug the bookkeeper and dropped a noisy kiss on her cheek. "You're a sweetheart, Bridget."

He paused on his way to the door. "You want a kiss, too, Jenny? Because I've got enough to go around, you know."

"Oh, I'm sure you have." She smiled at him politely. "But you'd better save your strength for filling those sandbags."

"Aw, shucks." He flashed a grin and fitted the wet cap on his head again. "Honey, you don't know what you're missing."

"Here, what's this? Is somebody flirting with my granddaughter?" Paddy asked from the doorway. "I can't allow this. The child's far too young and innocent for cowboys."

Jim laughed and paused briefly on his way outside to punch the older man affectionately on the shoulder. It was apparent that Paddy McKenna had won the hearts of everybody on the ranch.

He entered the room and sank onto the couch just vacated by the foreman, then gazed ruefully at his damp mud-stained jeans. "You have to give these people credit," he said. "They certainly know how to show a guest a good time."

That earned a chuckle from both women. Bridget got up and poured him a mug of coffee, handing it to him with a shy smile before she busied herself making a fresh pot.

"Are you sure you're not doing too much?" Jenny asked him. "Maybe you should take a break and relax for a while."

He laughed, a warm pleasant sound in the little office. "Jenny-girl, I can't remember when I've ever had so much fun. Battling the elements, fighting to survive... How often do city folks get the chance to do something like this?"

"Out here we battle the elements all the time," Bridget said quietly. "It wears people out, this constant struggle. It's just one thing after another, year after year."

Paddy's eyes crinkled with warmth as he looked at her. "But it makes you into fine people, Bridget. You folks living out here on the prairie, you're the salt of the earth."

The bookkeeper's cheeks flushed, and again Jenny was struck by how pretty she was. Bridget picked up a pen and began making entries in her ledger.

"You should be out there with us, Jenny," her grandfather said. "Poor Clay needs every hand he can get to fill sandbags."

"I can't stop what I'm doing and go out there to shovel sand, Grandpa," Jenny said. "I'm on salary. The government's paying me to do a job."

"I know, I know." He leaned back, smiling contritely, and took another gulp of coffee. "Even Maura's been helping this morning, you know. Until a few minutes ago she was shoveling right along with the rest of us. She can't work very fast, but she's certainly been trying, bless her heart."

He drained his cup, got up and headed for the door. "I'll see you ladies at lunch," he said, then clattered down the steps and headed back to the line of people working near the creek.

Bridget sat with her chin in her hand, sighing. "What a nice man," she murmured. "And *so* handsome."

Jenny gave her a teasing smile. "If I recall correctly, this is the second time you've said that very thing, Bridget. Do you have a crush on my grandpa, by any chance?"

But Bridget didn't smile back. Instead, she closed one of her ledgers with a little smack of impatience and reached for a fresh pile of invoices. "Well, I can tell you one thing," she said. "Maura Alderson certainly has a crush on that man. If your grandfather wasn't here, she'd no more be out filling sandbags than Teresa."

Jenny was amused, but decided to ignore the comment about her hostess. "Isn't Teresa helping at all?" she asked.

"Not that girl," Bridget said. "She claims she's got a sore back. If you ask me, she's a royal pain in the you-know-what."

Though privately Jenny agreed, she thought it might not be wise to express that opinion, either. Instead, she got up to help herself from the pot of freshly brewed coffee, then looked through the window at the sandbagging operation, seeing her grandfather's tall rangy body as he worked shoulder-to-shoulder with Clay Alderson.

"I really wish I could go out and help them," she said restlessly. "Maybe tomorrow if I get finished what I'm doing…"

"Now, don't let them make you feel guilty," Bridget said calmly. "You've got a job to do, and there's just no way to escape from it." Her face went bleak. "No way for any of us."

FOR THE REST OF THE DAY Jenny put aside all her tantalizing data about the auction sales and concentrated on finishing the rest of the audit, organizing her figures and typing data neatly onto the myriad forms she was required to file. Again she reminded herself it wasn't her job to find out where or how the funds were being stolen. All she had to do was show clear evidence of deliberate tax evasion, something worth passing on to the criminal-investigation division.

And when she'd presented the results of this audit, Jenny had no doubt that would happen.

Still, it took a conscious effort of will to leave the trail of the missing money and return to filling out forms regarding staff expenses and payroll, gas-well revenues and the enormous cost of maintaining a herd of bison on a prairie ranch.

Shortly after four o'clock, Bridget left the office to go see what she could do to prepare her little house for the worst if the dikes weren't able to contain the rushing water at flood crest.

The bookkeeper reappeared half an hour later, cheeks pink within the hood of her raincoat.

"Jenny, I'm supposed to tell you everybody's working on the dike, even Polly and Joe, so there'll be no dinner at the big house tonight. We're all eating down in the cook shack."

"Thanks, Bridget." Jenny looked up from the printer, which chattered away as it spewed out masses of paper. "That's the little tin-roofed building next to the barn, right?"

"Yes, and we'll be eating in shifts so people can keep working. Drop by whenever you get hungry."

Jenny looked at her watch. "I'll be finished here in about fifteen minutes, and then I'm going to help shovel sand for a while. Tell my grandpa not to work too hard, all right?"

Bridget gave her a wistful smile. "I'd be afraid to say any such thing, and you know it. Besides, he doesn't seem like a man who can be told what to do, does he?"

"Well, I've certainly never had much success at it," Jenny said dryly.

She longed to ask where Clay was and what he was doing, but resisted the urge. Bridget closed the door and left, splashing back through the puddles in the direction of the sandbagging crew.

At five o'clock Jenny completed her work for the day, locked her papers in a desk drawer and stored her computer files under the password she'd created, then tidied the office and went outside.

Rain continued to fall, a relentless drizzle that flowed away in muddy streams on the waterlogged soil. Through the mist she could see a massive shape parked near the corral, and recognized it as a cattle liner backed up to one of the loading chutes. A dark hooded figure was perched on one of the corral rails, talking to somebody out of sight in the pen below.

Intrigued, Jenny skirted around a deep puddle of water and approached the truck. The person on the corral rail was Teresa, wearing a black plastic hooded rain cape. Her white face was expressionless.

Jenny climbed the corral rails and stood next to the girl, looking into the corral.

A burly man young was leaning against the fence, apparently flirting with the unresponsive Teresa. He wore a cap emblazoned with the logo of the trucking firm, and despite the cold and rain, a sleeveless T-shirt. The cloth was plastered to his muscular body, and his tanned arms sported several tattoos, mostly of snakes and daggers.

"Hi," Jenny said.

"This is the tax auditor," Teresa said coldly. "I told you she was here."

The young man glanced up at Jenny and grinned, showing a missing front tooth. "I'm Gordie," he said, gesturing at the cattle liner. "I drive the truck."

"So you do lot of the hauling for the ranch?" Jenny asked.

"Most of it. I like coming out here." The young trucker looked up at Teresa with a significant glance. "The company's real good."

The girl rewarded him with a lofty humorless smile, then stared into the rainy corral again.

So Gordie, too, appeared to be smitten by Teresa. Jenny couldn't understand the strange young woman's appeal. Teresa must give off some kind of pheromone that was attractive only to men.

While Jenny was thinking about Michael Alderson's girlfriend, a mass of dark shapes materialized through the misty corral, moving toward the loading chute. About a dozen small cows, their hides slick with moisture, eyes rolling in fear, were driven onto the ramp by Joe Dagg and a couple other cowboys. They plodded into the truck and Gordie trotted up the ramp to move them to the front, then enclosed them behind a partition.

Joe and his helpers went back into the corral and reappeared with a group of bulls, several of them limping badly. Jenny watched in fascination as the massive animals were driven up the ramp with much shouting and swearing, and locked in the center of the cattle liner by young Gordie.

Suddenly Joe and the other ranch workers flattened themselves against the corral rails and stared down an alley barred by heavy rails. Jenny, too, tensed and held her breath as Clay walked toward her, leading the bay stallion by a leather halter.

The big horse was covered with a trailer blanket and his eyes were blindfolded. He moved with exaggerated caution, his sightless head thrown erect, steps high and nervous. Clay kept to one side of him, watching the horse warily from under his hat brim.

Jim Cole brought up the rear, holding a portable

gate to shield his body and standing close behind the
big horse as Clay led him up the ramp.

When they reached the top of the loading chute,
the stallion smelled the imprisoned animals in the
truck and tossed his head, then swung his body vi-
ciously in the rancher's direction.

Jenny tensed and watched in an agony of fear as
Clay vanished between the stallion and the fence. But
he emerged after a moment, straddling the top rail,
and leaned down to deftly unfasten the halter rope as
Jim pressed forward from the rear with his wooden
barrier. Together they guided the big animal into the
truck, then Gordie sprang forward to latch the gate.

"Thank God that's done, at least," Clay said while
Jenny watched him in silence.

"I'm not unloading that big bugger," the trucker
warned. "I don't want my head sliced open."

"Jim's going along with you," Clay told the
trucker. "We'll let the stallion out at the corral in the
community pasture. Hopefully he'll be all right there
for a couple of days. Joe's going to drive up and get
you, Jim. Come on, boys," he added, coiling the halter rope. "We've got lots of work to do yet."

With a brief glance at Jenny, he went off with the
other cowboys, leaving his foreman, Joe Dagg and
the young trucker near the fence with the two women.

"Well," Jim said at last, "if we're going, we'd
best get on the road. Come on, Joe."

The driver gave Teresa another adoring glance,
then headed for the cab of his truck. "I gotta fill out
this shipping form," he called over his shoulder.

Jim watched him go, then paused by the fence to

mutter something to Teresa. She bent low to respond. Jenny watched curiously, wondering what they were saying, especially when Cole gestured at the young trucker and seemed angry. Teresa managed to look even more sullen than usual. She turned her head away and ignored the foreman, her jaw set stubbornly.

"Here's the trucking slip," the driver called. "Who wants to take it to the office?"

Joe was already moving toward one of the ranch pickups, deep in conversation with Jim Cole as they prepared to follow the cattle liner out of the valley. Teresa ignored the question, glaring at the corral with a brooding expression.

"I'll take it," Jenny volunteered.

"Okay," Gordie said, still watching Teresa from the shelter of his opened truck door. He scribbled something on a pad. "You wanna sign it, too?"

Jenny looked up at Teresa, who continued to ignore her.

"Sure, I guess I can sign it," Jenny said.

She scribbled her signature on the form, then waited as Gordie tore a yellow slip from the pad and handed it to her. Jenny folded the paper hastily and put it in her pocket before it could get soaked, watching while the driver climbed inside and put the cattle liner in gear.

He pulled away from the loading chute, turned around and lumbered out of the yard with fountains of water gushing from beneath his heavy tires. The other two men followed in a pickup.

When they were gone, Teresa climbed down from

the fence and headed toward the house, ignoring Jenny as if she didn't exist.

Jenny fell into step with her, trying to sound casual. "Do you often come down to watch them loading cattle?" she asked.

Teresa gave one of her characteristic shrugs. "Sometimes. Gordie's more interesting than most of the jerks around here."

"I see."

More interesting than Michael, your boyfriend, and the reason you're living out here in the first place? Jenny wanted to ask.

Instead, she turned aside when their paths diverged and stood in the rain watching as Teresa plodded off toward the ranch house, her shoulders hunched, hands plunged deep in the pockets of her cape.

She looked so bored and miserable that Jenny felt a twinge of sympathy for her. Again she wondered why the girl stayed.

Still thoughtful, Jenny went back to the office, took the yellow trucking slip from her pocket and put it on Bridget's desk.

About to leave the office, she turned on a sudden impulse and went back to glance at the shipping form. Then she lifted the paper and examined it carefully, studying the column where Gordie had listed the total number of animals loaded on the truck.

Suddenly dry-mouthed with excitement, she hurried across the room, unlocked her temporary desk and took out a handful of the other papers, comparing them with the trucker's slip.

All at once she realized how the embezzlement had

been managed. It was going to take a lot more sleuthing and some serious number crunching to prove her theory. But Jenny knew that by the end of another day, she would not only know how the money had been stolen, she was going to have a pretty good idea who'd done it.

CHAPTER FOURTEEN

NIGHT FELL across the prairie and the rain increased its tempo, streaming down from the coulees, flowing through the darkness into the swollen waterways.

"My God," Joe Dagg said to Bridget across the table in the cook shack. "I never seen a rain like this in my life. Have you, Bridget? So much bloody rain, it's hard to figure where it all comes from."

The others ranged along the rough pine table nodded wearily and concentrated on their plates. Rain pounded on the tin roof like small shotgun blasts, making conversation difficult. And most of these people were too tired to talk much even if they could make themselves heard.

Bridget murmured something to the old cowboy in reply and picked listlessly at her plateful of chili and hash browns.

It seemed her life had been difficult and terrifying for such a long time she could hardly remember being happy. But the troubles had only started, of course, back in the fall with Maura's investment tip and her ill-advised venture into the stock market.

Losing her nest egg had been a dreadful, soul-destroying thing, and not because money was so important to Bridget. What tortured her was the knowledge that she'd been greedy and foolish, and as a result had squandered both her hard-won independence and all her dreams for the future.

She'd long been accustomed to a life of loneliness and hard work, and she could even have made the best of her financial misfortune. But this tax auditor was something else again, this quiet woman who was going through the ranch books, rooting out all Bridget's sins and errors and exposing them, one by one, to the light of day so everybody would soon be able to see how she'd betrayed her employer.

And now this flood coming down on them like a judgment, sweeping away all the hopes and dreams of the Alderson family, along with her own.

Maura sat across the table from Bridget, next to Paddy McKenna whose handsome bald head was tilted courteously to one side, listening to something his bright little hostess was telling him over the thunder of the rain.

Paddy caught Bridget's eye and smiled, his face creasing warmly with good-natured humor before he returned to his conversation with Maura.

Bridget sighed again and took a mouthful of potato, wondering how it would feel to be like Maura, so secure in her attractiveness, able to flirt and enrapture a man even in the midst of this awful crisis.

As if responding to Bridget's thoughts, Maura, too, looked up and smiled, then gave her friend a mischievous wink. Suddenly the years fell away and Maura looked just as she had when she and Bridget were young girls growing up on neighboring ranches.

Maura had hardly changed at all in more than sixty

years. She'd always been small, quick-moving and mercurial, with a cheerful knowledge of her appeal to men, coupled with a warm generous nature that made women like her, as well.

At this moment Bridget wanted to hate the woman, but she couldn't. Not even while Maura was monopolizing and charming the very man Bridget found more attractive than anybody she'd met since her husband died more than thirty years ago.

Bridget glanced down the length of the table. About twenty people sat eating, most of them in the damp, mud-stained clothes they'd been wearing while they worked on the sandbag dike.

Only a few, like Teresa, looked dry and clean. Of course, Teresa had just wandered down from the ranch house a few minutes ago.

Maura leaned across the table at that moment, also looking at Michael's girlfriend. "Are you going to help us shovel sand, Teresa?" she asked. "I'm sure Clay can use some extra hands."

Teresa shook her head and nibbled languidly at a slice of bread. "I can't shovel. My back's sore."

"Oh, dear, that's too bad," Maura said coldly. "Well, then, I think you'd better stay down here and help Polly and the others cook for the next shift. I understand they've got a mountain of potatoes to peel. That's a job you can do while you're sitting down."

Teresa gave her boyfriend's grandmother a brief malevolent glance. "I can't—"

Maura met the girl's eyes steadily. "Yes, I think you can," she said with steel in her voice. "This is a crisis, Teresa. We need everybody on the ranch helping out, and that includes you.''

On Maura's other side, Allan chuckled and looked up with an impudent grin. "Teresa's got kitchen duty!'' he said. "Hey, Teresa, too bad your back's so sore. I'd rather fill sandbags than peel potatoes any day.''

Teresa glared at the laughing young man with open hostility, then glanced at Michael as if looking for support. But Clay's other son ate in silence, ignoring the conversation.

Bridget, who'd always had a warm place in her heart for Michael, knew the boy was thinking about his dike of hay bales. He was fretting over its construction and brooding about whether it would hold when the flood crest hit or be a huge waste of time and manpower and expense.

Michael Alderson lived for his father's praise, Bridget knew. He'd feel terrible if the dike washed away and the hay meadow flooded, even though he was working as hard as he could to get the job done.

And Teresa certainly wouldn't be any help or support to him, Bridget thought in annoyance. She'd seldom even seen the girl give her boyfriend a kind word, let alone the kind of comfort and encouragement a man needed from his partner.

But poor Clay. He was the one who really needed comfort and encouragement, and he was the loneliest of them all.

Bridget glanced across the table at her employer. He ate silently, looking so weary and troubled that her heart was wrung with sympathy. She could hardly bear to think about everything he was enduring right now.

She wondered what he was thinking, but his face was impossible to read. When would this terrible crisis pass so their lives could get back to normal? She sighed and began to pick at her food again.

CLAY FELT BRIDGET'S worried glance and tried without success to summon a reassuring smile for her. He took a sip of coffee and mechanically buttered another slice of bread, realizing she was in agony over something. He needed to talk with her and find out what the trouble was, try to set her mind at rest. But he just couldn't find the time. There was no time for anything but this gargantuan battle he was fighting, and increasingly he doubted if was going to win.

Involuntarily he glanced at Jenny who sat a few places down the table across from him, listening to something Jim Cole was telling her. She'd been working on the dike for a couple of hours and her clothes were as wet and soiled as his own. Clay noticed a little smear of dried mud on one of her cheeks. He found himself yearning to reach out and wipe it away.

More and more he wanted to touch this woman, to hold her and find comfort in her body. The longings puzzled him, because he would have thought such urges would be the furthest thing from his mind in the midst of a crisis like the one he faced. He was so tired right now that he didn't even want to bother with the patient rituals of courtship and all the things a man had to say and do to get close to a woman. He wanted Jenny McKenna in his bed, wrapped tight in his arms, lying beneath him while the rain drummed on the roof and he lost himself over and over again in the sweetness of her body....

He shook his head and began to eat again, remembering that dreadful moment earlier in the day when he'd rushed into the barn and found her cowering in the manger while the stallion lashed out at her with his hooves.

Clay tensed and gripped his fork tightly.

That event had been so unsettling, so heartstopping, that he didn't like to think about it. Jenny's terror and the danger she was in had reminded him of—

No! he thought in anguish.

He couldn't let himself start thinking about little Suzy. Not now, while he had so many things to concentrate on.

Briefly he wondered about the audit and what Jenny was finding. In a normal world he would have been following the situation closely, checking on her progress to find out what was happening with the books.

But at this point he didn't even know if she'd found anything in her search. And she must be almost finished, because she'd mentioned winding up her audit tomorrow and heading back to the city.

Clay wondered if she still planned to do that, or if she'd stay at the ranch and continue to help as they waited for the flood crest to arrive. He knew her grandfather intended to stay on through the weekend, but maybe Jenny was still too conscious of her uncomfortable position as the tax auditor and wouldn't want to become too involved in their personal affairs.

I still need to talk to her, Clay decided. *Before she leaves, I've got to know what she's found.*

He resolved to find some time alone with Jenny that night, before the next day brought them all to the brink of disaster. Somehow he'd manage to question her and find out what she might have discovered.

She looked up at that moment and met his eyes gravely, while the foreman continued to joke and banter at her side.

Clay felt his heart lurch and turn over, his groin tighten with sexual desire. He'd never met a woman who had such an immediate powerful effect on him. It was all he could do to keep from shoving his chair aside, striding around the table and hauling her off to his bed.

But he only gave her a brief, courteous smile and finished the last of his meal, then got up and reached for his hat and slicker. His sons and most of the other workers followed him outside into the rain.

For a while all thoughts of the woman vanished from Clay's mind as he began to issue orders and make plans for the next stage of the battle.

BY THE TIME she'd worked on sandbag detail for a few hours after dinner, Jenny's body had hardened to the task and her mind wandered freely, helping to ease the grinding monotony.

She lifted and shoveled, lifted and shoveled, her movements spare and mechanical. As she worked she thought about the history of this beautiful old ranch and all the people who'd lived here over the years, trying to imagine what it must be like in normal times when they weren't faced with such a crisis. How privileged they were, she thought, to be able to live out here in this wild loveliness.

She felt a brief jolt of sadness and realized she was going to miss Cottonwood Creek tomorrow after she'd left. Nor was she likely to be welcomed back, Jenny thought grimly as she paused and leaned on the shovel for a moment to rest her back. Not after what she would soon have to report to her superiors.

But she didn't like to think about the ledgers and her painstaking audit, the worrisome discrepancies she'd brought to light. She brushed back a strand of hair and tucked it under her cap, looking around at her fellow workers. About forty people were filling sandbags along with her. Now that the animals were safely moved and the houses and outbuildings secured as best they could manage, Clay had put most of his staff to work on the dikes.

Michael was still in charge of the long dirt-covered barrier down in the hay meadow where Paddy had also gone to help, lending some of his engineering expertise, as well as a strong back and a fund of cheerful energy that kept the men's spirits up. Clay had assigned half a dozen more hands to his son's project, showing both his faith in the dike and his mounting desperation over the prospect of flooded hay meadows.

The rest of them were struggling to shore up the lower banks of the creek through the main ranch yard where barns, machine sheds and houses were most at risk.

Clay had ordered the dike built to a height of three feet over the past few days, but the water already lapped near the top of the piled sandbags, washing over in places, and they still had almost twenty-four hours until the river crested. Jenny and the others were scrambling to add another three feet, a task that seemed impossible unless they could find more workers.

And people had to sleep. They couldn't keep going at this pace or they'd simply drop. Still, it was amazing what people could accomplish when they all worked together. Slowly but surely, the stack of heavy plastic sandbags was rising all along the length of the creek.

If only they'd had another couple of days' warning, maybe they could have beaten the floodwaters. But as it was, Jenny didn't see how the ranch could be saved.

What a tragedy to lose so much of what a family had worked more than a century to build.

"It's ten o'clock, people," Clay called through the darkness. "I want everybody to take six hours off and try to get some sleep. Be back out here at dawn to start work again, all right?"

Some of the workers protested, reluctant to give up so many precious hours. These people, after all, were in danger of losing their own homes, as well as their livelihood.

But Clay waved off their objections. "None of you will be any good to us if you're overtired and sick," he told them. "Tomorrow's the day when we'll need all hands on deck, rested enough to work twelve hours without stopping. If you've managed to grab some sleep during the day, you can keep working. Otherwise it's time to go home and go to bed."

Talking quietly amongst themselves, tense with worry, the ranch hands stored their shovels in the barn and filed off. Jenny did the same, trudging through the rain to the big house.

Nobody seemed to be around when she got there. The kitchen was silent and she couldn't hear a television set anywhere, not even a scrap of music or conversation from upstairs. The family members were either still out working or else sleeping the few hours they could manage to snatch before tomorrow's dawn.

Jenny stepped out of her wet boots and hung her jacket and cap by the door. She tiptoed through the hallway and up the back stairs to her room, trying not to make any noise. In her room she tugged off her sodden jeans with a sigh of relief, then took her shampoo, hair dryer and cosmetics bag and went into the bathroom to have a shower.

For a long time she stood and turned under the streaming jets, feeling the heat and driving force of the water beginning to revive her weary muscles. The pleasure was almost mesmerizing after so many hours of toil in the cold and darkness. She ran her hands down the length of her body, conscious of her physical self, surprised by a strong, pulsing sexuality.

Clay's face came into her mind and she couldn't push it away. She imagined him cupping her breasts and touching the erect nipples, then stroking her waist, her abdomen and thighs slowly, lingeringly.

She continued to soap herself dreamily, thinking about his slanted cheekbones and piercing eyes, his finely shaped mouth, those competent hands with their callused palms. Those hands touching the most intimate part of her, making her feel so good…

She shook herself and stepped out of the shower, then wrapped a towel around her hair and used another to dry her body. She avoided her reflection in the mirror, shocked and distressed by her wayward lustful thoughts. This was so unlike her, to be dreaming and fantasizing about any man, let alone one she was investigating in the course of her job. But she couldn't seem to get his image out of her mind, or forget the times he'd held and kissed her, the way it had felt to be in his arms with his hard body pressing against hers.

Again Jenny wrestled her thoughts under control, took the dryer and began to ply it on her damp hair, so close to the mirror that she couldn't avoid looking at her troubled face.

I'm worn out, she thought. *And I'm worried about the damned audit. I need to get away from this place as soon as I can.*

She frowned at her image in the mirror, wondering if she could leave when she finished the books in the morning. Jenny had already completed her portion of the audit to her satisfaction. If there'd been nothing wrong in the ledgers or tax forms, she would have needed another day to tidy up the rest of the forms.

As it was, her job required her to pass the audit

higher up if she was certain a fraud had been committed. But she was so tantalizingly close to figuring out who'd actually stolen the money, even though that sort of detective work wasn't part of her job. Besides, she argued, how could anybody drive away when it was the weekend and the Alderson family were in such a state of crisis, needing all the help they could muster? Especially since they'd been so hospitable to her during her stay. It would be a shabby way to behave.

But I can't stay here, Jenny thought in despair. *If I spend any more time with the man, I'm going to fall apart completely.*

Still, the argument continued, there was small danger of anything happening, no matter how attractive she found her host. Absorbed as he was in the battle with the oncoming flood, Clay Alderson hardly had the time or energy to seduce a visiting tax auditor, even if he wanted to.

She finished drying her hair and left it loose around her face, then padded naked into the other room, took her plaid nightshirt from a drawer and pulled it over her head.

The shower had revived her, made her feel restless and unable to sleep although she was physically tired. She moved quietly around the room, packing and tidying her belongings in case she did decide to leave the following day. Finally she looked at a small pile of books on the dresser, trying to decide which one she wanted to read.

Clay had brought her the novels from his own library, telling her they were all ones he'd enjoyed. She lingered over the bright dust jackets, surprised again at how similar their tastes were. Every book was one she would have enjoyed reading. Wistfully, she pictured a world where there were no floods or tax audits. She imagined herself sitting at the big dining-room table with Clay, laughing and talking as they discussed books and shared ideas.

Maybe later they'd go out for a walk together in the mellow prairie twilight and play with the kittens for a while. Then they'd come back to the house and climb the stairs together to his big master bedroom. Clay would close the door behind them and turn to her with that unsmiling intense look that made her shiver with anticipation. He'd take her in his arms and lift her, carry her toward the bed...

Jenny's cheeks warmed at the pictures filling her mind. She snatched one of the books at random, put the light out and climbed into bed, then turned on her lamp and tried to concentrate on the printed pages.

But the words blurred in front of her eyes. The casement window stood open a few inches and the curtain fluttered in the damp wind. Shadows danced on the walls, huge and soft in the diffused light.

Suddenly Jenny heard a muffled knock at the door. She frowned and strained to listen. The sound came again, difficult to hear above the steady pounding of the rain.

She slipped from the bed, crossed the room and paused with her hand on the knob. "Who is it?" she asked softly.

"It's Clay. I need to talk to you for a minute if that's all right."

Jenny's heart began to pound. She looked around for a housecoat or something to cover herself, but she hadn't bothered to pack anything so bulky for this brief summer trip. Oh, well, her nightshirt was a modest garment, hanging almost to her knees, with elbow-length sleeves.

She opened the door and looked out. Clay stood in his moccasins in the dim light of the hallway, wearing jeans and a white T-shirt. He, too, had just showered, and smelled pleasantly of soap and shaving cream. His big body was taut with fatigue, his eyes darkly shadowed. He carried a tray with a cut-glass whiskey bottle, a couple of glasses and a plateful of crackers and cheese.

"Want a snack?" he asked. "I'm starving."

"But I—"

"It's not the way it looks," he told her. "This is a business discussion, Jenny. I want to talk about the audit."

CHAPTER FIFTEEN

JENNY REALIZED suddenly that she was, in fact, very hungry. Still, she was reluctant—no, afraid—to let him into her room.

"I won't stay long," he said. "We all need to get some sleep. I just wanted to ask you a few questions and I thought we might as well combine the two activities. Eating and talking, I mean," he added with a weary grin.

She saw how tired he looked and felt guilty at her own thoughts. Nodding wordlessly, she stood aside and let him in, then closed the door behind him while he carried the tray over to the dresser.

He set it down, then sprawled in an armchair near the window. "I hope I didn't wake you," he said, gesturing at her lamp and the rumpled bedcovers.

"I was reading." Jenny paused awkwardly, wondering what to do. He'd already taken the only chair in the room, and the floorboards were chilly on her bare feet.

At last, trying to look casual, she climbed back into bed and pulled the covers up around her waist, grateful for the girlish modesty of her nightshirt.

But her host didn't seem at all uncomfortable.

"Which book is that?" he asked, leaning over to peer at the cover. Jenny held it up so he could see.

Clay nodded and settled back, uncapping the whiskey bottle. "I liked that one. The mystery was really well done. I didn't figure out who the killer was until the last chapter."

"Don't tell me," Jenny said hastily. "I just started it."

He laughed. "Good. Then you'll have to take it home with you and finish it, and that'll give me an excuse to see you again."

She looked down nervously at her hands, folded on the bedspread.

"Would you like a drink?" Clay asked.

She hesitated, then nodded. "All right, but just a small one, please. I don't usually like to drink whiskey without mix."

"Neither do I, but I couldn't find anything in the fridge and I didn't want to bother Polly." He poured an inch of whiskey into a heavy tumbler and reached over to hand it to her.

Jenny accepted the drink and sipped, feeling the rich warmth coursing down her throat.

Clay leaned back, dark head resting wearily against the back of the chair. "It's hard to believe there'll ever be a time when I can think about nice ordinary things like picking up borrowed books," he said. "Right now I feel like I'm going to be fighting this damned war for the rest of my life."

She took another taste of the golden liquor, her heart wrung with sympathy.

Clay gathered himself together with a visible effort

and handed her the plateful of crackers and cheese. Jenny took a couple and munched gratefully, surprised by how cozy and pleasant it felt to be with him, even in a situation as intimate as this one.

In his absence she worried all the time about her professional relationship with this man and how it might be affected by her attraction to him. But all the strain seemed to fall away when they were actually together. At the moment she didn't feel at all like a government auditor, just a woman spending time with a man whose company she enjoyed.

"This is like a picnic, isn't it?" he said, echoing her thoughts. "It feels so nice and cozy when everybody else is asleep and we're gobbling up all the snacks."

"I've always loved picnics."

"Me, too."

Jenny laughed, then sobered. "What chance do you have of surviving this flood?" she asked. "Realistically, I mean."

"Realistically?" He took a long swallow of his whiskey. "Slim to none," he said at last. "If the crest is a bit lower than they're projecting, and if we can streamline our technique tomorrow to get more work done, and if the rain happens to stop, we could just squeak by."

"And if not?"

He sighed, "God, I don't even like to think about it. The cost would be horrendous. At least nine of the houses could flood, and most of the major outbuildings. We can't sandbag all of them. And the hay meadows..."

He picked up several crackers and ate them along with hefty wedges of cheese. Jenny realized he must have sliced the cheddar himself, and none too skillfully. She imagined him all alone down in the kitchen, preparing his hasty late-night snack. The thought made her smile and feel another dangerous surge of warmth.

"Do you have insurance?" she asked.

He raised his eyebrows. "You mean there's actually something about my financial affairs you don't already know?"

"I saw quite a few insurance premiums listed in the expense ledger," she said calmly. "But I don't know what kind of coverage you have."

"Well, I'm afraid it's not very much. Most of the houses carry a bit of insurance, but I don't have any on the outbuildings, and you can't even get flood insurance on a standing hay crop. It's going to be a disaster. I'll probably have to sell some land to cover the damages."

"Are you really reluctant to do that?" Jenny asked.

"I think all ranchers hate selling land. It's so hard to get pasture, especially in a usable block. When you have to let it slip away again to pay the bills, that really hurts."

She nodded and took another sip of whiskey, thinking about all that missing cash and the consequences when it was finally tracked down.

She turned aside hastily to take more of the cheese and crackers, afraid he might be able to read her thoughts again. But he was leaning back in the chair with his eyes closed. She stole a glance at his tanned features, the clean line of his cheek and jaw, the surprising thickness and length of his eyelashes.

He looked up suddenly and found her watching him. Their eyes met and held for a long time until she looked away.

"I appreciate your help, Jenny," he said, raising his glass in her direction. "It's good of you and your grandfather to work so hard on our behalf."

"We're glad to be able to do something," Jenny said, feeling more treacherous than ever.

Because Paddy might be helping the people at Cottonwood Creek in the midst of this crisis, but she was spending her days scouring the books for discrepancies that could land this beleaguered rancher in jail.

"The books aren't looking good, are they?" he asked quietly.

She fitted a bit of cheese on top of a cracker, her hands suddenly tense. "I can't really discuss it with you at this point," she said. "When I've finished and filed my report, you'll be able to—"

He looked too tired to press the issue. Instead, he waved a hand and took another cracker. "I think I knew there was something wrong," he said. "Even before Saul told me about the dropping revenues, I had a feeling the books were off-kilter. But we've been so busy these past couple of years, I guess I didn't pay as much attention as I should have."

Jenny listened in silence, wanting to believe him.

"And every time I tried to talk about the books," he went on, "it seemed to upset Bridget. She's been unhappy about something lately. I know I should have talked to her, but there's always so damned much to do around here I just kept letting it slide and hoping things would get back on course."

"The bookkeeping is a big job for Bridget," Jenny said after a brief uncomfortable silence. "This ranch is a complicated operation, especially now that so many things are computerized. I think she might be getting a little out of her depth."

"I know. I should hire a professional to do the books, but it's a touchy situation. I need to keep providing a home for Bridget, and she wouldn't want to accept charity. She'd demand to keep working."

For the first time Jenny began to realize the awkwardness of his position as an employer. The people who worked for Clay Alderson didn't simply give him a few hours of their time every day. They devoted their lives to this place.

And that kind of lifelong loyalty demanded a return.

"So, do you want a job?" he asked her with a tired smile.

"Me?" she said, startled.

"Why not?" His dark eyes rested on her thoughtfully. "You like it out here, right? And you're certainly qualified. I'll offer you housing and a good salary. You can take over management of the office and let Bridget be your assistant. I'll give you whatever you need in the way of computers and equipment."

"You're serious." She stared at him in amazement.

"Damn right I'm serious. If I've got problems with my books, then it's time I hired somebody who can do the job properly without hurting Bridget's feelings or throwing her out into the cold."

"But I have a job already," she said. "I can't just…leave."

"Why not? Do you really like working up in that crowded room with all those other people and not even having an office with a window?"

With his usual unnerving accuracy, he'd put his finger on the very things Jenny most disliked about her job. She began to feel defensive, almost frightened.

"I manage to get out of the office a lot of the time," she said. "I have to do quite a few on-site audits like this one."

"I see." He watched her over the rim of his glass. "Well, my offer stands. I'll give you a house to live in and a better salary than you're earning now. And as a bonus," he added, his face lighting with one of his rare smiles, "you'll have all the running room you could ever wish for."

Jenny smiled back in spite of herself. For a moment she pictured what he was offering, let herself imagine living out here and managing the books and payroll, going for long walks in the evening, reading by a cozy fireplace when the winter winds howled and snow drifted across the prairie.

She felt a harsh stab of longing and suppressed it firmly, wondering if this job offer was some kind of bribe. Maybe the next demand would be that she keep quiet about what she'd found in the books.

She glanced at her host in suspicion, but he was still smiling dreamily as he sprawled in the chair.

"This is so good," he said.

"What's good?"

"Everything." He waved his glass to indicate the soft pool of light cast by her lamp, the drinks and food, the curtain lifting gently on the breeze and the steady whisper of raindrops in the vine beyond the window. "It feels wonderful to sit and talk with somebody at the end of a hard day."

All her suspicions vanished in another treacherous rush of sympathy. The man worked so hard to provide for all these people who depended on him, and then spent his evenings alone.

Her emotions must have shown on her face, because he leaned over and touched one of her hands, then gripped it in his own. "You're such a nice person, Jenny," he said quietly.

"No," she whispered, looking down at their linked hands. "I'm not."

He got up, set the tray of food and the glasses aside and lowered himself onto the bed next to her, still holding her hand.

Jenny opened her mouth to protest, but couldn't seem to find the words. Instead, she moved over a little to make room for him.

"You're lonely, too, aren't you?" he said gently, reaching up to stoke her cheek. "It's hard to believe that a woman so beautiful could ever be lonely."

"Please, don't say things like that." She tried to move away from him. "We shouldn't…"

He ran his fingers under her chin and lifted her face. He was so close she could see jewel-like flecks of green and gold in the brown depths of his eyes.

"Yes, you're beautiful, Jenny," he whispered. "In every way."

"Clay, please…"

But his gaze was direct and compelling, almost hypnotic. And she couldn't doubt his sincerity. This man really, truly believed she was beautiful. It seemed incredible to her, but it was true. She didn't think any man, even Steve, had ever looked at her with such a heady mixture of desire and admiration. Her mind swam with a tangled whirl of emotions.

He twisted to face her, putting his hands on her shoulders, sliding them down her back. "How long has it been since a man told you how lovely you are?"

She didn't answer, only nestled in his embrace, clinging to him, burying her face in his chest.

"You're as lonely as I am," he murmured against her cheek. "Aren't you?"

She nodded into the warm cotton of his shirt.

He moved closer on the bed, drawing her more securely into his arms, bending to kiss her cheek. "Such a sweet lovely woman, and all alone," he whispered huskily. "It doesn't seem right."

Jenny understood with despairing certainty that if she didn't stop this now, immediately, there'd be no turning back.

Her whole body was on fire. She ached for the man, yearned to feel his mouth and hands, his strong naked body moving on hers…

"Do you want me to go away?" he murmured softly, his lips close against her ear. "I'll leave now if you say the word."

He's under investigation! a small voice screamed inside her head.

But he's so…and I keep feeling…

The man's probably guilty of tax fraud, and you're the auditor!

Under any other circumstances, Jenny would certainly have listened to that warning voice. But tonight it was somehow drowned out by the roar of rising floodwaters, the sense of imminent disaster, the pounding rain beyond the window.

And the troubling sexual desire that had haunted her since she'd first looked at Clay Alderson, complicated by a woman's age-old yearning to give comfort and ease to a man when he was in the midst of a crisis.

She pulled away and looked at him with the frankness that was part of her nature. "We shouldn't be doing this, Clay. It's wrong for us even to think about it."

"Wrong?" he asked hoarsely. "To love each other for a while and find some warmth in the storm? Tell me, Jenny, how can it be wrong?"

Deep in her mind that urgent voice continued to scream its warning, but Jenny was no longer even listening. She put her hands on each side of Clay's face, gazing at him hungrily as if she could never get enough of looking at him.

She reached up with her thumb to stroke one of his cheekbones, surprised by the silky feel of his tanned skin. Everything about this man was so finely made, so appealing.…

Clay caught her hand and kissed the fingers, then took her thumb between his teeth and bit down gently, looking into her eyes all the while.

"I could gobble you up," he said. "I've wanted to since the first time I saw you sitting across the table from me in that restaurant."

Jenny's stomach tightened with excitement and desire. Keeping her eyes on him, she got up and stepped away from the bed, then with calm deliberation, pulled the nightshirt over her head and stood facing him, completely naked.

Clay drew a sharp breath. He got to his feet, as well, then reached out to touch her breasts, ran his fingers down the curve of her waist and over the slight flare of her hips.

"Beautiful," he whispered again, staring at her. "Jenny, you really are."

Perhaps it was the whiskey, driving away all her inhibitions. Or the strange intimacy of their situation, like two people clinging to a life raft while disaster loomed in the darkness surrounding them.

Whatever the reason, Jenny didn't feel at all uncomfortable or self-conscious under his gaze. She felt cherished and desired, more secure about herself and her body than she'd ever felt with Steve.

In fact, her former fiancé had often pointed out little imperfections in her, as if she were a racehorse he was thinking of buying. She would have been reluctant to stand naked in front of him like this.

"Steve...my boyfriend didn't used to think so," she heard herself saying. "He always told me my feet were too long and thin, and my breasts were too small, and my—"

"Steve was an idiot," Clay interrupted her, sweeping her into his arms. "Let's not talk about him anymore. What man could look at a goddess and find fault?"

Suddenly, inexplicably, Jenny began to feel wonderful. She was drunk with happiness, on fire with a lusty wanton kind of playfulness she'd never experienced before.

"So," she whispered, smiling against his chest, "are you a god? Because otherwise I'll have to ask you to leave my bedchamber immediately. So come on, let's have a look at you."

He chuckled, his breath warm on her cheek "Oh, Jenny, I'm just a broken-down old cowboy. You're going to be disappointed."

"I doubt that."

She tugged at his shirt, pulling it over his head to reveal a pair of broad shoulders and a lean, hard-muscled torso. His chest was matted with dark curly hair that ran down the center of his flat abdomen and disappeared under his belt.

Jenny's fingers toyed with the line of dark hair, her hand straying lower and lower until it dipped inside the waistband of his jeans. She felt him shiver, then she grasped the zipper and lowered it, finally kneeling to tug his jeans down and off his ankles.

He stood naked before her except for his shorts, his desire alarmingly evident. She touched him there, tentatively, wonderingly, and his response was to groan and pull her body hard against his.

"See what you do to me, Jenny," he gasped, then pulled her onto the bed, discarded his shorts and lay holding her.

Jenny was surprised by how easy it was to be with

him this way. She felt as if she'd known him for years, not just days, and sensed he felt the same way.

He knelt above Jenny and began to kiss her with feathery-light brushes of his lips that began at her forehead and ears, moved over her face and neck and progressed downward, over her breasts, her abdomen...

Jenny shuddered with arousal. His mouth and hands were building her to a fever pitch, a height of passion she'd never known and was afraid to reach.

Then, so gently that she didn't realize how it happened, he was inside her. He seemed to fill her body with a rich silken warmth that moved and thrust with infinite tenderness, soothing and exciting her at the same time.

She tensed, trying to push the confusion away, to retain a grasp of where she was and what was happening to her.

"Is everything all right?" he asked in her ear. "Should we be using something, Jenny?"

"Using...?" She struggled to concentrate on what he was saying. "No, no," she said faintly. "It's all right. Don't stop. Please don't stop..."

He kept stroking gently, his mouth roaming her face and breasts, his hand reaching between them to keep stimulating her.

"You're fighting it, sweetheart," he whispered. "Relax. Trust me."

"But I've never..."

He paused. "You've never climaxed?"

She wasn't afraid to answer, because she knew it was possible to tell this man anything.

"I always faked it," she whispered. "Steve was so upset if I didn't, but it never seemed to happen so I just—"

He kissed her to stop her talking, then continued with his patient lovemaking. Gradually Jenny abandoned herself to pleasure, gave up fighting her deep fear of losing control. A rich warmth spread through her body, a feeling of hushed imminence. Then, abruptly, the world exploded, vibrating crazily. She moaned aloud, dazed by pleasure.

When she recovered her senses, Jenny was locked in his arms, panting, while her body quivered in rhythmic bursts of sensation.

Clay laughed softly and cradled her, studying her face with searching tenderness. "That wasn't bad considering we're both dead tired from hard physical labor. Wait till we've had a rest and see what we can do."

Jenny couldn't speak, couldn't even summon the strength to smile.

Still, a part of her mind was already beginning to return to sanity, to tell her that no matter how wonderful he was or how much she loved being in his arms, there would be no "next time" for her and Clay Alderson.

She felt hot tears stinging behind her eyelids and blinked them away rapidly, hoping he wouldn't see.

But she needn't have worried. Clay was already falling asleep, his face soft with contentment as he gathered her into his arms, curved his long body around hers and settled against the pillows.

CHAPTER SIXTEEN

THE FIRST LIGHT OF DAWN glimmered through the slats of the window blinds, casting narrow shafts across their bed. Clay awoke and lay still for a moment, wondering why he felt so good.

Then he remembered and smiled, easing his arm out from under Jenny's body so he wouldn't disturb her. He leaned up on one elbow and studied her.

What a woman she was! So lovely and intelligent, so warm and generous....

Her face was peaceful and childlike in sleep, and a pale blue vein pulsed in her temple. Clay leaned forward to brush it gently with his lips, then drew away again, thinking about her surprising boldness when she'd undressed in front of him, her passion and sweetness, the winsome playfulness of her lovemaking.

And yet, incredibly, she'd never experienced true sexual fulfillment until now.

His face hardened briefly.

What a selfish bastard that boyfriend of hers must have been, taking his own satisfaction and not being concerned about the needs of such a wonderful woman.

She was like a garden of pleasure, filled with so

much richness that a man could spend a lifetime in her arms and still want more of her.

That's what I intend to do, sweetheart, Clay promised her silently. *I'm going to devote my whole life to making you happy. Every day from now on…*

But gradually the reality of his life and responsibilities began to intrude on those loving thoughts. He slipped from bed, dressed in his scattered clothes and crossed to the window, studying the horizon with a practiced eye.

The rain had let up, but judging from the leaden clouds already massing in front of the sun, it looked as if it could start again at any moment. And the creek was higher than he'd ever seen it, thundering along between the sandbag dikes. When he opened the casement and leaned out for a better look, his heart began to pound heavily in alarm.

The lazy little waterway he'd known all his life had changed to a raging monster. The water was high and muddy, whipped into crests by the wind. It carried all kinds of debris, including uprooted trees and scraps of lumber torn from wrecked buildings. Here and there he could see the carcasses of drowned animals, even cattle and horses, being dragged along by the current, and big metal gas tanks that bobbed like corks on the surface of the water.

For the first time, the water had risen high enough to threaten the little cemetery. They hadn't built the dike beyond the main ranch yard, and silver fingers of water now crept across the valley, lapping almost at the foot of the wrought-iron fence.

He thought about Suzy's grave.

At last he left the window and moved close to Jenny's bed again, silent in his leather moccasins as he gazed down at her sleeping face. He hated to slip away from her like this after their first night of love-making, without a word or a kiss to let her know how deeply he cherished her. Maybe he could leave something for her.

Clay looked helplessly around the room. The perfect gift would be a bouquet of chrysanthemums from the garden, he thought. That was what she reminded him of, a tall bronze chrysanthemum, sun-kissed and rich with sweetness.

But he could hardly go down and start picking flowers when he had a flood to battle.

Besides, the garden flowers were wet from the rain. He pictured a bedraggled spray of chrysanthemums soaking her pillow, and thought how she'd laugh with him over that image.

His lips curved into a smile and it was all he could do not to throw off his clothes again, climb into bed and take her in his arms. But finally he tore a leaf from the notebook on her desk and selected a pen from the cup nearby.

He hesitated, wondering what to say. At last he wrote simply, "Good morning, sweetheart, I love you."

He folded the note and put it on the pillow near her cheek, then tucked the covers up around her shoulders, gathered his tray and the empty whiskey glasses and quietly left the room.

JENNY STIRRED, lost in a pleasantly erotic dream. She and Clay were all alone, far out on the prairie somewhere, the sun blazing down on their naked bodies. They lay on a soft carpet of grass that shone emerald green, though the land all around was parched and dry.

She wanted to ask him where this bit of greenery came from, but she couldn't find the words to speak because his lovemaking was so tender, so passionate, it took her breath away.

Something rustled under her cheek. "Clay," she murmured into his bare shoulder. "Clay, I think there's a—"

She awoke abruptly to find herself alone. The disappointment was so intense she almost cried. She sat up, hugging her knees, and peered around the room. There was no sign of him, not a trace of his clothing or their late-night tryst.

Maybe I dreamed the whole thing, she thought hopefully.

But she knew she wasn't imagining the warm sated feeling of her body. To say nothing of the fact that her nightshirt was crumpled on the floor and she was completely naked.

"Oh, no," she whispered. "Dear God, what have I done?"

She saw the paper folded on her pillow. With trembling hands she opened it. As she read it, tears filled her eyes and her hands began to tremble.

Jenny could hardly believe the situation she found herself in. For years she'd prided herself on being levelheaded and sensible, not doing the kind of rash things that could ruin your life.

Now suddenly, at almost thirty-one, she was be-
having like a complete idiot. In the space of a few
days she'd found herself falling into a relationship
with the most unsuitable man in the world, the subject
of her audit, then having unprotected sex with him.
True, the time of the month meant little likelihood of
her getting pregnant, but still...

It was unthinkable. She couldn't begin to understand what was wrong with her, but she was determined to get away from Cottonwood Creek as soon
as she could decently make her escape.

Still, she couldn't forget the sweetness of the rainy
night and their rich lovemaking, their shared joy and
passion, and the shuddering pleasure of her own release.

Jenny flung herself from the bed, dressed hastily
and went downstairs to find the kitchen empty, the
big house silent and deserted.

It was only seven o'clock, but everybody was apparently outside already, working on the dikes. She
felt a mixture of relief at not having to meet Clay this
morning, and a growing worry over the flood.

The situation at the ranch must be even grimmer
than yesterday if they were all working so hard. Again
she wondered if she could actually bring herself to
drive away in the midst of such a crisis.

And what would she tell her grandfather?

*I had to leave, Grandpa. I slept with the man, you
see, and it was an awful thing for me to do under the
circumstances. So I couldn't hang around, even
though they were in such trouble...*

"Oh, hell," Jenny muttered wearily.

She cleared away her dishes, tidied the kitchen and left the house, trudging down past the boiling creek waters toward the office. The sandbag crew were hard at work beyond the barn. She peered at the group and made out Clay's broad shoulders and gray Stetson as he worked on the line with the rest of his employees. Her heart beat faster and she hurried through the lane of sheltering trees, wondering what she was going to say to the man when she encountered him.

But she needn't have worried. Nobody, Bridget included, came to the office all morning. She worked alone at the computer, trying to ignore the ominous rumble of the rising water but feeling sick with fear.

By late morning, she'd discovered more than she needed to know about the missing revenues at Cottonwood Creek ranch. It was, in fact, a fairly straightforward embezzlement scheme, but still hard to detect unless you had some idea what to look for.

At regular intervals over the past two years, some of the trucking slips had been altered to show fewer cattle shipped to a particular auction. Then a matching set of papers had been removed from the auction-yard receipts, both the sales slips for certain lots of cattle and the corresponding checks.

It was actually a form of rustling, with paper being stolen, instead of animals. When the whole transaction was completed, there was no way to trace the missing cattle unless you ran a spreadsheet on all the numbers shipped, cross-checked the various auction dates and were able to pick out the discrepancies.

When she knew what to look for, Jenny could even find the alterations on the trucking slips. They hadn't been done all that skillfully, but of course nobody had ever thought to check the numbers on the bills of lading because the checks and sales slips had tallied, so the accountants had no idea there might be a problem.

Jenny worked grimly, not even stopping for lunch. She punched numbers and checked totals, trying not to think about what she was doing. But the facts became clearer and clearer as the day went by.

Within another few hours she was able to trace the missing revenues to certain cattle sales and to check them against the sales slips and trucker's bills for those auctions. Practically everybody on the ranch seemed to have signed the trucking forms at one time or another, even Teresa.

But every time money was missing from the auction revenues, it was Clay himself who'd attended the livestock sale and signed the receipts.

Clay Alderson was the guilty party. Beyond a doubt, he was the tax thief who'd stolen so expertly from his own revenues.

JENNY FINISHED with the books and logged her data, printed out the last of the spreadsheets and locked them in her briefcase, then went back up to the house. It was getting late in the day and she was hungry, but there was still nobody around.

Feeling hollow and miserable, she wandered downstairs to the kitchen and made herself a sandwich, then put on her boots and cap and walked across the yard to join the sandbagging crew.

There was no sign of Clay, but it didn't matter

anymore whether she stayed or left. She might as well help them battle the flood, because nothing could happen now to change the reality of what she'd found.

Clay Alderson was going to jail, and she was going to be the one to send him.

She felt an aching sadness so deep she could hardly keep from bursting into tears. Mechanically she shoveled sand next to her grandfather as the light began to fade and twilight rolled in, and with it more rain.

"I'm starved," Paddy said, leaning wearily on his shovel, his face flushed with exertion. "Want to come over to the cookhouse with me, Jenny?"

She shook her head, keeping her face averted. "I ate a sandwich at the house just a little while ago. Does anybody know where Clay is?" she asked with forced casualness.

Next to Paddy, Maura and Bridget labored side by side, filling sandbags. Maura leaned forward to look at Jenny, her pert face smeared with mud.

"Clay's up at the cemetery," she said. "He left a couple of hours ago, took a load of sand and said he was going to try to protect a few of the graves."

"Poor Clay," Bridget murmured. "This is all so..."

Her voice broke and Maura slipped a comforting arm around her.

Jenny glanced into the distance, but the outer edge of the ranch yard was blocked by cottonwood trees. "I think I'll go over there for a minute," she said. "I need to ask him something."

She put her shovel down, then thought better of it and carried it with her as she trudged down the line past the weary crew, conscious of their growing hope-lessness as the waters continued to rise.

She reached the edge of the trees where the trail opened out toward the cemetery. Jenny huddled in the shadows for a moment, watching.

Clay had dumped a truckload of wet sand near the gate. He was working like a man possessed, filling the slippery plastic sacks and mounding them along the base of the fence, trying to protect the little com-pound.

But despite his strength and unflagging energy, the task was huge and he was only one man.

She stood at the edge of the trees, still unseen, her heart torn by conflicting emotions. It was the first time she'd been alone with the man since their passionate night of lovemaking, but the cold twilight seemed to have washed all those memories away.

No tenderness remained in this grim world, nothing but the approaching darkness, the thunder of the water and the danger that stalked all of them in the next few hours.

And Jenny's dreadful knowledge that Clay Ander-son was a skillful tax cheat who would soon be pay-ing for his crimes.

He turned at the moment, squinted toward the trees and then smiled, his teeth flashing white against his tired muddy face.

"Jenny," he called, waving an arm. "I haven't seen you all day. Come and give me a hug."

She moved toward him reluctantly and allowed him to fold her in a damp embrace, even let him kiss her mouth a couple of times before she pulled away and looked down at the little pile of sandbags.

"Clay," she whispered, turning aside so she couldn't see the planes of his face, the blunt cheekbones beaded with moisture, the long eyelashes starred with raindrops. "This is all so…"

"What?" He rested an arm around her shoulder and leaned against the fence post.

"It's so hopeless," she murmured, her breath catching on the words.

"What's so hopeless, sweetheart?" he asked, giving her another hug.

Everything, she wanted to stay. *Trying to save this ranch and your little cemetery. Trying to save your own reputation when it's already too late.*

"I can do this," he said, gesturing toward the cemetery. "One more course of sandbags and it should be safe." He fixed his gaze on her. "Do you think you could spare a few minutes to help me?"

"Sure," she said tonelessly. "Why not?"

His dark eyes under the hat brim were puzzled, but she turned away without comment to lift her shovel.

They began to work, by now quite accustomed to the process of filling, tying and stacking the sandbags. They exchanged scraps of meaningless small talk, neither able to find the energy for more.

"Thank you, Jenny," Clay said at last, standing and removing his hat to run a hand through his hair. "I think that's probably enough. Couldn't have managed without you."

Jenny stood numbly beside him, leaning on her shovel. She looked at the rows of neat graves behind their protective dike, and the little marble headstone with its sad inscription.

"Was she your daughter?" she said at last, not daring to look at the man beside her.

"Yes," he said after an awkward silence. "She... Her name was Suzy. She died when she was two years old."

He turned away then, one hand covering his eyes, shoulders heaving in a sob.

"Clay," she whispered, putting her arm around him with automatic sympathy.

"I loved her so much," he said brokenly. "She was the sweetest little thing. Blond and chubby, happy all the time. And she was so smart. You should have heard the way she..."

He flexed his jaw and stared blindly into the darkness.

"What happened to her, Clay?"

"I never... talk about it," he said simply. "I don't tell anybody, Jenny."

"Maybe it would be better if you did."

He shook his head from side to side like an animal in pain and gathered her closer into his arms. After a long time, still gazing emptily into the darkness, he bent toward her and began to talk.

"It was about this time of year, late in June. There'd been some pretty good rains and we were already mowing the hay meadows. Suzy liked to hang around when I worked, and I made a pet of her, took her everywhere with me in the truck and around the ranch. After she learned to walk, she used to run along behind me all the time, chattering and asking a thousand questions.''

He looked down at Jenny with a sad smile. ''When I first saw you walking with Bridget—slowing your pace to match hers—it reminded me of having Suzy trailing along next to me. I always had to do the same thing so her little legs could keep up.''

Jenny smiled and squeezed his arm encouragingly. The results of the tax audit had, temporarily at least, fled her mind.

Clay's answering smile faded and his face twisted with emotion as he went on. ''She liked to play in the meadows when the hay was tall. I guess to her it was a kid-size forest full of magical things. She'd take her dolls out there and spread them around, and you couldn't even see the top of her head. But you could hear her talking and singing to the dolls....''

His voice broke and he seemed unable to speak. Jenny glanced up at his rigid jaw, then stroked his cheek with a gentle hand.

''Clay?'' she murmured. ''What happened?''

''The mowing machine ran over her. Poor Joe was driving, and had no idea she was in there. I didn't, either. I thought she was in the house with her mother for her afternoon nap.''

Jenny's hand flew to her mouth. She stared up at him in horror. ''Oh my God, Clay...''

''She died in my arms,'' he said. ''I could feel the moment when her little spirit went away. I'll never forget it.''

Jenny looked again at the pink marble headstone and wiped at the tears streaming down her face.

"Eleanor blamed me," Clay went on, gripping the fence rail, his knuckles white. "She said no decent man would raise his children in such godforsaken place. Said that if we were living a normal kind of life, Suzy wouldn't have died."

"But that's not fair!"

"She said if I really cared about my sons, I'd sell the ranch and move to the city and raise them where they could be safe and have decent opportunities. I refused, and soon afterward Eleanor left, still blaming me for everything."

Jenny looked up at him in disbelief. "She left you *then*? While you were both still grieving for your little girl?"

"I suppose she did, but I hardly even noticed when Eleanor left. I was so…"

Suddenly he began to cry in earnest, with deep wrenching sobs that shook his whole body. Jenny wondered if he'd ever had the chance to mourn openly for his lost child, or if these feelings had been bottled up for ten long years.

She put her arms around him and held him, whispering words of comfort while he lowered his head to her shoulder and went on crying. In her arms she could feel both his strength and his weariness, and the terrible aching pain he'd never been able to share.

"Clay," she murmured, all her earlier resolve completely forgotten now. "Clay, darling. I'm so sorry. So very sorry."

She stroked his hair, his cheeks, wiping away his tears and lifting her hand to taste the salt on her fingers, her heart overflowing with love. They clung together in silence for a long while.

"Thank you," he said at last, his voice hoarse. "Thank you so much for being the sweet understanding woman you are. I love you Jenny."

Now that the emotional moment was behind them, Jenny's caution began to return. No matter how much she craved the feeling of being in his arms and holding him close, it still wasn't the right thing for her to be doing. Especially when—

"Do you love me?" he asked. "When this nightmare is over, Jenny..." He touched her cheek and gave her a weary smile that tore at her heart. "Will I ever have a chance to come courting like a normal guy?" he asked.

"Clay..." She avoided his eyes, moving away from him and his muddy dike.

"What is it?"

She took a deep breath. "I've finished the audit."

She could see the way he tensed, clenching his hands suddenly into fists.

"I see," he said after a long silence. "And I take it everything's not okay."

"No," she said quietly. "It's not okay."

He stared at the river, saw a dead cow in the muddy foaming water. The corpse was grossly bloated and misshapen, legs flailing in the air.

"So have you tracked down the guilty party?" he asked.

"It's not my job to determine guilt or innocence, just to uncover proof of fiscal irregularities."

"I know." Clay gave her a shrewd glance. "But

you're a really smart girl, Jenny. I'm sure you have some suspicions.''

"Yes," she said, her heart beginning to pound. "I have some suspicions."

He jammed his hands into his jacket pocket. All at once the atmosphere between them seemed electric with danger, charged with caution.

Nobody would ever guess, Jenny thought miserably, that just a few minutes ago this man had been wrapped in her arms, pouring out the torrent of grief he'd kept hidden for a decade. Now the pair of them were like wary antagonists, watching each other's every move.

"So who did it?" he said at last. "Who stole all that money?"

"I think..."

She hesitated, wondering if she should go on.

After all, this wasn't her business. Criminal investigation and prosecution of tax fraud were done by others, not by the on-site auditor. But Jenny felt she owed Clay Anderson the truth. After the tender moment just passed and the sweetness of their lovemaking the previous night, she wanted him to hear it from her, not some bureaucrat in a suit.

Besides, others would be talking to him soon enough.

"I think I know who stole the money, Clay," she said. "And all the investigations I've done help to confirm my suspicions."

Looking down at the muddy water, keeping her voice deliberately expressionless, Jenny told him what she'd discovered. She described how the sales slips, checks and altered trucking slips had all been used to embezzle revenues from cattle auctions so cleverly the ruse was all but untraceable.

Finally, in a low halting voice she told him how every single lot of cattle had been stolen while he, personally, was in attendance at the auctions.

Then she fell silent, gripping her hands together, staring at the creek. After a long tense moment she forced herself to look up into his stricken face, the incredulous pain of his eyes.

"Jenny," he whispered, "you really believe that? You honestly think *I* did it? How could you call me a thief after the way we loved each other last night?"

All the tension and drudgery of the past few days washed over her in a dark wave of fatigue. "Oh, Clay…how do I know that's even true?" she asked bitterly. "Maybe you only seduced me so you could invalidate the results of my audit."

"Is that what you really think of me?" he asked, his voice soft and steely. He reached out to grasp her arm, so tightly she winced. "Is it, Jenny?"

Their eyes met with a harsh challenge, but she refused to answer him. At last she pulled herself free, picked up her shovel, walked away from him toward the tunnel beneath the cottonwoods.

She almost expected him to come running after her, to seize her and try to argue, to defend himself against her accusations.

If he had any words to say in his defense, Jenny was anxious to hear them. She wanted to listen to and believe his protestations of innocence. She wanted nothing more in all the world than to know this man wasn't guilty of a deliberate fraud.

She hesitated for a long time at the edge of the path, but he didn't follow her. At last, without looking back, she plunged into the dark tunnel and headed back to the ranch yard.

CHAPTER SEVENTEEN

THE LEAVES OF the cottonwood trees enclosed her like a shroud. It was close to midnight, the rain had stopped and the moon shone fitfully through billowing clouds, casting a ghostly glow across the valley. The only sound was the creek, now a broad river that rushed and foamed along just beyond the growth of trees at her side.

The flood crest had finally arrived.

Jenny edged through the trees on her left to look at the silvered water thundering past. The bank at this point was quite high, so she could stand safely and watch. Still, the waters lapped almost at her feet, in places where the creek had been fifteen feet lower when she'd first arrived at the ranch.

The power of the flood was awesome. It boiled through the steep narrow channel, roaring and rumbling, louder than a freight train. Whitecaps curled above the crest of the water.

To Jenny's awestruck eyes they looked like the manes and tails of a herd of wild horses, galloping wildly through the valley. The flood was both terrifying and surprisingly beautiful. She could hardly imagine where so much water was coming from, especially in this prairie valley where the creek was usually just a lazy trickle.

Whole trees bobbed on the surface of the water, rising slowly, turning and being sucked under like matchsticks. She could even see the wrecked skeletons of small buildings, floating pieces of automobiles and big metal gas tanks that drifted past her and vanished into the darkness. With increasing frequency she also saw the carcasses of dead cattle and horses, sad reminders of the fragility of life in the face of such a disaster.

Suddenly Jenny heard something over the roar of the water, a sound that came from behind her on the trail. Though muffled, it seemed vaguely menacing. She whirled and stared into the dripping trees, her heart pounding.

"Clay?" she called. "Clay, is that you?"

There was no answer, but still she had the feeling somebody was close by, watching and waiting. "Who's there?" she called, louder this time, her voice a thin, panicky sound, barely carrying over the crash of the water.

Again no response, but she heard a twig snapping, someone moving in the shrubbery. The bile rising in her throat, Jenny remembered that gunshot thudding into the tree next to her, just a few feet from where she now stood.

And the frenzied hot breath of the trapped stallion, his hooves crashing above her head.

The hair prickled on the nape of her neck and stood straight up on her chilled forearms. She moved back onto the pathway with a brave attempt at casualness and began to walk rapidly along it, heading down the tunnel toward the well-lit safety of the ranch yard where people still worked to fill and stack sandbags.

The unseen presence stayed close, moving through the dense shrubbery at her side, not even trying to keep silent any longer. Jenny knew beyond a shadow of a doubt that somebody was stalking her, and that if he decided to attack she would be helpless. Nobody would ever hear her scream over the relentless thunder of the floodwaters.

Involuntarily she thought of Clay's dark face and penetrating eyes, and his look of shock and pained outrage a few minutes ago when she'd told him the results of the audit.

It would have been easy for him to follow her into the trees.

And it wasn't the first time. She frowned, trying to remember as she hastened her steps.

The rancher had also been nearby during both those other "accidents," after the gunshots and the incident in the barn with the stallion.

She still hated to suspect Clay Alderson of such calculated treachery, but this situation was so terrifying she couldn't put the thoughts aside. She whimpered aloud in fear and quickened her steps, then remembered the shovel. All this time she'd been clutching it in her hand, not even realizing she had a weapon, and a sturdy serviceable one at that.

She stopped and gripped the worn wooden handle, holding the shovel up in front of her as she turned to scan the dense brush at her side.

"Who are you?" she called, summoning all her courage to keep her voice steady. "What do you want? Clay, if that's you in those trees, come out and talk to me. I really think you owe it to me to explain what's going on, because I..."

The rustling sound came closer. A couple of branches waved in front of her horrified eyes, then stilled. Her unseen stalker was right in there, just beyond the path a few feet to her side. Now he lurked in silence, watching and listening.

Jenny lifted the shovel again and cast a glance in both directions along the leafy tunnel. Behind her the water screamed and pounded against the bank. A cold rivulet spilled over and crept across her feet. More water followed, and she realized that even the highest bank had been breached.

Water was soon going to flow everywhere. By daybreak most of the ranch would be washed away.

Again the leaves rustled and stilled. She fought her panic and tried to stay calm. At least she knew what direction the attack would come from, if it came at all. She was blocked from behind by the swollen creek, so her only opportunity for escape lay along the narrow path.

She had two options—drop the shovel and run, or stand and fight.

Her mouth was dry with fear, and her heart pounded heavily. But in spite of her fear she felt a rising boldness, and a fierce wave of anger. Like a trapped animal she raised her head, backed toward the creek and shouted defiantly, "Come and get me! Just try it, and you'll see what happens. Why won't you come out and fight, you coward? You don't—"

Her demand was answered. A dark shape hurtled

out of the trees and launched itself at her. She was conscious of a strong body crashing into hers, of hands gripping her shoulders and a frenzied breath that was as hot and terrifying on her cheek as the stallion's had been.

The shovel, which had felt so sturdy and reliable in her hands, was grabbed like a toy and wrenched away from her before she knew it. Jenny and her assailant were locked in a macabre dance, swaying back and forth on the moonlit path, so close together that she had no idea who was attacking her.

She was conscious only of lean strength, of wet denim and iron hands and a fear so choking and urgent she could hardly breathe. She fought and kicked, writhing in the other's grasp, trying to beat with her fists or find a bit of exposed flesh to bite.

To her alarm she could feel herself being forced slowly backward. With sickening horror, she finally understood what was happening.

"No!" she screamed. "No, please…"

But at that moment they reached the water's edge. Jenny felt her body being lifted and flung into the swirling depths.

HOURS SEEMED TO PASS, though it probably couldn't have been more than a few minutes. Jenny was sucked under like a bit of flotsam in a whirlpool, forced downward into crushing darkness while waterborne debris pounded against her body.

Just when it felt as if her lungs would burst, she was thrown back up to the surface and found herself clinging to a drifting piece of wood—a ragged section of fence, she realized as her fingers clamped around it.

She raised her head to scream but there was nobody to hear, just the silver face of the moon, from which the clouds had parted as if to mock her.

She shouted again, then took a deep breath as she was pulled under once more, down into the foul depths of the water. When she came back to the surface, she flung the wet hair from her eyes and tried wildly to sight one of the banks, hoping to swim to safety. But there seemed to be no bank anywhere, just miles of water gleaming like dull silver in the night, frosted with whitecaps of dirty foam.

And she was moving so fast now, being carried like a toy on the crest of the flood. Again the current sucked her down. She came up spitting and increasingly exhausted, still clinging to the scrap of lumber.

For the first time she began to think seriously about dying, what it was going to be like. She even thought of Steve for a fleeting moment, wondering if he'd had enough time to know what was happening to him before the avalanche carried him away.

"I don't want to die!" she shouted to the black unheeding sky.

Steve's image was soon replaced by another. Jenny had a sudden vivid picture of Clay Alderson's face, his dark eyes, his powerful hands and body.

She felt, for some reason, warmed and deeply comforted.

Then the water closed over her head again and she plunged down, down, all the way to the creek bed where her feet dragged against the rocks. Her lungs swelled and burned until she was forced to let her breath out. Dirty water flooded in and choked her, made her sick and light-headed. She came back to the surface coughing and retching, and knew she was going to die.

Her body was too weakened from the pummeling of waterlogged debris, and from the influx of muddy water in her lungs. She couldn't fight to stay afloat anymore, couldn't even breathe properly, and the whole world was beginning to turn misty red in front of her eyes.

Through the blood-tinted haze she heard a noise that registered faintly in her ears. It seemed to be a voice calling her name, urging her to hang on.

But she floundered and went underwater, thinking with curious detachment that she'd never been so cold and tired in her life. It would be such a relief to let go and allow the waters to close over her head forever. They'd carry her down to some warm place where she wouldn't have to struggle anymore....

"Jenny," the voice shouted again. "Jenny, I'm here! I'm coming to get you!"

She drifted and turned with the current, floating faceup for a while, still clinging to her bit of lumber. Then she was sucked beneath the surface once more and couldn't hear the voice.

Maybe she'd just imagined it, or dreamed that Paddy was coming to rescue her.

At the thought of her grandfather, Jenny had a brief moment of new resolve. Paddy wouldn't want her to die alone in this muddy water. He loved her. She had to make an attempt for Paddy's sake.

She fought her way back to the surface and gasped for breath. But her lungs burned like fire, and she was too weak to keep herself afloat.

Again she felt herself yearning for those restful depths. Maybe there was a magic doorway down there, through which she could pass into green fields starred with wildflowers and find blissful rest....

"No!" she screamed, and began to cough in violent spasms. "I won't die," she cried. "I don't want—"

"Jenny!" The voice was closer, stronger.

She gripped her scrap of wood, trying to see through grit-reddened eyes.

A sleek dark head broke the surface of the water near her. She felt a man's strong fingers grip her upper arms, tightly, painfully. Moonlight drifted from behind a cloud again and she recognized Clay, his black hair plastered to his skull.

"No!" Jenny screamed. She pulled vainly at his hands, still locked on her upper arms. "No, you can't kill me. I won't let you!"

The effort of speech was too much. She fell into a paroxysm of coughing and began to sink, almost unconscious, but his hands jerked her up. He started pulling at her, dragging her through the rushing water.

In her tired and panic-stricken mind, Jenny was no longer conscious of anything but the need to survive. She knew he was trying to kill her, that he was going to maneuver her into shallow water, then drown her and hide her corpse where it could never be recovered. She couldn't allow that to happen.

She had to stay awake and keep fighting with every ounce of strength in her body.

"No!" she screamed again, turning over to kick against him furiously, though she was coughing and retching and the fierce effort almost made her pass out.

But his grip on one of her arms still held, and he kept tugging at her. She floundered and struggled to keep herself upright so she could see his face.

"I...hate you!" she panted, wiping the wet hair from her face and staring wildly into his eyes. "You stole all that money...from your own ranch...and then tried to kill me. You even made love to me...so I wouldn't tell. You're just a...filthy liar. And I won't...let you kill me."

She began to flail and struggle again, then leaned over to sink her teeth into the hand that grasped her arm, making him shout in pain.

When she looked up, his face was wet and dripping, his eyelashes clustered in dark stars. He bobbed in the water, gazed at her with a look of frantic sorrow and shook his head.

"I'm sorry, Jenny," he said. "I'm so sorry I have to do this."

He raised his hand and struck her. She felt herself black out, then return, seconds—hours?—later to dim consciousness. She was aware of being pulled through the water, finally dragged painfully onshore in the darkness. The moon had vanished again, but illumination was supplied by a set of truck headlights.

Her attacker left her lying rumpled in a mass of pain while he rummaged in the truck. Jenny watched with bleary eyes as he hurried back and spread something on the grass and mud of the riverbank. It appeared to be an old horse blanket, stained and dirty.

He lifted Jenny and put her facedown on the blanket. Her nostrils were filled with the rank scent of horses and dried sweat. She shuddered, remembering the hooves of the stallion.

They were miles from anywhere, alone in this howling wilderness. Clay was going to kill her and hide her body. Nobody would ever find her, because he must know a thousand places on the desolate prairie to conceal a woman's corpse.

She was amazed to find that her mind could keep working and thinking, even though her body was paralyzed with cold and shock. She couldn't feel anything, didn't even know if her arms and legs were intact. Still, she remained very much aware of what was happening to her.

She was lying on her stomach while he sat astride her and pressed hard on her back, with a deliberate rhythmic firmness. She retched deeply, her mouth and throat burning.

"Stop." She choked. "Please stop. I can't...bear any more."

But he ignored her protests and kept on pounding her back, grim with purpose. The pain became too great to bear, and she began to drift in and out of consciousness.

She only knew that she longed for death. Maybe if she stopped talking and fighting, he'd just kill her and be done with it.

She pillowed her head on her arms and closed her

eyes. He shouted something in her ear, but she didn't care anymore.

Her tormentor bent close to her again, still yelling urgently.

Jenny blocked out his voice and fell asleep. To her pleasure she found herself dreaming of that familiar green oasis on the prairie. It was a lovely place, carpeted in rich green, ringed with trees and splashed with wildflowers. She sighed in bliss, recognizing the place, then tensed, even in her dream, when Clay walked over the prairie toward her.

"No," she muttered. "Not him. I don't want him here…"

The man had tried to kill her at least three times. Even now, in some other dimension, she knew that he continued to beat and pound at her. Yet still she dreamed about him.

"Get out of my dream," she whispered, her face pressed hard against the horse blanket that was now soaked with foul creek water coughed from her lungs. "Get away from me, you bastard.…"

But in her dream he was taking her clothes off, stroking her body, looking down at her with passionate intensity while he caressed her breasts, then bent to nuzzle them with his mouth.

JENNY AWOKE AGAIN and stirred painfully, trying to understand what was happening.

The nightmare time in the swollen creek—was that real? Did it happen? Or had she dreamed the whole thing? She was in a bed of some kind, but it wasn't her own. Her body was totally naked. And, she realized in horror, somebody else was with her, a man who held her in strong bare arms. She lay with her back curled into his warmth while he wrapped himself around her, chin resting on top of her head, hands closed over her chest.

She coughed and her lungs burned like fire. A deep chill gripped her, making her shudder and moan.

"Oh, God," she whimpered in agony, pulling weakly at the enclosing arms. "What happened? Where am I?"

"Jenny," a voice said at her ear. "Sweetheart, are you all right?"

"I'm cold," she said as plaintively as a child. "Who are you?"

Part of her mind retained enough awareness to register the absurdity of the situation.

What a question to ask of a naked man who was in bed with you, and wrapped all around you!

But nothing seemed to make sense anymore. Her mother bustled in, wearing her pink apron patterned with yellow chicks and teapots.

"Get out of bed, Jenny," she said. "It's time to clean your room."

"But, Mommy, I can't," Jenny whispered. "This man won't let me go."

"What are you saying?" the man asked.

"Go away." She struggled to release herself. "Mommy says you have to go away."

The effort of speech made her throat burn more than ever. Her voice as so hoarse and raspy that she could hardly understand it herself.

"Don't try to talk, Jenny," the man enveloping her

said. "Just rest. We're hoping the helicopter will get here soon to take you away, but in the meantime you have to stay warm. We need to raise your body temperature. You probably have hypothermia. I'm holding you like this because it's the best way to keep you warm."

Only part of his speech made any impression on her.

Helicopter? I can't go away in a helicopter, she wanted to tell him. *I have to clean my room before Mommy comes back....*

Paddy came striding into the room, looking strange because he wasn't bald, but had a full head of luxurious blond hair. He pushed the handlebars of a bicycle with pink training wheels.

"It's all yours, kitten," he said. "Why don't you hop on?"

Jenny was both frightened and excited. "But Grandpa," she said, "I can't learn to ride it now. I'm sick. My chest hurts and I'm so cold..."

Another long spasm gripped her body. She shuddered and coughed, then fell back limply into the man's comforting embrace.

"Don't try to talk, sweetheart," the man whispered. "You're sick and delirious. Just relax. Try to sleep until the doctors get here."

Through mists of confusion she recognized the man's voice.

"You're Clay," she muttered accusingly over her shoulder. "That's who you are."

"Of course I am. Now rest, sweetheart. You've been through hell."

She coughed harshly, then looked down in alarm as a fresh trickle of muddy creek water seeped from her mouth into the pillow.

"You tried to kill me," she muttered. "You pushed me into the water and then came back to finish the job."

She struggled and tried to get out of his arms, but he held her tight and she was too weak to resist. Her head felt light and cottony, as if she'd been given some kind of drug.

"Jenny," he whispered, cuddling her, "how can you say that?"

"You stole the money," she said. "You hid it so you wouldn't have to pay taxes, and you knew I'd find out. So you tried to kill me. Three times," she added.

"Three times?"

"You shot at me the other day. And then that horse...and the water..."

Clay held her in silence, his face hidden behind her. She could feel the hard-muscled warmth of his arms and chest, the silky nakedness of his legs, even his bare feet rubbing against hers, trying to warm her.

"Jenny, how could I ever want to hurt you? I love you."

She wrenched herself from his arms and with a supreme effort raised onto one elbow to look down at him, then at the room they were in.

He lay back on the pillows, his hair stiff with dried creek water. There were dark bruises on his face and shoulders.

The room must be his own, Jenny thought in bleary

confusion. She saw wooden panels, rows of books and a closet that stood partly open, filled with cotton shirts and jeans.

"Lie down," he said, reaching for her. "You're supposed to lie still and let me keep you warm. We have to raise your body temperature, and this is the only way to do it."

"You're a liar." She struggled to focus on him. "You're a liar and cheat. You pretended to care about me so I wouldn't report what you did."

His face twisted in pain and he rolled his head on the pillow. "Jenny, Jenny," he murmured huskily, "don't say things like that. Don't say anything until you're feeling better."

Dark clouds massed and billowed inside her mind. "I hate you," she said, coughing. "I never want to talk to you again."

But she felt so chilled, and the air on her shoulders was like ice. His image kept slipping away, replaced by hazy memories of childhood, of her parents, of long-ago birthday parties and school outings.

"I hate you," she whispered, summoning the last of her energy.

She thought she saw tears sparkling in his dark eyes and flowing down his cheeks. But she couldn't be sure because the waters closed over her head and dragged her down into the silent warmth, and she knew nothing more.

CHAPTER EIGHTEEN

THE NEXT MORNING Bridget walked across the ranch yard to the office, moving though a weird, dreamlike landscape shrouded in mist from the swollen creek. The place was awash in mud, but the dikes had held. It was a miracle, the way they'd been spared.

Nothing in the valley had flooded, not even the little cemetery. The flood crest had come and gone through Clay Alderson's ranch property, and its only casualty had been poor sweet Jenny, almost swept to her death on the raging tide.

Bridget shuddered and pushed open the office door, looking up in surprise as she removed her rubber boots. A square white envelope lay on her desk, addressed simply, "Clay." She crossed the room to pick it up.

The last she'd heard, Clay was still in Calgary at the hospital, waiting to see if Jenny was going to be all right after inhaling all that muddy water and coming so close to drowning.

Just then Bridget glanced up and saw her employer in the doorway, his eyes like black hollows in his face. He came in without speaking and went straight to the coffeemaker, then began to prepare a fresh pot.

"How is she?" Bridget asked.

"The doctors think she's going to be all right, but it'll be a while before she's fully conscious. Most of the problem now is a bad case of pneumonia from the dirty water in her lungs. Paddy's staying at the hospital." He stared out the window, waiting for the coffee to drip through the filter. "He said he'd call if there was any change."

"There's a letter here for you," she said. "I don't know who it's from."

He sank wearily into a chair. "Could you open it for me?"

Bridget obeyed, removing a few sheets of folded paper. A check fluttered out of the envelope and landed on her desk.

As she read the letter, struggling to understand, she began to feel light-headed and wondered if she might be going to faint.

"Bridget?" Clay asked when he saw her face. He got up and hurried across the room. "What is it?"

Wordlessly she held up the sheets of paper. Clay took them and read the beginning of the letter, then leaned against her desk, passing his hand over his eyes.

"It was Jim Cole," Bridget muttered, staring at the pages in Clay's hand. "It was him all the time. He stole all that money. He says he thought Cottonwood Creek would never miss it."

"Never miss it," Clay echoed, his voice uneven. "The damned fool. Why didn't he just ask me if he needed money?"

Bridget gestured at the letter. "He says he wanted to buy a ranch of his own."

"I trusted that man," Clay said, looking shaken and sick. "We've worked together for ten years. Bridget, he was the best foreman a rancher could ask for."

Bridget nodded, fighting back tears of sympathy.

Suddenly his face hardened and he turned to stare at her. "And when Cole embezzled the money, he tried to make me look like the guilty party. He only took money from sales that I attended."

"I know."

"Even Jenny was fooled by him. And he says...he says here that Teresa helped him."

"He says they've been lovers ever since she came to the ranch. I can't say I'm all that surprised," Bridget added grimly, "but it's going to be hard for poor Michael."

"At least Cole took her with him when he left." Clay looked at the letter in distaste. "God, I can't believe this. It's like I've been living through a nightmare for weeks and can't seem to wake up."

"Why do you think he ran away? Just because he thought Jenny was going to catch him?"

"I think Jenny was right," Clay said grimly. "She kept saying somebody pushed her into the water last night. But she thought it was me."

"You?" Bridget asked, stunned.

"The bastard knew she was getting close, and he had to make his getaway before she caught him. He tried to kill Jenny, just for money."

"But he didn't take the money, Clay."

"He didn't?"

Bridget lifted the check that had fallen on her desk.

"This is a check for three hundred and forty thousand dollars. That's probably every penny he stole. It doesn't make sense."

"Sure it does," Clay said. "Think about it, Bridget. Everything changed for Jim after I pulled Jenny out of the river. He was afraid she could identify him. And if he was caught, he had a better chance of lying his way out of an attempted-murder charge if he wasn't also carrying all that stolen money. He's just a coward, after all."

He leaned over to pick up the check.

"My God," he muttered.

He and Bridget gazed at each other while the tractors moved back and forth beyond the window, taking apart the sandbag dikes. Finally Clay crossed to the coffeemaker and filled two mugs, one of which he handed to Bridget. Then he sat on the vinyl couch next to her desk and fixed her with an intent look.

"We need to talk, Bridget," he said.

"Now?" Her heart sank and she looked down nervously at her desk. "When you're so tired?"

"Yes, now," he said quietly. "Most of my worst troubles, it seems, have come from not tending to things when I knew there were problems. Although God knows I never suspected…"

He fell silent for a moment, then cleared his throat and went on. "This job," he began gently. "It's getting to be too hard for you, isn't it?"

Bridget wiped at the tears that rolled down her cheeks. "I should have pointed out the errors in the books long ago, before he took all that money," she said. "It's my fault, Clay."

"How can it be your fault? You never stole anything from me."

"But I saw the money disappearing! I didn't tell you about it because I was afraid you'd realize I was too old and slow to do a proper job of the books anymore. All those computers…"

Her voice trailed off unhappily while Clay watched her in thoughtful silence. "What would you really like to do next, Bridget?" he asked. "If you could have any wish for the future, what would it be?"

She wrestled her emotions under control and stared out the window, thinking. "I'd want to quit my job and live in Calgary in a nice house with a yard for the dogs. I'd be able to walk to the library and the store and go to bingo on Fridays. That's really all I want."

"Well, you've worked here a long time and you're hardly a spendthrift. You must have enough saved to do that easily. If you don't," Clay added, "then maybe I can help with the balance."

His gentle concern was almost more than she could bear. Finally, halting and reluctant, Bridget told him all about her foray into the stock market and the foolish loss of her nest egg, which had now doomed her to a life of poverty.

Clays face hardened as he listened.

"My mother," he said darkly, "really needs to do some serious thinking about her life."

"I can't blame Maura for my troubles," Bridget said loyally. "She wanted me to sell. It's my own fault for being so greedy."

"Oh, Bridget." Clay gave her a sad smile and patted her shoulder, bringing her to the verge of tears again. "We'll talk about this later, all right?" he said. "I need to call the police, and then get some sleep."

She nodded in wordless misery as he left the office, striding up the path toward the house.

JENNY AWOKE to light and warmth. Sunshine dazzled in her eyes. She turned her face away, blinking.

Somebody moved near the bed, then blended into the square of light and reached up. A shade fell, dimming the room, and Jenny felt a surge of relief.

She tried to express her thanks, but where her tongue and throat had once been, there was nothing but raw fiery pain.

"Don't try to talk just yet." A woman in a blue smock leaned over the bed and smiled, reaching out to adjust something near Jenny's cheek. "Your throat's going to be very sore for a few days. And we have you on a respirator to give those poor lungs a rest, but you're going to be just fine."

Jenny watched in bleary confusion. The woman was plump and gray-haired. She looked warmly pleasant in spite of the crisp uniform, much like Bridget. The nurse smiled again and made some notes on a clipboard before she left the room, silent on her white rubber-soled soles.

Alone in the dimness, Jenny reached up with a cautious experimental hand and touched the plastic tubes at her nose, then looked at the IV drip attached to her left arm.

She was in a hospital, but she had no memory of

coming here. The attack and those frantic moments in the creek seemed like a distant scrap of nightmare.

And Clay holding her afterward, naked in his bed—had that really happened?

The only thing that seemed real, oddly enough, was her dream of him, the green oasis on the prairie and his arms enclosing her, his lips caressing…

She shuddered and closed her eyes, then opened them again when a familiar voice spoke her name.

Paddy stood at the side of the bed looking down at her, his face creased with loving concern. As soon as he became aware of her gaze, the worried look was replaced by a jaunty smile.

"Well, well. Finally woke up, you lazy girl," he said. "It's about time."

He was carrying a vase of white daisies. "More flowers," he said ruefully. "Just what you need, Jenny-girl."

She watched in confusion, following with her eyes as he carried the vase to a dresser crowded with other flowers. Jenny squinted at them in surprise.

"So, do you want to know who sent all these?" he asked.

She nodded.

"Love and kisses from Lisa and the girls." Paddy read and replaced cards. "Hurry and get well from Bridget. An obscenely huge bouquet from the Alderson family, full of good wishes, and another from your boss urging you to take as long as you need. One from your mother and Stan down in Florida, and one from Mrs. Cummings next door. You're a very popular girl."

Aren't there any flowers from Clay?

But she couldn't speak. Paddy smiled and bent to kiss her. "Don't try to say anything," he said. "I'll be back tomorrow, and they tell me the respirator should be gone soon so we can talk. Go back to sleep, Jenny-girl. I'm taking good care of all your pets."

She reached out weakly to hold him, to ask him the question that was uppermost in her mind. But he took her hand and squeezed it, then replaced it on the cover.

"I'll see you tomorrow, dear," he said huskily.

AFTER A COUPLE OF DAYS of sunshine and frenzied cleanup, the ranch yard at Cottonwood Creek bore almost no signs of the recent flood. The workers had dismantled all their dikes, except for Michael's, which would be upgraded and remain permanently in place along the hay meadow.

They emptied the sand from the bags and hauled everything away. Waterlogged debris along the edge of the creek was raked into piles and burned, and stones were hauled in to fill the spots where the bank had eroded.

Even the weather changed abruptly, turning from warm to hot almost overnight. It was still June, but the sun blazed warmly from a sky as blue as lapis lazuli. The winds were stilled and the far horizon shone hard and bright, as if no drop of rain had ever fallen.

The prairie grasses, nourished by the recent downpour, rolled to the horizon in a rich carpet of pale green and gold. Cattle grazed placidly, calves frolicked and played near their mothers, and wildflowers danced on the warm air currents.

Everywhere there was a sense of rebirth and second chances, and a relief that was almost palpable. Even Bridget's heart was a bit lighter as she sat at her desk on a sunny morning and looked out her window at the sweeping expanse of prairie.

Things were working out well for everybody, she thought. And it was such a relief not to have Teresa's surly presence in the office anymore.

Bridget's face creased with unhappiness at the memory of Michael's ex-girlfriend and the handsome ranch foreman. She wondered what was going to happen to them. What a foolish risk to take for lust and greed, she thought. How could anybody be so—

But before she could complete her thought, two people appeared in the distance, strolling up the path leading from the creek to the ranch house.

It was Paddy McKenna and Maura.

Clay's mother wore a jumpsuit of bright pink crinkle cotton with a matching sun hat, and looked about ten times as attractive as any woman her age had a right to be. Paddy, too, was very attractive. Tall and handsome, he wore crisp khakis and a blue short-sleeved golf shirt. Now that Jenny was on the mend, he seemed happy and relieved. He bent his head to hear something Maura said, touching her elbow solicitously, then threw back his head and laughed.

Bridget felt a wave of pain that went beyond envy. She could hardly bear to see them together. Until now, she'd never really known what it meant to be deeply attracted to a man. Even her love for Hal, her long-dead husband, seemed like a frail, girlish thing compared with this raging torrent of emotion. But Paddy McKenna was with Maura Alderson, her best friend, and both seemed to be making it clear the situation was not about to change. Bridget didn't know how to cope with her pain. She'd have to leave the ranch, of course; she'd known that for some long time.

The problem was, she had nowhere to go. She could never find another job at her age, and her retirement money was all gone.

Her thoughts floundered along the same old treadmill, weary and hopeless.

BRIDGET WAS WORKING AGAIN, copying figures from trucking invoices onto the ranch ledger and brooding about how close they'd all come to disaster, when a long shadow fell across the floorboards.

It was Paddy McKenna, still wearing the neat khakis and the blue golf shirt, looking even more handsome at close range. Bridget's heart began to thunder and, maddeningly, her cheeks turned bright pink.

You'd think, she told herself furiously, *that after a woman reached sixty, she should be able to quit blushing like an idiot whenever a man looked at her!*

But he was so handsome and sexy, and she adored him with such hopeless secret passion....

"Hello, Bridget," he said, helping himself to coffee. "Do you by any chance have some cookies for a hungry visitor?"

Wordlessly she offered him the tin of crispy oatmeal cookies, then got up from her desk to make another pot of coffee.

"I believe you're looking slimmer, Bridget," he said, settling on the old vinyl couch with a sigh of contentment.

Bridget's hands began to shake as she measured coffee grounds into the filter.

"I've lost...about five pounds," she murmured. "All this flood and...everything else..."

She turned her old wedding ring nervously on her finger. The thin gold band slipped around with ease.

"Well, it's very becoming," Paddy said from behind her. "But you shouldn't lose any more. You're perfect just the way you are."

Bridget's nervousness turned to painful embarrassment. She was beginning to find the conversation actively distressing.

"Where's Maura?" she asked, glancing timidly at the office door.

Paddy waved a hand in dismissal. "I think she went off somewhere with Allan for the rest of the day. Anyway," he added with a warm smile, "it's you I wanted to talk with, Bridget."

"Me?" She hesitated awkwardly in the middle of the room, carrying her coffee.

"Are you very busy?" Paddy asked. "Could you sit down and visit for a while?"

Bridget glanced longingly at the pile of invoices on her desk, wishing she could plead overwork and send Paddy away before she made a complete fool of herself. But the stack of paper looked pitifully small, and the rest of her desk was clear.

"I...suppose I could talk for a minute." She sank into a chair, wondering what he wanted.

Probably, she thought bitterly, he was ready to buy a ring for Maura, and he wanted her advice on whether it should be a diamond or a sapphire. Men had always loved to give jewelry to Maura Alderson.

"I wondered if you might have dinner in town with me this weekend," he said. "Jenny should be home by then, and we could all—"

Bridget gaped at him, stunned. "Dinner? she asked. "With *you?*"

It was Paddy's turn to shift nervously and look shy. "If you'd rather not..."

"But of course I'd love to have dinner with you," Bridget said. "I just...I don't know why you're asking me."

Paddy threw his head back and laughed heartily. "Why, Bridget, I'm asking you because you're the woman I'd like to spend my time with. Didn't you know that?"

It had to be some kind of cruel joke. But why would Paddy McKenna be cruel to her when he treated everybody else with such kindness and consideration?

"You really didn't know, did you?" he mused. "And all this time I've been wearing my heart on my sleeve like a schoolboy. Everybody on the ranch seems to know how I feel except you."

She shook her head in confusion. "But...but you and Maura..."

"Maura Alderson is a fine woman," he said. "And a very smart one. When Jenny first came here and mentioned her grandfather, Maura realized I was probably the same man you'd been interested in for years through those newspaper clippings. So she arranged to get me out here and let me meet you, hoping to do a bit of matchmaking.''

''Matchmaking?'' Bridget echoed, feeling faint.

''Yes, and her efforts succeeded beyond her wildest expectations. On my side, at least,'' he added, smiling at her.

Bridget was speechless. She felt so stupid, sitting like a dumbstruck rabbit and trying to comprehend what he was saying.

''But,'' Paddy said, his smile fading, ''if you don't feel the same, Bridget, then it's no problem. I'll just keep this our little secret and not talk about it anymore. I won't bother you again.''

He got to his feet and moved toward the door, looking crushed.

''No, wait!'' Bridget ran and grasped his arm. ''I'm sorry to be rude, but this is all so... I just can't believe...''

''What can't you believe?'' Paddy stood and gazed down at her searchingly. ''That you're the kind of woman who could turn a man's heart upside down, Bridget? Because you surely are.''

She gazed into his eyes, thinking how joyfully a woman could drown in those rich blue depths. ''But I have no money at all,'' she whispered, feeling silly but wanting him to know the whole truth about her dreadful mistake. ''I gambled on the stock market and lost everything. I'm such a...''

Paddy put his arms around her and patted her back

comfortingly. "Bridget," he murmured against her hair, "don't worry about it. I don't care about your money. All I want from you is your companionship."

She drew away and looked down at the little alligator sewn above his shirt pocket. Surely, Bridget thought, dazed with happiness, it was the most beautiful alligator she'd ever seen.

"So do you think you might be willing to have dinner with Jenny and me?" Paddy asked again.

Bridget smiled, feeling wonderful. She felt slim and graceful, as sparkling and pretty as a teenage girl with a new boyfriend.

"I think I'd love to," she said demurely.

Paddy laughed and drew her into his arms again, chuckling. She nestled against him and saw a sudden vision of her young husband watching them. Hal smiled and winked at her, nodding his approval. Bridget smiled back. After a moment she wiggled the golden wedding band from her finger and slipped it unobtrusively into her pocket.

"Well, Maura wins again," Paddy murmured against her hair.

Bridget drew away to look up at him.

"Maura bet me ten dollars you'd say yes," he told Bridget. "I thought you'd never want to go out with an old man like me, but she bet on you."

"Maura would bet on anything," Bridget said, laughing.

"Not anymore. In fact, that was her last bet. Since the flood Maura's begun to worry about her life and the effect on her grandsons of all that gambling. She's decided to give it up forever. And you know what?" Paddy said with a grin. "I believe she will."

He put an arm around Bridget's shoulders and led her toward the vinyl couch, settling cozily next to her as if they had all the time in the world and a million things to talk about.

And so they did, Bridget thought, nestling against him. So they did.

CHAPTER NINETEEN

JENNY AWOKE AGAIN in a faint half light, feeling much stronger. Metal carts clattered down the hallways and voices called cheerfully.

"Breakfast time," the nurse told her. "How are you today?"

Jenny raised her free hand and tried to smile.

The nurse looked at her keenly, checked her pulse and listened to her chest with a stethoscope. "Looks like we're ready for all those tubes to come out," she said. "I'll be right back."

She returned with a sober young doctor in horn-rimmed glasses who examined Jenny, then helped the nurse remove the breathing apparatus.

Jenny endured the pain and discomfort stoically, relieved when all the tubes were gone and she felt like a person again, independent and breathing on her own. Every new breath sent a stab of agony knifing into her lungs, but even that seemed bracing.

It was so good to be alive.

The doctor smiled at her. "You're a very strong woman," he said. "You've done amazingly well."

She didn't know what to say and was glad when he left.

The nurse brought her some red gelatin and a dish

of ice cream and propped her up so she could eat. The coolness felt soothing on Jenny's raw throat, but she could only manage a few bites before weariness overcame her and she drifted off to sleep again.

When she next awoke, Paddy was in the room. He sat quietly in the armchair by the window, leafing through a magazine.

"Hi," she whispered.

He set the magazine aside and got up, coming over to hold her hand.

"Hi there," he said. "How's my girl? You sure look a whole lot better without those tubes in your face."

She smiled and squeezed his hand. "What happened, Grandpa?"

"Well, to start with, you came close to drowning. And the next day you developed pneumonia from all the creek water in your lungs, and that was almost worse than the flood."

"Pneumonia?" she asked, dazed. "How long have I been here?"

"It's been three days since you went into the water, Jen. You've been drifting in and out of consciousness ever since. Mostly out. It's the drugs, they tell me."

"Three days," she said in wonder. "I can't believe it. Grandpa, what did…"

She remembered the water closing over her head, the debris battering her, the sickening fear as her lungs filled with water. And Clay pounding at her, yelling at her…

"He saved my life, didn't he?" she whispered.

"He surely did. God, what a man he is." Paddy's face contorted with emotion.

"Tell me what happened, Grandpa."

"Clay said he was finishing the sandbag dike at the cemetery, loading his truck when he heard you scream. He saw you in the water so he got into his truck and drove downstream as fast as he could to a place where the creek widened and the current wasn't as fast. He tied a rope around his waist and attached it to the bumper of the truck, then swam out to get you."

She watched her grandfather's face in silence, trying to understand.

"By the time he got you to shore you were already in bad shape. He did his best to get the water out of your lungs. Then he brought you up to the ranch house and we called the paramedics. They said you had to be kept warm while they brought the helicopter out. They told us the best way to do it was for somebody to get into bed with you and hold you." Paddy grinned. "And for maximum effect, you should both be naked."

"Naked?"

"Yep. And Clay volunteered. He didn't seem to mind at all."

Jenny felt her cheeks redden. "But he…"

An awkward silence fell while the nurse came in to check Jenny's pulse and blood pressure.

"Not too long," she told Paddy, who smiled at her warmly. "She's still not strong."

He nodded and got up to leave, but Jenny caught his hand. "Don't go yet, Grandpa," she whispered hoarsely. "Tell me the rest. I want to know everything."

"Well, you were unconscious by the time the paramedics arrived and loaded you on the helicopter. They said there was no doubt Clay saved your life."

"Grandpa..." She coughed, wincing at the pain. "Somebody pushed me into that water," she said. "I didn't imagine it."

"Of course you didn't. But," he added quietly, "it surely wasn't Clay who pushed you, sweetie."

Her chest tightened with another harsh spasm. "He...he told you what I said?"

Paddy nodded, looking grave. "The poor man was heartbroken to know you thought that of him."

"Who pushed me? Do you know?"

Paddy settled back in the chair and glanced out the window. "The next morning, after you were taken away and the floodwater crested and started to go down, Clay and Bridget found a letter on the desk in the office."

"What kind of letter?"

"It was from the foreman."

"Jim Cole?" she asked, her eyes wide with shock.

Paddy told her about the foreman's letter, and his check for all the embezzled cash.

"And the creek?" she whispered. "It was Jim Cole who threw me into the water?"

"Jim didn't say anything about that, but Clay assumes he panicked because he knew you were getting close to the truth. After he realized you hadn't drowned, he was sure you'd be able to identify him. That's why he ran. And I suppose he refunded the money hoping they might go easy on him, since attempted murder is a whole different ball game from fraud.''

Jenny stared at the ceiling, trying to come to grips with all those harsh terrible things she'd said to Clay Alderson.

''There was another letter, Jenny,'' her grandfather said gently. ''From Teresa. She left it in their room for Michael. He wouldn't show it to anybody, but apparently she called him all kinds of names, told him he was a poor excuse for a man and that she was leaving with Jim. It seems she and Cole have been lovers ever since she arrived at the ranch last year.''

Jenny remembered the girl's pale face and scornful bored face, her languid manner.

''Oh, dear. Poor Michael,'' she murmured. ''How's he taking it?''

''He's getting over the shock and beginning to look almost happy again. We think perhaps the spell Teresa had him under is finally broken.''

''So she was part of the embezzlement scheme? She was helping to steal the money?''

''It appears so. Jim Cole recruited her soon after she arrived because he needed help to alter the trucking slips and lift some of the checks from the ranch office after Clay took cattle to auction. The whole thing's out in the open now.''

''Does anybody know where they are? Jim and Teresa, I mean?''

''They were caught yesterday at an American border crossing and shipped back to Calgary. They're being held for trial, but nobody's sure what the charge is going to be since he refunded the money.''

"But he tried to kill me! Probably more than once,'' she added grimly, remembering the gunshots and the stallion in the barn.

"He's never admitted pushing you into the water. And you probably can't press charges,'' Paddy said gently, ''since you didn't get a good look at him. You actually thought Clay did it.''

Jenny couldn't bear to think any more about how wrong she'd been and how unfairly she'd accused Clay who'd risked his life to save hers.

But there were other painful realities to consider.

"The ranch,'' she whispered. ''What happened to it, Grandpa? Is everything flooded?''

His face broke into a sunny smile. ''Well, honey, that's the best news of all. Michael's dike held, so there was just a trickle of water in the hay meadows. And all those sandbags of ours protected the ranch yard. The water only broke through farther down, just past that channel where you—''

He stopped abruptly, swallowing hard, and Jenny reached out to take his hand. Paddy squeezed it and smiled at her.

"Anyhow,'' he went on, clearing his throat, ''the water broke through down there, but it didn't damage anything except a couple of empty pastures. Even the cemetery's pretty much intact.''

"Oh, Grandpa,'' Jenny breathed, her eyes stinging with tears. ''That's so wonderful. They must all be...'' She couldn't go on. She kept thinking about

Clay's arms around her, his naked body against hers, his stricken face when she accused him.

"I was out there yesterday," Paddy said. "Life's almost back to normal."

She had to ask, because not knowing was the greatest pain of all. "What about Clay?" she whispered, so low that Paddy had to bend near the bed to hear.

"What about him, Jen?"

"Does he hate me? Has he…said anything to you?"

Paddy shook his head and moved away to peer out the window. Jenny, who knew him well, could see the tension in his broad shoulders.

"He didn't say much, except to tell me what happened and that you believed he was the one who'd been trying to hurt you. He's a reserved man, Jenny. He doesn't let his feelings show."

Paddy came back to the bed and looked down at her gravely.

"I need to call him," she said. "I have to apologize for the things I said."

Paddy shook his head. "I don't think that's going to help, dear," he said gently. "Clay doesn't care about what you said. He's all torn up over what you *felt*. And he's right, isn't he?"

Jenny closed her eyes to block out her grandfather's wise creased face.

Of course Clay was right. How could you ever apologize to somebody for accusing him of treachery, theft and attempted murder? Especially when it was the same person you'd held in your arms, made love and cuddled and laughed with, exchanged secrets…

She moaned in pain and rolled her head weakly on the pillow.

Paddy sat nearby, holding her hand as he waited for her storm of emotion to pass.

"At least," he told her finally, "some good things have come of all this."

Jenny heard a strange note in his voice and forced herself to look up at him. "What's that, Grandpa?"

"For one thing, Clay got all his money back. He's very relieved to have that cash in hand and feel prosperous again, even after settling his affairs with the tax department. And there's…" Paddy looked out the window, almost shyly.

Jenny pushed aside her own troubles and gave him a curious glance. "Grandpa?" she asked. "What were you going to say?"

"Well, Jen, it's sort of a miracle." He smiled, his face suddenly radiant. "Seems I've found the woman of my dreams."

"The woman of your… Grandpa! Really?" Jenny reached out to grasp his arm.

"I just can't stay away from that ranch," Paddy said, beaming. "And you'd better hurry up and get well, Jenny-girl," he added, moving around the end of the bed. "Because from now on, life is going to be a whole lot different for all of us."

He strode toward the door, blew her a smiling kiss and left quietly. Jenny lay staring at the closed door, her mind whirling.

Things were going to be a lot different.…

If her grandfather had really fallen in love with Maura Alderson, that was certainly true. Maura would never leave the beautiful old ranch house, so Paddy would probably sell his home in the city and move to Cottonwood Creek.

That meant Jenny would hardly ever see her grandfather anymore, unless he came to Calgary for visits.

After the way she'd behaved, she would certainly never again set foot on the Cottonwood Creek ranch. The mere prospect of seeing Clay was too painful and embarrassing to contemplate.

Jenny moaned and felt the tears gather in her eyes again, wondering why she cried so easily since the accident. She told herself it must be the drugs they were giving her; they had some kind of weakening effect on her system.

But her sorrow went far deeper, and she knew it. Her greatest shame was how quick she'd been to accuse Clay, and the reasons for her behavior. She suspected she'd been afraid of her own emotions, especially the love that was growing in her heart at such an alarming rate. She didn't want to be swept away by love—or lose her memories of Steve, which had always been comforting and easy to control.

But the soaring sexual passion that Clay had brought to her life... She was terrified of such abandonment, of yielding and losing herself in a wild tumult of emotion. Especially when she'd already known the pain of loss. Once before she'd allowed herself to love, and a man had been torn from her without warning.

She couldn't risk that again. And so she'd accused

Clay at the first opportunity. Knowing how much she cared for him, she should have been loyal and fair, prepared to give the man a chance to prove himself.

Instead, she was a cowardly and contemptible woman, and she deserved to lose him.

Only now, at the realization of her loss, did Jenny understand how truly and completely she loved the man. Over the brief intense time they'd spent together, she had come to recognize him as her soul mate, her intellectual equal, her partner and playmate.

Clay Alderson was the man she was supposed to hold through life, and she'd driven him away. She'd probably never see him again, except at awkward formal occasions if Paddy and Maura Alderson became a couple.

Bitter tears welled up in her eyes and trickled down the sides of her face, soaking quietly into the pillow. The nurse appeared, soundless in her thick-soled shoes. Jenny swallowed and looked up at her, feeling guilty and embarrassed.

"Don't you worry," the nurse said soothingly, patting her hair. "You just go ahead and have a good cry. It's a normal reaction to shock, and it'll do you a world of good."

She bent nearer, looking sober and concerned. "There's nothing else wrong, is there, honey? Just a touch of the blues?"

Jenny nodded, unable to speak.

"Well, then," the nurse said briskly, "we won't worry about it, will we?" She began to plump the pillows, turning them so they presented an inviting expanse of soft coolness.

"Thank you," Jenny murmured, her voice husky.

"And maybe tonight," the nurse went on, "that handsome hubby of yours will be back for a visit. Now *that's* certainly something to look forward to, isn't it?" she said with a wink and a meaningful smile.

"My husband?" Jenny looked up blankly.

The nurse hesitated, her cheeks pink with confusion.

"Wasn't that your husband? That tall dark cowboy who came in with you the first day? My goodness, he never left your side for ten hours, except to come down to the nurses' station and demand attention from the doctors. And believe me," she added with a reminiscent smile, "he got attention. We had people running all over the hospital looking after you."

Jenny stared up at her, wide-eyed and silent.

"We all just assumed he was your husband," the nurse went on, "because he seemed so upset and worried. But after you started to stabilize, he left and went back to his ranch. I happen to know for a fact that a few of the girls on the evening shift are really hoping he'll be coming to visit tonight."

"No, he won't," Jenny said, turning to gaze out the window through eyes blurred with tears. "He'll never come back."

The nurse hesitated, looking flustered. "But isn't he…"

Jenny shook her head and closed her eyes, so miserable she couldn't find any more words to speak.

At last the nurse adjusted the water jug on Jenny's bedside table, then bustled from the room, leaving

Jenny staring out the window, watching clouds drifting like dandelion fluff across a sky of summer blue.

BRIDGET SAT AT HER DESK, humming as she entered invoice amounts in the ledgers. She wore a pink cotton dress sprigged with flowers, and felt about sixteen years old. Life was wonderful, she thought, smiling as she sipped tea from one of Maura's thin china cups. Truly wonderful.

Clay came in at that moment, also looking better than he had for a long time. He wore faded jeans, a baseball cap and a white T-shirt, and his bare arms were tanned and muscular.

"That sunshine sure feels good," he said, helping himself to a mug of coffee. "I think the yearlings are putting on about twenty pounds a day with all the green grass they're eating."

Bridget watched him with loving concern. Despite the cheerfulness of his words, there was still something about the man that worried her. She could see a pain glimmer in his eyes sometimes when he thought nobody was watching.

"Clay," she said gently.

"What?"

"You should call her."

"And say what?"

Bridget made an exasperated gesture. "For goodness' sake, what does any man say to a woman he cares about? Ask her out for dinner. She's getting out of the hospital tomorrow. Go to the city and take her out on a nice dress-up date."

He sprawled on the couch and extended his booted

feet, sipping the coffee. "She thought I was a thief, Bridget. She honestly believed I was the kind of man who'd steal from the tax department and then seduce and bully a woman to keep her from telling."

"It was an awful time for all of us," Bridget said. "Poor Jenny was a stranger here, and terrified by what was happening. No wonder she got confused. The least you could do is call her."

He got up and moved to the window, looking out with a brooding expression.

"Don't lecture me, Bridget," he said, then turned with a smile to soften his words. "I'll do something about it. But only when I'm sure that she..."

He fell silent, watching Paddy McKenna who sat on a flat rock at the edge of the ranch yard, observing a pair of whooping cranes through binoculars.

"When you're sure of what?"

Clay turned to his bookkeeper. "I don't even know how she feels. I'm not going to bother her if she still hates me."

"She never hated you!" Bridget declared. "Jenny was just confused and really scared. No wonder, with all the things that were going on. Poor girl," she added with feeling.

Clay nodded thoughtfully and put his coffee mug down. "So, has Jim Cole's check finally cleared the bank?" he asked.

"I got the confirmation today from Saul's office. More than two hundred thousand dollars will be left after the back taxes are paid. You're rich, Clay."

"Rich," he said with a bitter smile.

"So what are you going to do with all that money?"

"Drill a new well on Sagebrush Flats," he said. "And I was thinking…"

What?" Bridget asked when he paused. "What else will you do with the money?"

He flashed one of his rare smiles, then gazed out the window again, his dark face softening. "Maybe I'll have a picnic."

"A picnic?" she asked in astonishment.

Paddy came in at that moment, carrying the binoculars. Bridget felt her heart flutter.

"What's going on here?" he asked Clay. "Are you flirting with my girl again?"

Clay grinned. "Sorry, Paddy. She's looking so pretty these days I just can't leave her alone."

"She certainly is," Paddy said. "And I've come to escort her to the ranch house for lunch."

Bridget got up to take his arm, thrilled by his touch, and the three of them left the office together.

Halfway to the ranch house, she realized that she still hadn't asked Clay what he meant about spending some of his newfound wealth on a *picnic,* of all things.

CHAPTER TWENTY

JENNY RECOVERED rapidly after her first few days in the hospital. Within a week she was back at home, where Paddy irritated her by treating her like an invalid.

"I'm fine, Grandpa," she told him. "I don't need to be pampered and waited on. I just need a little time to feel strong again."

But he ignored her protests and insisted on cooking all the meals, even coming downstairs to tidy her apartment and do her laundry so she could rest. After a while Jenny gave up and let him do what he wanted.

Paddy seemed almost ridiculously happy. By now, Jenny realized that it was Bridget he loved, not Maura Alderson, and she rejoiced with him in his renewed contentment.

Lisa stopped by to let her know what was happening at the office and keep her current on new tax audits. She told Jenny that Clay Alderson's accountant had paid the ranch's tax arrears in full and the file was closed.

On her third day at home, Jenny got up the nerve to call the ranch. Bridget answered, clearly delighted to hear from her, and told Jenny that Clay had made a quick trip to Texas to return the vicious bay stallion to its owners. He was expected back the following week.

Jenny chatted a while and then hung up, both relieved and disappointed.

Late at night when she lay sleepless in bed and listened to the traffic rumbling by on the street, she remembered that dark rainy night in the guest bedroom at the ranch house. The image was so clear she could almost feel the warmth of his skin, hear the wind rustling the trees outside the window and his murmurs of pleasure as he made love to her.

She moaned and rolled over, burying her face in the pillow to keep from crying.

On the weekend Paddy brought Bridget to the house for a visit. Jenny embraced the older woman, then stood back to take in Bridget's glowing smile "It's good to see you! she said. "How is... everyone?"

"We're all just fine," Bridget said. "Maura and the boys send their love, and so do Joe and Polly."

The omission of Clay was so pointed that Jenny felt her cheeks warming with distress. She turned away quickly to check the teapot while Paddy cast her a quick glance and crossed the kitchen to take a bowl of fruit salad from his fridge.

"I'm looking for a new apartment," Jenny told Bridget. "Grandpa tells me you're hoping to move into the basement around the first of September."

Bridget made a gesture of alarm. "Oh, but I don't mean to push you out, Jenny. You can stay here as long as you want."

Jenny smiled and hugged her again. "Don't worry,

Bridget. I've been meaning to move out for a long time, but I've always just been too lazy to get around to it. This is the perfect opportunity. I'm going to be happy, to live somewhere a little higher up where I can...where I can see a bit of open space.''

She crossed to the china cabinet to get Paddy's best teacups.

''Well,'' Bridget said, ''that's just wonderful. Everything's working out so well. Clay says he's planning to hire a new bookkeeper so I won't have to spend another winter at the ranch, and Paddy and I—''

She broke off, smiling. Paddy placed a hand on her shoulder fondly and she reached up to pat it. Jenny watched them, touched by their obvious happiness, then lifted the teapot with unsteady hands.

''Has Clay... has he already found somebody to do the books?'' she asked, trying to keep her voice casual.

Bridget and Paddy exchanged glances. ''I'm not sure,'' Bridget said, accepting a cup and saucer. ''But I think he has somebody in mind. We'll be talking about it more when he gets back from Texas.''

Jenny nodded and sank into the opposite chair, staring moodily out the window.

THE NEXT WEEK Jenny went back to the office and buried herself in ledgers and accounts, tax files and new abstracts, working so furiously that Lisa expressed concern.

''Hey, take it easy, Jen,'' she said on a beautiful morning in early July, pausing by her desk with an armful of folders. "You're going to kill yourself. You still look a little pale, you know. And you've lost weight, too."

"I'm fine," Jenny said. "I need to work, Lisa. It's good therapy. Don't worry about me."

Lisa dumped the folders on her desk, looking unconvinced, and went off to buy a box of doughnuts.

When she was gone, Jenny sat alone and stared at the papers on her desk. She had a thousand things to do but she couldn't bring herself to tackle any of them.

All of it seemed meaningless—the job, the crowded city existence, her entire life....

Lowering her head onto her folded arms, she gave herself over to tears. Her desolation was almost unbearable.

She loved him so much. If only he'd call, send a note, give some indication that he forgave her and bore her no hard feelings. She could even live without him, if she knew he didn't hate her.

True, the nurse said he'd come and sat by her hospital bed for ten hours until she was out of danger. But there'd been nothing since.

Maybe she'd call again tonight. He had to be back from Texas by now.

Jenny thought about his dark eyes and finely shaped mouth, his lean muscular body, those beautiful hands. She shivered and rolled her head on her arms, marveling that she'd once fancied herself in love with a vain shallow man like Steve Marshall. She hadn't even known what the word meant. In those days she'd been a child, dazzled by the idea of being in love.

But now that she was a woman and knew the truth, it was too late.

Jenny raised her head and dabbed her eyes with a tissue. Then she took a small hand mirror from the top drawer of her desk and stared at her reflection in brooding silence.

Today was her thirty-first birthday.

Nobody had remembered, of course. Paddy would probably have said something if he'd been at home, but her grandfather had gone away, as he did frequently these days, to spend a few days at Cottonwood Creek where he was training for an upcoming triathlon. He loved running and biking on the open prairie and enjoyed being close to Bridget.

The thought of her grandfather out at the ranch, socializing with all the residents and seeing Clay every day, made Jenny feel more alone and excluded than ever.

Her mother might call tonight and wish her a happy birthday, or perhaps a card would arrive from Florida in tomorrow's mail, but that was cold comfort.

She replaced the mirror, sighed and pulled a stack of files toward her.

"Hey, Jen." Lisa popped her head around the divider, looking pleased and mysterious. "Clarence wants to see you up in his office."

"Why?"

"Beats me." Lisa vanished again, grinning.

Jenny pushed herself away from her desk and trudged upstairs to her supervisor's office, glancing out the window as she went. The sky was blue and cloudless. A pair of birds circled and dipped on the warm air currents above the city, then drifted off across the plains.

Jenny envied them with all her heart.

The elderly supervisor sat behind his desk, looking amused about something. He took off his glasses and rubbed his temples as she entered the office.

"Well, well. Good morning, Jenny," he said. "How are you?"

"I'm fine." Jenny sank into one of the chairs opposite his desk.

"Feeling better?"

"I'm much better now," Jenny said. "Thank you for asking."

"I understand it's your birthday today."

"How did you know that?" she asked, startled.

He beamed, the overhead lights glistening on his bald scalp. "Let's just say a little bird told me. You can have the rest of the day off."

"I don't need a day off," Jenny said, puzzled by his manner. "I've just come back to work."

The supervisor smiled again, looking as mysterious as Lisa had. He reached under his desk and took out a parcel wrapped in plastic, which he handed to her.

"You can change in my washroom." He indicated an oak door on the far side of the room.

She stared at the parcel in her hands. "Clarence...what's this all about?"

"Go and change, Jenny. You're making a little field trip."

Still baffled, she carried the package into his executive washroom, opening it to find a pair of her own jeans, along with a plaid shirt and some socks and running shoes.

She stared at the clothes in growing confusion. Whatever was going on, her grandfather was clearly involved in the conspiracy. He had to be the one who'd gathered these clothes.

Jenny dressed and came back out, carrying her folded work clothes in the plastic wrapping.

The supervisor eyed her with warm approval. "Good," he said. "Now, go on up to the roof."

"The *roof?*" she asked blankly. "What's on the roof?"

"You'll see. You can leave that stuff here," he added, indicating the package in her hand, "and pick it up later. Happy birthday, Jenny."

Still dazed and uncertain, Jenny climbed a flight of service stars and went out onto the flat roof of the office building. A helicopter sat there, its blades rotating slowly in the warm summer air.

The pilot waved to her and she climbed aboard, her heart beginning to pound as they lifted from the roof and whirled off over the city.

The prairie spread beneath her, vast and shimmering in the morning sunlight. Jenny gazed out the window in tense silence, hardly daring to breathe. The pilot frowned at the rolling landscape beneath them, scored by deep coulees and windswept ridges. He consulted a map, then circled and lowered the aircraft to the ground.

"This is the place," he shouted to Jenny over the roar of the engine. "I'm supposed to leave you here and take off."

Numbly she climbed out of the helicopter and watched as it rose and drifted away, fading to a distant speck in the blue arch of sky. Then she looked around and gasped in amazement, feeling a warm thrill of recognition.

She stood in a bower of greenery, an oasis in the sea of bleached grass and sage.

This was the magical glade where, in Jenny's dreams, Clay had held her and caressed her body with such tenderness. Water bubbled in invisible springs nearby, and young cottonwood trees swayed in the wind. All around for miles in every direction, she saw nothing but open spaces and here and there the shapes of grazing cattle.

But she wasn't dreaming anymore. This green bower was real, and it was the most wonderful place on earth. She was alone but unafraid, just happy and breathless with an excitement she hardly dared to analyze. She sat under one of the trees and looked down the hillside at the wide sweep of land, waiting.

Within ten minutes she could see a rider far off to the west approaching at an easy gallop. As he drew nearer, she could make out his big sorrel horse, and another that he led behind him on a halter rope. The second horse was also saddled and carried a bulky pack.

Jenny watched with tears streaming down her cheeks and a tremulous smile on her lips. She brushed at her face and composed herself, scrambling to her feet.

He rode up to the sunny glade, dismounted and tied both horses to one of the cottonwoods, then crossed the grass to stand gazing at her, his eyes dark and searching under the hat brim.

"Clay," she whispered.

God, he was a beautiful sight. She reached out blindly, conscious of nothing but the need to hold him, to feel him in her arms.

He stepped nearer, tossed his hat aside and gathered her close, laughing softly.

"It's so good to see you," he said. "I wasn't sure you'd ever want to be with me again, so I had to kidnap you."

"Oh, Clay... I'm so sorry..."

He silenced her with a kiss. "Happy birthday," he said huskily. "I've got a picnic in those saddlebags, Jenny. Champagne and everything. Wait till you see."

"But Clay," she protested, "it must have been so expensive. That helicopter..."

"I'm feeling flush these days." He drew away and gazed warmly at her. "I've got a whole lot of money I never even knew about. Besides," he added with a teasing grin, "this is business. I'll have to check with my auditor, but it's probably even a tax writeoff."

"Business?"

While she watched, he strode back to the second horse and drew a bright Navajo blanket from one of the packs, spreading it carefully on the grass. He took off his boots and stretched out on the blanket, relaxing in the sun.

"Come and lie here beside me," he said.

Jenny crossed the grass and looked down at him, then sank to her knees. "Clay, what's going on?"

"We're having an employment interview," he told her solemnly, though his eyes sparkled with laughter. "I'm looking for a financial manager, and I think you might be interested."

"What are the qualifications?" she asked, then trembled as he reached up with a lazy hand and began to unbutton her shirt.

"Well, you have to sleep with the boss every night," he said.

Jenny pretended to consider. "I could probably do that."

He pulled her into his arms and kissed her. "And," he whispered against her hair, "you'd have to give him a couple of babies..."

"I could do that, too."

"Jenny McKenna," he said, chuckling as he rolled on top of her and kissed her lustily, "I think you're hired."

She laughed with him, lost in the wonder of his nearness. And this time, the only flood that mattered was the sunshine pouring down on them and the love that filled her heart.

MEN at WORK

All work and no play?
Not these men!

July 1998
MACKENZIE'S LADY by Dallas Schulze

Undercover agent Mackenzie Donahue's
lazy smile and deep blue eyes were his best
weapons. But after rescuing—and kissing!—
damsel in distress Holly Reynolds, how could
he betray her by spying on her brother?

August 1998
MISS LIZ'S PASSION by Sherryl Woods

Todd Lewis could put up a building with ease,
but quailed at the sight of a classroom! Still,
Liz Gentry, his son's teacher, was no battle-ax,
and soon Todd started planning some
extracurricular activities of his own....

September 1998
A CLASSIC ENCOUNTER
by Emilie Richards

Doctor Chris Matthews was intelligent, sexy
and *very* good with his hands—which made
him all the more dangerous to single mom
Lizette St. Hilaire. So how long could she
resist Chris's special brand of TLC?

Available at your favorite retail outlet!

MEN AT WORK™

 HARLEQUIN®   Silhouette®

Look us up on-line at: http://www.romance.net   PMAW2

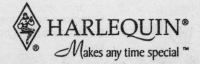

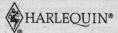

HARLEQUIN®

Not The Same Old Story!

HARLEQUIN 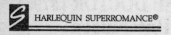 PRESENTS®

Exciting, glamorous romance stories that take readers around the world.

Harlequin Romance®

Sparkling, fresh and tender love stories that bring you pure romance.

HARLEQUIN®
Temptation

Bold and adventurous—Temptation is strong women, bad boys, great sex!

HARLEQUIN SUPERROMANCE®

Provocative and realistic stories that celebrate life and love.

AMERICAN ◆ ROMANCE®

Contemporary fairy tales—where anything is possible and where dreams come true.

HARLEQUIN®
INTRIGUE®

Heart-stopping, suspenseful adventures that combine the best of romance and mystery.

Humorous and romantic stories that capture the lighter side of love.

HARLEQUIN SUPERROMANCE®

FAMILY MAN

In 1998, can you have it all?

**Garrett Lock is a family man who *wants* it all.
So does Sherry Campbell.
They want love, family, work and success—
everything!**

Garrett's son is the most important thing in his life; for Sherry
it's her job as a college counselor. When Garrett becomes her
boss and eventually her lover—*and* her love!—they both find
that there's more than one way to get what you want.

With a little bit of compromise and a lot of trust...you *can*
have it all!

Watch for HAVING IT ALL (#800)
by Roz Denny Fox,
available August 1998
wherever Harlequin books are sold.

HARLEQUIN SUPERROMANCE®

COMING NEXT MONTH